WAR DECLARED!

Theodore Roscoe

Satan's Vengeance

BY CARROLL JOHN DALY

*The Viper: The Complete Cases of
Madame Storey, Volume 2*

BY HULBERT FOOTNER

*The Sapphire Smile: The Adventures
of Peter the Brazen, Volume 4*

BY LORING BRENT

*The Curse of Capistrano and Other Adventures:
The Johnston McCulley Omnibus, Volume 2*

BY JOHNSTON MCCULLEY

*The Man Who Mastered Time and Other
Adventures: The Ray Cummings Omnibus*

BY RAY CUMMINGS

*The Guns of the American: The
Adventures of Norcross, Volume 2*

BY W. WIRT

Trailin'

BY MAX BRAND

The Return of the Night Wind

BY VARICK VANARDY

*The Fetish Fighters and Other Adventures: The
F.V.W. Mason Foreign Legion Stories Omnibus*

BY F.V.W. MASON

WAR DECLARED!

THEODORE ROSCOE

ILLUSTRATED BY

SAMUEL CAHAN

COVER BY

C.C. BEALL

STEEGER BOOKS • 2020

PUBLISHING HISTORY

"War Declared!" originally appeared in the April 27, May 4, 11, 18, 25, and June 1 & 8, 1935 issues of *Argosy* magazine (Vol. 255, No. 2–Vol. 256, No. 2). Copyright © 1935 by The Frank A. Munsey Company. Copyright renewed © 1962 and assigned to Steeger Properties, LLC. All rights reserved.

Fe-fi-fo-fum,
I smell the blood of a war to come.
Legions alive will soon be dead.
I'll grind their bones to make my bread.
              Mother Goose, 1936.
       Song of The Armament Maker—

CHAPTER I

JULY, 1936

TWILIGHT SHADOWED OVER Teutony, and omens were afoot in the dusk. Suspense. The air over Europe was charged with it, as it had been charged throughout that hot July day. All day John Keats had suffered that tension in the back of his mind; that "here it comes" feeling he'd known as a boy squirming on the curbstone, waiting for the circus parade. That sensation you had in a theater when the signal buzzed in the orchestra pit, the houselights dimmed, the audience strained forward in hush, the curtain started up. First-string newspaper men have a nose for such things. That is why they are first-string newspaper men, and that was why John Keats was in the Teutonic capital.

The assignment was routine stuff, but the mood was something he couldn't put his finger on. Like the feeling he'd had that morning away down there in Transylvania, when he had entered that tower room and the tall dark man turned slowly from the fireplace to meet him. Queer, that morning. An interview that had started with dead silence and ended with a shot.

There were only the four of them in the room—the mute Negro whose eyes were like the dog's; the Great Dane; the dark figure in front of the fire; and John Keats, correspondent, Universe News. But there had always been something morbid to

1

*There was history
in that tableau.*

Keats about a huge dog, and the room, itself, stood around like a
presentiment. A tower room, long and lofted. Below the Gothic
windows dropped beetling walls, mossy dark bartizans, a deep
moat, stagnant tarns and forested mountain. Garganoff Keep.

Flying over Transylvania in the great Intercontinental
Airliner, he had looked down on the castle times before, and
something of its inner character had been communicated to
him even then. A frown congealed to stone atop a cliff; shadowy
towers with heads together in conspiracy.

Once through the lower reception hall with its crush of lack-

ies and castle attendants—once beckoned past the Russian
secretary who wore a spongy wen on the base of his head, he had
invaded the dismal quietude of a catacomb. A maze of corridors,
staircases, galleries, following the heels of the Blackamoor while
the mastiff sniffed his trouser cuffs. Then at long last the tower
room where the black-robed figure waited before the fireplace,
back toward his visitors.

"Count Vasil Garganoff," the Negro lipped at Keats.

The tall dark figure wheeled around so slowly from the fireplace, as if his balance were difficult from wine and any moment
he might fall, that John Keats eyed him in a sort of fascination,
really wanting to glance around over his shoulder. The room had
a way of creeping at his back. Candles glimmered in sconces
up the tall walls, and a bony chandelier swooped down from
the cavernous ceiling, burning high and dim in the gloom like
a Christmas tree suspended in mirage. The fireplace was chilly

as a grate in a mortuary chapel, a flat-topped ebony desk with an invalid's wheelchair behind it was like a coffin waiting its inheritor, and high-backed imperial chairs along the wall were mourners carved in black wood.

John Keats found himself fidgeting in a chair. Damn it, he was fussing like a cub reporter at his first inquest. Suppose this Balkan recluse was the richest miser in creation, the so-styled Mystery Man of Europe? Keats had interviewed eccentrics before, all the way from Mussolini to George Bernard Shaw. He grinned without enthusiasm at the dog watching him with its sorrowful Negro eyes and the Negro watching him with sorrowful dog eyes, and began to remember stories he'd heard.

In London—"See Garganoff? Not a chance. He keeps himself shut up in that castle like a pearl in a clam."

In Rome—"Only a handful of people have ever seen the great munitions king face to face."

In Belgrade—"It is said his mother, the Countess Hertha, kept him locked up as a child and gave him this hermit complex. It was she who built the tremendous cannon factories and left him the business."

In Bucharest—"Why, he once refused a royal command to appear before Queen Marie. But twice in his life has he left the Keep."

In the village below the mountain where the smallest of the great Hertha Gun Works factories belched smoke by day and fire by night—"I wouldn't go up to his castle, sir, for a million *kronen!*" That was Popescu, the plump innkeeper, crossing himself nervously and wagging dire ominations. "The brave Crusaders, sir, six hundred years ago, they wouldn't stop at the place. As for *him* up there—all my life in this village I never set eye on Vasil Garganoff. They say he lives alone in the north tower with a Negro servant, a Russian and a monstrous dog. That he never goes out save at night. That he's sick. Sick! You know what the village thinks, sir?"

JOHN KEATS had listened to the village's thoughts. Popescu confided them in a gaudy whisper. "We think it strange, we do. The old Countess Hertha never allowing visitors to see the boy, years ago. The way now he never goes out but in the dead of night, and then only to walk alone in his private gardens. I'm not saying I believe it, sir, but these mountains—did you never hear of the *loup-garou,* the werewolf, sir? And there's a story that the black man, the Russian and the dog are sorcerers. And *him!* But it's got to be nights of no moon and a fair-haired child they've caught—he can drink the blood of a little boy and regain his youth, yes, sir. Change himself into a girl or a little child—*Loup-garou*—"

Well, that was a new name for armament manufacturers. John Keats had chuckled. That forgotten corner of Rumania, those Transylvanian mountains had always been the home of Dracula stories. Old wives' tales filtering down the forest from the rich overlord's castle, and Rumanian peasants not the least superstitious of their class.

But Popescu's words echoed to mind as this tall dark figure faced about from the fireplace and tottered stiffly to the wheel-chair behind the coffin-like desk. He almost creaked, this anchorite Crœsus, stiff-jointed in a black Inverness cape, more a shroud than a mantle, the folds loosely enveloping the old man from collar to floor, the hem swishing on the carpet like the cloak of a bishop. The black columns of cloth gave the fellow's head an undersized appearance, making him taller than he was. Concealed under the dark robing, his arms appeared to be folded; the Negro had to help him down. In the chair he collapsed full length, clumsily. There was some difficulty with the legs under the black cape.

"You are the American, John Keats?"

The voice, anticipated as a somber rumbling, was bloodless, thin in the throat, as if the speaker suffered tonsilitis. John Keats made formal acknowledgment of his card. "At your service, Count Garganoff."

The man said, "Good," without looking up. Then he lifted a

gaze from the desk-top to fix it on Keats; the room deepened in hush, the only sound was the ivory clicking of the dog's breath-less tongue. John Keats told himself that if this was the face you must wear after gathering yourself a billion dollars and shutting yourself up with it in a castle, he'd stick to his hundred a week.

NEVER HAD he confronted a face as extraordinary. Some-how it was old, and at the same time (he knew he was imagining this) Count Garganoff's countenance was inexplicably young. An animated death mask, wisps of puerile blond hair crown-ing a domish forehead without a wrinkle. The chin with its dab of straw-colored goatee was smooth, round. Under colorless eyelashes the eyes were sparrow beady; an English monocle fixed under one brow as if it had grown there, and a candle-flame mirrored in the glass wavered like a pale moon caught in the lens of an astronomer. Without a trace of emaciation, the face wore the shocking pallor of complete senescence, but in that deathly white mask the mouth was full-lipped, carmine, the lips glossy as exposed veins, lurid as make-up on a dying girl.

Caught staring, Keats forced his eyes to shift at the decora-tion hooked at the old man's collar—ribbon of blue supporting a golden badge, double-headed eagle and crucifix. The Order of St. Andrew of Russia.

"You are admiring my decoration," Garganoff observed, his voice reminding Keats of the reedy huskings of a polite mario-nette. "Sent me by Czar Nicholas many years ago. However, you did not call on me to talk of decorations. My secretary informs me you have made repeated efforts to arrange an interview. Why do you wish to see me?"

"Well, your Excellency," Keats began a professional tone, "the Universe News has been publishing interviews with all the important men of Europe, and we—"

"I know all that, young man, please come to the point."

"As I advised your secretary," Keats blandly ignored asperity in the old man's attitude, "I'm on my way to report the conference between Baron Von Speer and Victor Gatreau, meeting at the Hotel Metropole in the Teutonic capital tonight."

"You wish to know if I will attend?"

"The press understands you were invited by Monsieur Gatreau. We feel this unusual parley, coming at a time when Europe is dangerously—"

"I," the red lips snapped, "am not going. You may inform your papers Count Garganoff is unacquainted with the diplomats involved or the purpose of their camarilla. Why the Esperench minister should invite me to dine with him and the Teuton premier in any hotel, I don't know. As I am ill—quite incapacitated with rheumatism—a trip to Teutony at this time would be impossible. I wish these blundering statesmen would let me alone. And now you've had your answer, my dear young sir, will you permit me to ask *you* a few questions?"

The Dane growled a faint drumroll out of its throat, and Keats controlled an impulse to pull his shoes under his chair. "Over a great many years," the squeaky voice was going on, "I have granted but four interviews. Do you know why I have arranged this one with you?"

Keats' eyebrows were unable to conceal his surprise. "Universe News will appreciate your confidence, sir."

"I am not talking for publication. I wished to talk with *you.*"

The red lips parodied an ingratiating smile. "I wished to speak with you, my dear young sir, because some of your recently syndicated articles in the press have commanded my respect and attention. Particularly your diligent work in disclosing certain arms scandals, graft, interlocking directorates between various European and American armament firms. You've gone a long way to prove that arms makers have fostered, even started wars in an effort to create markets for their wares."

THE TROGLODYTE was purring at him now. Keats said warily, "I'm only a reporter, Count Garganoff, trying to do my job."

Garganoff nodded pleasantly. "And a very shrewd job it is, my

dear young sir. I thoroughly enjoyed your articles on the Briey
scandal, Krupp and the Thyssens, also your assertion that many
cannon makers controlled newspapers and inspired the reading
public to warlike opinion.*

"I've been most interested," Garganoff pursued softly, "in your
literary attacks on my own Hertha Gun Works."

The dog drumrolled in its throat. Keats' lips stiffened. "I would
hardly have called them attacks, your Excellency."

"Ha! But for a long time articles written by you have hinted
that my agents were stirring up border scares to stimulate sales. I
refer to that assassination last month in the Kingdom of Helvania."

"I made no accusations," Keats said warily. "I only reported
the truth, that the assassins were from Transylvania, and one of
them had once been an employee of your torpedo plant."

The candle flickered in the monocle. "You are considered an
authority on Helvanian state affairs?"

"I haven't covered Helvania for five years, your Excellency."

The old man made a sound in his nose. "But you are well
aware that my Hertha Works have not been supplying Helvania
with munitions. I don't like cynical inferences that my company
tries to stir up warlike emotions. The reputation of the Hertha
Gun Works is, in a way, my reputation. I like to say my business
has been founded on honor. However," he paused judiciously to
gather irony in his tone, "I greatly admire your insight in ferret-

---

* AUTHOR's NOTE: During the World War the Briey Iron Fields, owned by Comite
des Forges of France was captured by Germany. Authorities claim without this iron
supply Germany could not have continued the war. Time and again French generals
moved to bomb or recapture Briey. Always the order was countermanded by hidden
powers behind the line; not once was Briey assaulted until finally taken by Pershing. Did
munition makers want the war to go on?... After the war, Krupp of Germany sued British gunmakers for a royalty on hand-grenade patents. The Royalties were paid. Krupp
collects profit on a device used to slay his own countrymen.... The Thyssen interests
of Germany sold arms and cavalry horses to the Allies through Holland. Exposed and
fined by angry Germans, they were later excused by the Kaiser's government... Many
newspapers, European and American, are controlled by munition companies. Comite
des Forges operated papers in Paris, Nobel Dynamite in Sweden, etc. Papers never
notable for editorials on peace.

ing out the faults of my competitors. It has caused me to respect so bold and facile a pen."

The monocle winked. Screwing his body in the wheelchair, Garganoff made a jerky nod at the Negro. The Nubian's hand flicked in and out of his liveried jacket, produced a dove-colored envelope, flipped it carelessly on the desk. The envelope skated across the polish; came to rest an inch from the edge, exactly in front of John Keats.

Keats could feel his mouth going dry. A sleepy heaviness lay on his eyelids. Casually he picked up the envelope. His pupils dwindled.

Garganoff blinked his bead eye. "From one who admires your literary talent," he said squeakily, hitching his long body in the wheelchair.

The envelope was bulky. Unsealed. Keats pried back the flap with a thumb, grinned down at the contents. A crisp green slab belted with a fat rubber band. American currency. He fanned the edges with a finger, counting. One-thousand-dollar bills. Twenty of them.

His throat wanted a drink, and he said dryly, "I see," and shied the envelope back on the desk, not forgetting to tuck in the contents.

Garganoff nodded, apparently amused; made another head-bob at the black onyx footman behind his chair. Another envelope skidded at Keats. He waited a minute before touching, then picked it up with deliberation and a harder grin.

"Thirty thousand more," the black-robed figure purred, grimacing its death mask. "I am more than an admirer, my dear young friend. I am a patron. Surely fifty thousand dollars will compensate you for a long vacation—let's say a two-year leave of absence—from your strenuous literary activities."

KEATS SNAPPED his fingers and shot the envelope in a carom against its twin. His mouth worked pleasantly, but his voice had roughened. "Thanks. Generous. And of course the minute I stepped out of doors with that money on me, a Rumanian detective would haul me in, evidence and all, for black-mailing you."

Garganoff pouted, underlip outthrust, curling down over his goatee. "Come now. For an American you show a sense of European intrigue far beyond ordinary. You hardly do justice to the honor of a respected house."

Once more he jerked his head at his Ethiopian golem; and obedient to this mystic signal a third envelope sprouted from the African's velvet jacket and came sledding over the desk. Keats sighed; opening the bulged parcel. This time his eyes on the green sheaf of bills were dark, hot. Numbness assailed his temples. He knew Garganoff was watching closely. That peculiar sore-throat voice was speaking, altered in quality, sweetened.

"The third—and I am afraid, last—envelope. Fifty thousand dollars. Added to the others it will total a hundred thousand. I trust you will have a charming holiday."

Keats considered the packet, turning it in prickling fingers.

The sugared voice clucked, "Now then, now then, you needn't be afraid. You know the Gobell Dynamite Trust? You know their offer of the Gobell Peace Prize? As controlling stockholder, it becomes my privilege to make the award. You will find my secretary has prepared a statement for public announcement. As a committee of one, I have voted to increase the award, and have picked you as this year's winner in view of your zealous newspaper work on behalf of disarmaments."

John Keats stood up swiftly. Spearing out a hand, he snatched the envelopes, stuffed them into the pocket of his coat. Whipping on his hat brim low, he grunted, whirled, started for the door. Long strides took him the length of the room where the Negro and the Great Dane had outflanked him; the Negro bowing, holding open the door. But then, on the threshold, Keats spun. Confronting the room his face was suffused, jaw jutted, mouth drawn at one corner, eyes savage as quinine under the slanted hatbrim. With furious hands he tore the three envelopes from his pocket, sent them spinning back through algid candlelight.

"You can tell your committee of one that John Keats declines the prize without thanks."

The black-robed figure in the wheelchair had jelled. Engloomed in distant perspective, the face of Garganoff beyond the desk seemed to shrivel,

John Keats

age, the white features go cataleptic. One glassy eye was a candle, and only the scarlet lips moved. "I think you are making a great mistake, my dear young sir. I might even say, a dangerous mistake."

ON THE tower staircase Keats did not look back. Prickles continued on his forehead when he reached the reception chamber where the Russian secretary with the wen returned to him his automatic, apologizing in elegant Oxonian English, "Sorry to have asked it from you, old man. Count Garganoff permits no weapons on the premises, don't y' know."

In the entrance hall with its piffling crowd of footmen and foreigners, Keats was merciless with an elbow, and near the doors he jostled someone in a military cape who turned with a sharp expletive of protest, met eyes with Keats, then instantly melted in the crowd. Vague recognition in those fleet-glimpsed eyes disturbed Keats, but he hurried from the hall with a shrug, not caring if he'd slammed a rib from the King of Rumania. It was good to be out in the air. His bootheels drummed on a drawbridge, carried him rapidly down a courtyard. Hot sunlight baked the cobbles beyond an arched gate where Crazy Hooper, Universe News camera man and world's wildest air pilot, was waiting half asleep in a rented Mercedes sedan.

Keats woke the freckled eyelids with a snap. "Bucharest airport and step on it. I've got just time to catch that noon airliner for Teutony if I hope to cover that conference story tonight."

Crazy yawned, "Gee, and I got to catch a plane for Athens, Greece," unwinding like a cat, and stamping on the starter. The long car streaked out of the drive, hummed down a mountain road golden with sunshine. Woods went by like green soup and stray geese hollered, getting out of the way. Keats scowled at the landscape, then swung at his companion with a snarl.

"Listen, Crazy, you still carry that doctor's certificate on you? The one that proves you're sane?"

The lank freckled one at the wheel grinned. "Sure, buddy, and what's harrowing you?"

"A hundred grand," Keats snarled. "You'd better lend me that certificate. I'm the one ought to be carrying it."

The period to that sentence was a glassy jangle. The pane broke in the sedan's rear window, and an invisible bee passed between them and on out through the windshield, leaving a penny-sized hole and a little whorl of cracks. Crazy draped his chin on the steering wheel, and gasped, "Jerusalem!" two-wheeling the car at fifty on the turn. Looking back, Keats saw the highway behind was empty; pool-green woods and a yellow ribbon of deserted road. But a mile behind on the mountain a little dark cluster of towers made shadows against the sun. That was all.

CHAPTER II

FOUL SKY!

WELL, THE MORNING had started off with that bang, but this acuteness in the atmosphere of the Teutonic capital, this peculiar awareness that came over John Keats as he watched the city from the hotel terrace, was something else. Garganoff Keep, those Transylvanian mountains, were a million miles away; he had angrily dismissed the episode from his mind. Nothing but a squeaking old tycoon trying to bribe the press, and ghost stories plus a medieval castle had exaggerated the melodrama. More than likely the bullet had been the stray shot of a pheasant hunter or some fool Communist.

But a feeling of impending events, a big story about to break, persisted. The dusk had an air of bated expectancy that bothered his skin. Keats scolded himself mentally, "What's come over me tonight? I'm nervous as a fiddler's foot. If I hadn't been so darned Puritanic I'd be out of this dizzy European merry-go-round and no more dumb assignments from the Big Boss."

The Big Boss's wire was in his pocket. *Interview Garganoff. Cover Conference Between Von Speer and Gatreau.*

Lord, but he was sick of interviews and conferences. Sick of dashing from one country to the next, playing Peeping Tom for the press, listening to statesmen spread the same old oil. Take the pair who were up in the hotel now, wining and dining behind locked doors like a couple of gods on Olympus, getting a little stewy on champagne and words, talking of countries as if they were cuts of pie. He could vision the futile headlines.

13

"Foreign Minister of Esperance Confers with Premier of Teutony."
And the story: "The fiery minister from the Republic across
the Rhine repaired at once from Tempelhof airdome to the
Hotel Metropole for his unofficial rendezvous with the Teuton
Premier. Gatreau, famous for his patriotic speeches, his noto-
riously savage temper and record for duels, meets Baron Von
Speer, stern-jawed, many-uniformed Iron Premier second only
to Schnitzler in power over the Central Empire. Conversations
of extraordinary and private nature take place over friendly
dinner table. Because Vasil Garganoff, Rumanian arms king,
was also invited, it is believed the discussion may have bearing
on the armament race reaching a climax between Esperance and
Teutony. Garganoff, ill, will not attend—"

So what? Gatreau had promised startling revelations for the
press immediately after his talk with Von Speer, but nothing
was liable to come of it save higher taxes for everybody. Keats
scowled across the hotel terrace at breathless, hot-yellow dusk
from a sky early darkened by a threat of rain. Wanting relief from
a furnace-hot day, the city was holding its breath. Yet it seemed
to him as if springs somewhere had been wound another notch,
and the world was going faster. The crowds on the avenue, the
darting taxis, the dodging pedestrians, the methodical police
whistles, everything was hurry, hurry, hurry, and he wondered if
that wasn't dangerous when people were going Nowhere.

KEATS EASED his shoulders in the confinement of his sticky
dinner coat and watched arc lamps constellate the lindens of the
park opposite the hotel. Over there the foliage looked thirsty.
A stiff-necked statue of Emperor Ludwig stared down with
disapproval at a sprinkler playing on a scarlet canna bed. Pigeons
hopped near the shower; lavender pigeons and white pigeons,
fat and pompous as the delegates to the Brewers Convention
who came jostling up the terrace to crowd the hotel lobby with
gutturals and stomachs.

Not a normal July heat, but a dead, torpid haze clung in the
twilight, and in this heat people were hurrying Nowhere like

the electric letters that ran around and around the edge of a
roof down the block, chasing themselves off the lighted track
only to reappear in the same hustling procession. Keats watched
the electric sign. *Nach dem Rasieren—TARR—Keine trockene
Haut—Keine Flechten—Kein Spannen*—Ad for shaving lotion
or something. The words looked leaden, hot. What a language.
The letters moved with the same clicking, upright discipline that
characterized those Work Troopers you saw in motor lorries on
the avenue.

Youngsters in mustard-colored uniforms came down the
plaza in a jolting truck. They wore flat-crowned visored caps
with military chin straps that made Keats think of a coal miner's
cap back home, and each carried on shoulder a shining work-
man's spade. On the sleeve of each was a circular arm-band and
the famous Trefoil Insigne—that queer medieval symbol, a
squared black cross clover-leafed at the four tips—designating
the wearer a member of Schnitzler's Guard.

A banner flagging from the truck said, "We Were Born To
Die For Teutony." Everywhere in the country you saw these
boys, chopping timber, building roads, marching. He wondered
if all these people had been born to die for Teutony; the flat-
heeled, hurrying stenographers, the University Korps students
in drinking club caps, the small boys in gym pants bicycling
for some beach, the two Reichswehr officers strolling by, their
polished spike-helmets breasting the tide of derbies and straws
like a pair of little iron dreadnaughts cruising.

He stirred uneasily in his chair. Down toward the Potsdam-
merstrasse a tower clock pointed seven. Conference wouldn't be
over till nine, probably, and he'd have to wait. His glance idled
back to the park where a man had halted under a street lamp
to observe the pigeons. A stout individual in shapeless clothes,
the man was puffing a pipe the size of a small saxophone, and,
as Keats watched, he pulled a paper sack from his pocket and
tossed breadcrumbs while the fat birds squabbled around his
feet.

Keats grinned at the quaint figure, recognizing Anton Stehli, senior press correspondent from Switzerland. John Keats didn't know it then, but a time was coming when he was going to remember that picture. Afterwards, looking back through the dark binoculars of memory to that evening of portent, John Keats was going to focus his glass on incidents so trivial in themselves as to seem of no moment at the time, and mark how man's commonest gesture might drag him into a maelstrom.

There was Stehli, feeding pigeons under that lamp on the park. Then Alexandra Frantsovna with her little gilt-edged book—a little book that was to make more mystery for John Keats than could all the fury and drama between its covers. Then Nielsen sweating up the terrace in the heat; young Shepler's quest after handkerchiefs; Emmerich's stroll for cigarettes; Dubail, gesturing to touch a scar. A lift of the eyebrow, an unconscious turn of the head—that is the shape of Destiny. Tomorrow is an ambush built of yesterday's commonplaces, and Hell may start from a meaningless nod.

John Keats didn't know it then. He only watched an old man tossing crumbs, until a voice from across the café table on the terrace interrupted his reverie.

HE SWUNG at his table companion with a self conscious start, his grin apologizing, making him better looking than he was. "I'm sorry. I was watching Anton Stehli in the park over there. I—I'm afraid this heat is making me rude. What are you reading?"

Alexandra Frantsovna closed the little gilt-edged volume by her plate, and brushed it into her lap. "Just something to polish me up on my English. We dine together," she accused with a smile, "and for the past quarter hour you stare off at space as if I am not here. It is hardly flattering." She regarded him, elbow on cloth, chin in palm. "Something troubles you? I have not seen you before with so much—what?—the fidgets."

"But you've only seen me a few times, Alexandra Frantsovna."

"I should like it to be oftener."

He laughed, but, inwardly abashed, made a business of replenishing her glass with *kirchwasser.* The Russian girl's forthright way of speech had a trick of confusing him. Ever since Stalin had told the Japs to "keep their pig's snout out of his cabbage patch," John Keats had credited the Soviets with almost saying what they generally meant.

"You remember the first time we met?" she wondered.

"Sure. Kreuger's suicide. Paris. You beat us on the scoop."

"And last time I saw you, it was in Helvania."

"Almost five years ago. The coronation of Queen Roberta."

"Was she not charming?" the girl remembered. "You beat *us* on that scoop. You know, I always wondered how you got the inside story there—"

He shrugged. "Yankee luck; ever hear of it?"

"I should say," Alexandra Frantsovna smiled. "But I recall a story that you and the Queen were good friends. A romance, perhaps."

"That sounds like our superannuated snooper over the radio. Damn these Walter Busbies who know everybody's business but their own. What's a Queen to do with a common newspaper correspondent?"

For a moment the girl's fingers lightly covered his hand. "I am sorry, John-Keats," she hyphenated the name. "I did not know it meant anything to you."

"It didn't," he bit out. "Honestly, the way some people talk you'd think Europe was a novel by Anthony Hope. I don't believe in romancing out of your class."

"I did not think you Americans believed in class."

"You're thinking of Russia," he said severely, "there's no class there." But he took that back. Directly. She was leaning across the table toward him, and he couldn't help admiring softly moulded shoulders under a Pilgrim-wide collar of ivory lace. Class enough in that blue tea gown trimmed with Volga handwork or whatever it was. Most female journalists, Yankee or European, were liable to faint black mustaches and hobbyhorse eyes.

DECIDEDLY ALEXANDRA FRANTSOVNA'S eyes, gray-blue, smiling under the chic bit of veil, were not hobbyhorse; she did not wear a mustache. Hair curling from under her tight little hat caught an auburn spark from the terrace lamps; and he was suddenly conscious of shapely slimness that others at adjacent tables were turning to appreciate. He observed he was getting old.

"And just why did these diplomats have to pick this crowded hotel for a conference on the hottest night of the year?"

"Gatreau's doing," the girl explained. "Von Speer would not go to Esperance, so Gatreau insisted on a private hotel instead of a marble hall in the Reichspalast. All very secret it is, and nobody knows just why."

He jerked a thumb toward the lobby. "It's an oven in there. Jammed with secret police and brewers on convention. A lot of hot air."

"I got in this morning from Moscow, and it was all I could do to get a mop-cupboard at the end of the hall. I wish I were a man. You gentlemen of the press are lucky, all in the same room and in the conference suite."

"Like the Tower of Babel," Keats grunted. "Six of us in together. Dubail from the *Etoile*. Emmerich—*Illustrierte Tageblatt*. Old Stehli from Switzerland. Youngster named Shepler from the London *Observer*. And Nielsen of the Scandinavian press. He isn't here yet."

The Russian girl exclaimed, "All the first-string correspondents on the Continent. John-Keats, what is happening? You think war—"

He smiled at gravity in her eyes. "Dah. There's been going to be a war ever since the Armistice twenty years ago. Same old wolf."

"But this mysterious meeting between Gatreau and Von Speer—"

"Just talk. They're probably up there haggling an arms agreement. Teutony will have three wheels on a gun caisson if Esperance promises to sharpen only one edge of a bayonet. Signifying nothing."

"I feel it differently," the Russian girl said quietly. "Things are in a balance. Soldiers, soldiers marching everywhere. Europe is a working wine bottle. Somewhere the bottle is being shaken. All these assassinations, lately. Dolfuss. The Polish minister. The Rumanian. Barthou. King Alexander. Duke Michal in Helvania. All in the last several years. Another shake, I think, will pop the cork, John-Keats. But there is one man I could like to see assassinated."

"Who's that?" Keats grinned.

Her voice was low. "Baron Von Speer."

HIS GLANCE swerved uneasily. No telling who might be listening in this café crowd. Terrace tables were thickly populated with officers and one could be jailed in this country for such observations.

Alexandra Frantsovna was saying in a somber tone, "During the Great War Von Speer led a column of Uhlans through my father's village in Russia. His staff occupied our house, and I remember him as a fierce colonel with stiff mustaches and a shaved head. It was he who ordered my humble father shot. Now I am grown up, and must politely interview him for the Soviet papers—"

Glass doors opened suddenly on the balcony behind his chair, and Keats whipped to his feet with a warning glance at his companion. But the girl's closed lips were smiling again, and his own features brightened.

"Dubail! Emmerich! Shepler! We saved chairs for you—"

Arms linked, the three newcomers moved onto the terrace.

"*Sacré!*" That was Dubail, a dapper man, taller than was average among his countrymen, spruce with polished black hair, trim Latin mustache, jet eyes quick as a squirrel's. He advanced to the table, walking with a not ungraceful limp into lamplight that touched a thin scar, no deeper than a pock-mark, that made a faint pencil-line from left cheekbone to ear. His mouth was sardonic. "What surprise to find our confirmed American bachelor occupied with so charming a lady."

Keats introduced. "Alexandra Frantsovna—Raoul Dubail."

"I know her." The one-time Foreign Legion ace, who had dipped his sword in ink to become one of his nation's leading newswriters, gave the girl a slim hand. "Did not *mademoiselle* beat us on the Kreuger story?"

"And this is Paul Emmerich."

Emmerich bowed. Tallest of the group, he was direct contrast to his Gallic companion, blue-eyed, blond, meticulously shaved. There was gravity in his angular forehead, the upright flaxen head distinguished by a streak of gray on the crown, but his warm smile encouraged friendship. In his lapel he wore the bit of black and white ribbon which identified him as a World War veteran of the Kaiser's vanished day.

"Greeting, *fräulein*. We spent an evening once in Warsaw together covering the Pilsudski *putsch*. Allow me to present a new member in our ranks—Philip Shepler from London."

Alexandra Frantsovna gave the young Englishman a bright smile; and Keats wondered what rich uncle owning stock on Fleet Street had sent this lad into the battle-front of typewriters and headlines. The boy wore an eager expression enhanced by curly ginger hair and those pink cheeks so surprising in Britons reared on an island of watery skies and fog. You could almost see the diploma in Journalism with the ink just drying in his pocket.

THE BOY was admitting, "You knew, Miss Frantsovna, I always pictured Russian ladies as—well, in fur hats and fur-top boots doing that dance where they fold their arms and kick their heels along the floor."

She smiled, "And instead of that, we are so civilized in Moscow we ride in one of those terribly smelly American subways."

"Regard!" Dubail pointed from his chair. "Is that Anton Stehli over there in the park who feeds the pigeons?"

Keats nodded. "Been there half an hour."

"A character, that one," Dubail chuckled. "Prefers pigeons to people. Writes like Voltaire and goes about shabbier than Villon. You know he lives in a little Alpine cottage and breeds those birds? I think we need more like him in this world. Myself, I just came here from a delightful murder story in Brussels." He lifted a brow at Keats. "And you?"

Crazy Hooper

"From Bucharest."

"Where, then, is that elongated camera man who goes with you?"

"Crazy Hooper? Gone to Greece to film a church pageant."

"He should have come here," Paul Emmerich said in his carefully schooled voice, amused. "This brewery convention is every bit as red in the face. *Ach,* what heat. Perhaps our two statesmen will suffocate and we can all go swimming."

"An idea, Paul," Dubail suggested with a twinkle. "Maybe all our statesmen should suffocate, the way they smother Europe with empty words. 'Allo." He leaned from his chair. "Here comes our star reporter, Kurt Nielsen."

A Benz taxicab squealing to a halt at the pavement below brought red and gold bellhops swarming down the terrace to assault the opening door. But the gaunt man unfolding from the rear seat shooed them away, and proceeded up the incline carrying his big yellow kitbag for himself. Tweeds and linen spats, blackthorn stick crooked in arm, rakish cap, monocle in eye, the Swedish press correspondent had the air of a Hollywood celebrity making an entrance.

"These Swedes!" Dubail grimaced at Keats. "Rich as a bank and will not spend a tip to let a porter carry his luggage. Amazing fellow, this Nielsen. He has beat me to every big story in Europe for the last two years. One day he is in Rome. Tomorrow in Esthonia. How does he do it?"

"Money," Emmerich guessed. "His syndicate must pay him a fabulous allowance."

You got it for yellow journalist stuff, and Nielsen's articles were loud with jingo and war clouds. But the Swede was a crack writer, and Keats watched the gaunt man's progress up the terrace with a twinge of envy. Nielsen scanned the group at table with nods of recognition; set down his expensive bag and touched his temples with a pocket handkerchief.

"I say, it's hot enough in this city to boil water-pipes. Had a rotten train ride up from Stamboul." His manner conveyed genial self-assurance; the sort of man who knew how to draw off his gloves. His speech was cool, mild with its Scandinavian accent.

"How is the conference going? The press has reserved a room?"

"The Bureau managed our accommodations," Paul Emmerich offered. "I don't know who pulled the wires, but we're right in the conference suite."

"I'll take you up, Nielsen," Keats offered, pushing back his chair. "I left my pipe up there."

TOGETHER THEY entered the steaming lobby, and Keats steered the way up an Imperial staircase, across a dim-lit mezzanine to what once had been, in better days, a Royal Suite. Nielsen protested about humidity and trains and English kitbags, but with consistent thrift refused a bellboy. A press card let them past a brass-hatted officer into a private hall. Three doors in a row off this inner corridor; the middle door to a dining room standing closed, two wooden Reichswehr soldiers posted on guard. To the left the door hung ajar on a roomful of secret service men, and the door on the right opened into that chamber assigned to the press.

One of those Gay Nineties bedrooms, fusty as faded elegance, high-ceiled, gloomy, a big square box of a room trimmed in feverish red. Cots had been ranged along one wall, dormitory style, luggage was strewn in manful confusion, typewriters cluttered a table waiting tomorrow's headlines. Ordinarily rival newspaper men would prefer more elbow room, but the convention had taken all available space. Keats glared at two side windows that looked out on a brick court. Typical of European windows, they were closed. He opened them while Nielsen stowed his bag in a corner, unpacked a dinner coat, stripped out of tweeds and ducked into the bathroom for a shower.

Alone, Keats hunted his pipe, thoughts going bitter. He paused before a full-length mirror on a door at room's end to dourly contemplate an untouched portrait of John Keats. Why hadn't he taken that hundred grand from Garganoff this morning? Why hadn't he accepted the Gobell Peace Prize? If that weird old goblin wanted him to lay off the Hertha Gun Works—and that was a laugh, because he never had any dope on the Hertha Works—

Keats glared at the mirror, features stiffening, breath stopping. Then he dropped to one knee, electrified. Voices. Behind the door.

"We must tell all! All!" That was Gatreau's accented voice, faint through glass and wood, barely audible above the pour of the bathroom shower. "The fate of Europe depends on us, Von Speer."

That was the dining room in there! "The fate of Europe," came the Teuton Premier's guttural basso. "But we must obliterate this monster by another method—Teutony cannot disarm—when our spies tell us the Helvanian chemists are inventing a secret gas that can wipe out an army in one second—"

And Helvania the only country in Europe preaching disarmament! What a story *this* would make! Keats saw the door was locked, the keyhole sealed, and would have bartered his soul for a look into that room. Newspaper training wouldn't let him take his flattened ear from the panel.

"But think!" Gatreau's shrill pleading came thinly. "We cannot wait! The lives of millions of men depend—"

The voice faded to a blur on the lives of millions of men; and the life of one man almost faded to a blur at that moment. *Zang!* Something sharp streaked over John Keats' shoulder, ripped a stitch from his coat collar, made a ringing shiver of light against the door-jamb, dropped to the carpet. He made a cat's spring sideways, snatching up the knife as he spun. Mist broke on his forehead. The room was empty!

NOBODY THERE! Door to the hall was closed; Nielsen in the bathroom, shower running. Bathroom door hadn't opened; he'd have seen it in the full-length mirror. Table, luggage, cots— his eyes raced the chamber—the *windows!* "Damn!" Thick lace curtains were pinned back, panes raised, and in the blatantly lighted room he'd made a dandy target. Cutting an oath through set teeth, John Keats crossed the floor in a crouch, slowly reared his head above the nearest sill. A breath of torpid air sallied in from the dark court outside: a brick wall beyond was pitch save where parallelograms of light were cast by windows of the hotel. Fifty feet down was an alley, sheer drop on both sides, a dim chasm peopled with the shapes of ash cans.

Must have come from the roof across. Chimney pots were almost level with the bedroom windows, but scanning the black roofline, he could discover nothing. Wait! On a taller building beyond, high above the murmur of the street, a procession of little electric letters marched around a corner in the night. *Nach dem Rasieren—TARR—*and as the sign spelled itself out, a lambent shine came down across the chimney pots, picked out the peak of a gable, touched a shadow that detached itself from the silhouette of a chimney to move into deeper darkness.

Might be a cat or a head—there!—a man's head—no, a

woman's—somebody, anyway! Keats maneuvered a leap for his suitcase, found his Colt automatic, returned to the sill in a bound. Too late. A mouselike scurrying, and whoever that shadow was, it had gone.

In the bathroom the Swede was singing to the splash of water. Detectives muttered in the outer hall. Down below, the lobby was an undertone noise where the brewers chorused a drinking song. Next door the Foreign Minister of Esperance and the Premier of Teutony exclaimed over the fate of a continent and a secret gas that could wipe out armies; and John Keats, American, pulled down the bedroom shades and stood white-lipped, staring savagely at a six-inch thunderbolt that had severed thread from his collar.

He turned the knife in pallid fingers, careful of the razor-honed blade. Handle was stubby and heavy as solid silver, and there was a dime-sized trademark stamped in the hilt. When he made out that design, a cold muscle pulsed in his stomach and his legs felt weak. The hallmark was a double-headed eagle.

"Russian!"

A second he considered dashing for that neighboring roof, but water going off in the bathroom changed his intent. Dodging to his suitcase, he stowed the blade under a sheaf of shirts, and was at the sideboard when Nielsen stepped out in a towel. He discovered his pipe, stoked it while the Swede shrugged his long body into dinner clothes; together they left the suite and crossed the mezzanine. On the stairway Nielsen halted, looked down.

"I've got to locate the public stenographer before this brewery bunch date her for the evening. Did you ever see such a mess?"

The lobby was jammed with a crush of reddened faces. Handkerchiefs, in collars, the conventioneers were singing. The tall room boomed, red plush and gold. At lobby's end a Trefoil flag draped a heroic-sized portrait in oils of August Schnitzler. Men saluted the painting with its matinee-idol forehead and smear of mustache. Nielsen's monocle jeered.

"He'll have to work fast to keep those salutes. Start a war or something. Only way he can hold power and make 'em forget next winter's starvation. Well, I'll see you on the terrace. And who's the fair lady dining with the press?"

Keats cleared a cluttered throat. "Alexandra Frantsovna."

"From *Izvestia*, eh? Smart reporter. Seems to me I saw her two years ago in Spain. They'd arrested her as a Communist or something. She kissed the judge, you know, and got off. Damn clever, these Russians."

Keats masked his face with pipe-smoke and, his mind a dark whirl of thoughts with a knifeblade bright in the vortex, hurried out to the terrace. Anton Stehli had deserted his park pigeons to join Raoul Dubail at the table. But young Shepler, Emmerich and Alexandra Frantsovna were not there.

"LEFT ME sitting all alone until Stehli joined me," Dubail answered the casual question. "The English lad hurried down the avenue, saying he wanted to buy some handkerchiefs. Emmerich's gone down to the bar after cigarettes. Your lady friend, Frantsovna? She was paged in the lobby just after you escorted Nielsen upstairs. Where is the good Swede?"

"Inside finding himself a public stenographer."

"He should find a boilermaker," Stehli growled, bunching whiskered eyebrows at Keats, "the sort of junk he likes to write. Bah!"

Tilting back in his chair, Keats nodded at the old Swiss without hearing what was said. Two shaves in one day, and this last had been close. The barber had meant business with that Russian blade. He tried not to stare at Frantsovna's vacant chair where the girl had left her evening bag, gloves, the little gift-copy book. Hurried off without time to gather her things. And here was Shepler back, mopping pink cheeks and saying something about stores all closed; and Emmerich coming out of the lobby, tearing open a pack of Regattas, bowing formally at friends near by. Hot light streamed across the terrace as the lobby doors swung;

the plaza made a summer-night drone; everybody discussed the weather.

And presently Alexandra Frantsovna's slim figure came swinging through shadow and lampshine, trailed by the debonair Nielsen. As the girl took the chair at his elbow, Keats pretended attentiveness to an argument started between Emmerich and old Stehli. Plump face ruddy with intensity, the Swiss was thumping the cloth under Paul Emmerich's smile. Words and smoke poured from Stehli's mouth, from the gray mustache that pronged down over his lip like a hayrake, from the beaky nose, seemingly from polished blue eyes and ears.

"Look, Paul," he was puffing. "You know your country refused to pay its debts, yet it has secretly bought armaments. Tons of steel, ore—"

"And," came Emmerich's patient reply, "can Teutony stand unarmed while the Allies go on arming? Schnitzler only wants—"

Stehli said furiously, "Do not mention Schnitzler. Because I am a Jew I can hardly get alive through this country—"

Emmerich gestured sympathetically. *"Nein.* Myself, I have never approved of Schnitzler's anti-Semitic campaign. I wrote against it."

"But, Paul," Dubail put in, "your writings were never published. Only the fact your uncle is a Reichswehr general saved your job for you."

"Teutony was desperate, driven to desperate action," Emmerich defended quietly. "My country was starving, beaten, going to mental, physical and moral ruin. Schnitzler has ended all that. Unfortunate the Hebrews had to suffer, but is it not a law of life that a few must suffer for the good of the majority?"

Stehli snorted. "Schnitzler has not ended hunger here."

"Perhaps no. But he has taught the hungry to march with lifted head."

"March toward what?" the Swiss fumed. "March clanking toward an abyss, that is what. These boys in uniform with work shovels, I say they go out to dig their own graves, for tomorrow those shovels will be guns." The old man's scornful glare circled the table. "What is the matter with humanity? Regard Emmerich, here, and Raoul Dubail. As boys, classmates in a Holland university. Next, enemies fighting on opposite banks of the Rhine. Today the

Count Vasil Garganoff

best of comrades. Tomorrow—what? Perhaps dead. Carrion like my only son who was accidentally butchered by a stray shell during the last war. It is the fault of idiot statesmen like the fools upstairs. If *they* had to fight our wars, things would be different, I tell you. No, they sit in easy chairs and tell the rest of us to go. We ought to kill them before they start the next one, imbeciles like that."

Nielsen's voice drawled, "Only a spark will start it, too."

"I would not go," Stehli snarled. "I would kill no man."

"I've done all the fighting I will ever do," Raoul Dubail said with irony. "What avail? We are right back to where we were in Fourteen."

Paul Emmerich shook his head. "It is too bad, Raoul. I would not wish to go again, *nein*. A pity we must even think of it."

PIPE-SMOKE HURT in Keats' throat. Killing, killing, killing, Europe talked of nothing else. Across the table the British kid was listening with excited eyes; Nielsen yawned sleepily in the heat, saying he didn't care if the pack of fools blew themselves up or not; from the corner of an eye Keats saw Alexandra Frantsovna was calmly engaged with her book. Suddenly he wanted to get out of this, out of Teutony, out of Europe. That secret tension in the dusk was drawing tighter, unseen wires of tension humming like imaginary telegraph wires—or was that hallucinary vibration noise from the hotel foyer? He turned his head. That lobby wasn't singing! That was shouting. Yells!

Flashed open by sudden uproar, the lobby doors flew wide, a tan-whiskered man ran out on a gust of sound.

"Herr Emmerich! Herr Emmerich!" The man shook Emmerich in his grip, lips blurting a muffled stream of Teuton at the tall newspaper man's ear. Next minute he was gone; Emmerich turning to the table, his face the color of old bone.

"We had better get upstairs," he said in English, voice bleak from its effort for control. "That was a man from headquarters. Von Speer and Gatreau are finished. Locked in that room up there—they have shot each other to death—"

Dubail's hand, jerking to touch the scar on his cheek, was the only movement at the table. Nobody spoke. Stricken in his chair, John Keats saw a billow of clouds had massed on the skyline behind the distant tower clock, like figures silhouetted. Moon-face of the clock said nine. The clouds were iron. Miles in the night behind them, silent lightning flashed salmon and green. A moment the formation was revealed; four misty horsemen riding high in the night. Apocalypse—

Alexandra Frantsovna saw it, too. Her glance dropped to the little book transfixed in her hand, and she read in a whisper.

"So foul a sky cannot be cleared without a storm—"

Then everybody moved at once. Thunder smashed a hot pane in the sky, the riders whirled away, rain came down like black glass.

CHAPTER III

STORM!

EFFICIENCY. THAT IS the watchword of the Teuton police; and if any organization of humans may be described as an efficient machine, the term applies to the Bureau on the Alexanderplatz, from the lowest heel-snapping rookie to the highest scientist bisecting a dust atom under a microscope. Once the *Razzia,* the dragnet, is under way, the hunted criminal is a fly pursued by a Juggernaut. The *Meldwesen* card-index system demands a ticket of every citizen in the capital, a police-card autobiography for official reference. The *Razzia* may enter anywhere, arrest any and all without search warrant, haul them in for a check-up on the cards.

But for once the enormity of a crime almost jolted the precision of this law-enforcing colossus. Someone would pay for this hue and cry getting loose. Grim police guarded the mezzanine in the Hotel Metropole, fighting back the crowd, and brass helmets swarmed the lobby, bellowing for an order that wouldn't come. An iron-jawed police captain silenced the dining room of the Royal Suite with daggerish commands. Newspaper men must line against the wall without moving. First hand to touch anything would be under arrest. This crime came under Category 18a Section DG, "double murder by gunfire"—strictly under Homicide Squad No. 1, Commission on Ballistics.

Against the wall with his companions, John Keats watched the scene through a dizzy haze. Across the room inky rain slashed the window panes, and the air was suffocating with the smell of moist heat and stale food. Bathed in an aching electric glare, the dining room had that spurious quality of a stage set, one of those parody horrors in bad wax at a ten-cent museum. Sweat-rinsed faces of policemen paraded against a bilious wallpaper designed with cupids and roses, hot damask curtains and lace, and whatever appetite might have remained after a look at the wallpaper was speedily dissipated by the unwholesome aspect of the table centered in the room.

There was history in that tableau. A detective lieutenant was gravely writing it in a notebook, and a Reichswehr private ogled it with scared saucer eyes, posed before a door at room's end—the door John Keats had eavesdropped through from the bedroom side. These statesmen had been at dinner then, but they weren't dining now. The body of Victor Gatreau, Foreign Minister of Esperance, sprawled obliquely across his end of the table, black among crystals and napery and silver casseroles, the left side of his face in a dish of foamy cottage cheese, left arm outflung across a gravy boat, fallen as if dead drunk. Not drunk, but dead enough, with a .32 automatic death-gripped in his hand, blood in his Vandyke, blood running from a hole between his eyebrows.

Simulating another inebriate posture, Baron Von Speer, Teutony's Premier, was slopped down in full regimentals in his chair at table's head, chin on chest, mouth clamped under sandy V mustache, eyes rolled upward in his brain. His white and gold-frogged uniform, otherwise immaculate, was spattered from belt to collar as if by an exploding ketchup bottle; a bullet had shot the stem from his champagne goblet; another had chipped the Iron Cross at his throat. A third bullet had torn his right arm, and a fourth had punctured the tunic under his heart. Just beyond the reach of his hanging fingers, his Lüger pistol lay on the carpet.

SCOUTING THE room with amazed eyes, Keats counted four more bullet holes in the Valentine wallpaper behind the Premier's head, and what appeared to be another above the

sealed door behind Gatreau, a puncture high in the frame under
a closed transom. Von Speer had missed widely with that one.
Good God! Facing each other across this table, the Foreign
Minister of Esperance and the Premier of Teutony had shot it
out like a pair of Kentucky hill billies. Sarejevo was "filler copy"
by comparison.

It came to Keats' shocked mind that these bullets, instead of
stopping in bone and wood, were liable to ricochet around the
entire solar system.

Dimly he was aware of Alexandra Frantsovna staring and
white at his elbow. Dubail's black eyes shining under watchful lids. Nielsen's fascinated monocle. Emmerich, Stehli and
the British kid stunned colorless by these headlines. Then the
room tensioned as Homicide Squad and Commission on Ballistics, ambulance surgeons, medical examiners, Chief of Police
stamped in. Police Chief Wilhelm Von Guhle front and center,
a grizzled man in gray military cape, eyes savage with authority
under thundercloud brows. Yanking off his gauntlets, he gave
the presswriters a pugnacious glare.

"Hardly is it necessary for me to remind you of the need for
discretion in making public this delicate case. I charge you, be
careful in your dispatches." He whirled at the captain. "When
did this happen?"

"Between eight and nine o'clock, your Excellency."

"Who discovered the crime?"

"A waiter, Gustaf, and Lieutenant Waldersee, Detective
Korps."

"Lieutenant Waldersee, describe the circumstances."

The detective lieutenant consulted his notebook. "I am in
charge of the men assigned to guard the hotel. My operatives
are stationed throughout the building, and Reichswehr men
posted in the street outside. I have a picked contingent in that
drawing-room to the left; two soldiers guarded the dining room
door. Baron Von Speer and the Esperench minister entered the
dining room at three minutes of seven. Our Premier gave explicit

orders. Dinner to be served at seven-thirty. They must not be disturbed again until five of nine, when the waiter should come for the trays. The door was to be locked meantime. These orders were carried out."

"At exactly what time did you hear the shooting?"

"We did not hear the shooting, your Excellency."

"Gott in Himmel!" the Police Chief snarled. "Men in the next room? Soldiers at the door? Nobody heard the shooting?"

"The convention in the lobby was shouting and tramping, your Excellency. Also the hall door is very thick. I understand the room was chosen for this meeting as it was considered somewhat soundproof."

"That bedroom on the right? Who was stationed in there?"

"The press, your Excellency. The locked door at the end of this room opens into it. The newspaper people have entered and left the suite at will, otherwise no outsider was admitted."

Von Guhle whirled at the writers. "Any of you hear the shots?"

One after another they answered in negative, John Keats being last to shake his head. But so much was certain—the statesmen had been alive when he'd had an ear to that door. Later, if warranted, he could tell about it, but it might entail an accounting of the knife affair, and he wanted that to wait. No time for that little mystery with this story breaking.

VON GUHLE lashed out, "If news men heard no shooting I could hardly expect it of police detectives. Go on, Herr Leutnant."

"When the waiter came at five of nine for the trays there was no answer to his knock. I knocked, and when there was no response, unlocked the door and looked in. The waiter also saw into the room, and before we could stop him, ran screaming out to the mezzanine. The room was as you see it now. Nothing has been touched."

"Those windows were all down?"

"As you see them. Nothing has been touched, your Excellency."

Snapping grim directions, Von Guhle sent men swarming about the table, and it was a relief to have that evil dinner charade crowded out of view. Keats' head choked on the thought that if it hadn't been for the kindness of some guardian angel, this batch of bespectacled scientific bloodhounds might have been analyzing his carcass on the other side of that door. Instrument cases were opened. Voices buzzed around the table. A corpulent gentleman with eyes like candies in a cookie, wheeled around from his probing with a gruff report. He flicked a pink rubber glove professionally.

"Baron Von Speer, shot four times in chest, once in neck, in upper right shoulder and right forearm. Death immediate from shot in heart. Harumph. The Esperench minister, Gatreau, has a single wound, bullet lodged in brain, killed instantly."

A man who looked like a retired violin teacher trotted forward, plucking a jeweler's glass from his eye. "Your Excellency. I beg to report the bullet extracted from Baron Von Speer's right arm is of thirty-two caliber, obviously from the automatic pistol in the hand of the Minister, Gatreau. The gun is a Belgian ten-shot, thirty-two caliber, fired until empty."

"You examined the bullet from the transom behind Gatreau?"

"I have. With only a cursory examination I am positive it came from the Lüger, nine-millimeter caliber, found under Baron Von Speer's hand. The Premier's Lüger had fired two shots."

"Ja!" Von Guhle said angrily, "and no need to ask where our Premier's bullet is lodged. Lieutenant Waldersee! I want the Central Government on the wire at once. Stand by for dispatch to Esperench Embassy. Room to be cleared for inspection by the High Command. Post guards. Until further notice, nobody will enter this dining room. *Achtzung!"*

Police jolted to attention. The lobby was an undertone tumult, but a fly blundering across the ceiling for a look made the sound of a stone drill invading an Egyptian tomb. Von Guhle turned on the newswriters a face of iron, and his words, low, crisp, dispassionate, sounded a knell.

"Herren. Those bullets will tell your story. Baron Von Speer and the Esperench minister were closeted alone in this locked room. What happened is obvious. The room is hot, they discuss opposing policies, have a disagreement. Gatreau's temper is notorious. In a fit of rage he sprang to his feet, drew his automatic, fired many shots at Baron Von Speer. Although badly wounded, our Premier managed to draw his Lüger and fire twice in return, one shot going wild. Let it be clear that Gatreau fired *first,* however, and was therefore the aggressor."

An exclamation from one of the newspaper men. "One moment, your Excellency." It was Dubail, facing the Police Chief. "If it is not too much to ask, the *Etoile* papers would undoubtedly like to know how the Teuton police fix this grave responsibility on the Esperench Foreign Minister—"

Von Guhle nodded sternly. "That Gatreau fired first is evident from his emptied gun, the fact he had time to fire ten shots while Baron Von Speer fired only two. In a last second of firing each hit the other in a vital spot. The cause of their quarrel may only be discovered when the purpose of this secret meeting can be divulged. Our High Command will be informed at once; the Esperench government wired immediately. Baron Von Speer killed Gatreau in self defense. The minister of Esperance has murdered the Premier of Teutony." Voice crashing, the Police Chief whirled on his men. "Clear the room!"

Something cold and hollow took John Keats under the belt. Remembered words whispered to mind. Gatreau's voice, faint through that bedroom door. "We must tell all—the fate of Europe depends on us, Von Speer."

If the fate of Europe depended on those two statesmen telling something, then it looked as if Europe was once more out of luck!

TYPEWRITERS BANGED, in the bedroom next door to that

dinner party of death, in Alexandra Frantsovna's cubby across the mezzanine, in the public stenographer's booth, the noise was a miniature fire of machine guns.

Nielsen, of the Scandinavian Press, dictated smoothly, pausing only to smile at blond ringlets on the necknape of the hard-eyed stenographer.

"With Von Speer and Gatreau gunning each other to extinction over their coffee cups, the war clouds are darker than ever this stormy night. Teutony will certainly demand indemnity for the murder of the popular Iron Premier. Esperance is bound to demand further investigation. With Schnitzler and Teutony in their present moods, the world waits tomorrow morning's inquest—"

Alone in her small compartment, Alexandra Frantsovna sent her polished nails flying over the keys. "Why did Gatreau arrange this secret conference with Von Speer? Why did the Esperench minister insist on that private hotel dining room? Teutonic police claim a trap, and every indication points to Gatreau as the aggressor. Your correspondent for *Izvestia* has never witnessed so wild and confused a scene. The city tonight is maddened to fever pitch. With governments and chancellories rocking under this bombshell, the Capitalist Class will undoubtedly call on Labor to avenge the fiasco—"

Shaggy head engulfed in tobacco smoke, Anton Stehli of the Swiss Syndicate was writing: "How much better our statesmen have learned to settle their differences in private, politely shooting each other down at dinner instead of sending populations to war over their mistakes. Tonight in the Hotel Metropole the world has seen something akin to honest diplomacy—"

Black eyes racing across the copy, Raoul Dubail hammered his story for the Service *Etoile* and fifty papers across the Rhine. "There is absolutely no proof that Victor Gatreau started, and is therefore responsible for the dreadful tragedy witnessed in Teutony tonight. It seems entirely possible that Baron Von Speer may have fired first and missed; that our Foreign Minister, an expert duellist, then struck the Teuton Premier a number of times before hit by a second fatal shot in the head. Only the Teuton Police Chief's opinion supports this flimsy accusation against Esperance—"

Dubail

For the local *Tageblatt,* Paul Emmerich wrote in deliberate certainty: "There is absolutely no doubt that Gatreau, by firing first, started the tragic gunfight that ended tonight's conference with our Premier. The integrity and authority of Police Chief Von Guhle, quick to apprise the facts, is beyond question. Nevertheless, our neighboring country can hardly be held accountable for the deed of an envoy who may suddenly have gone insane—"

Sweating, head aching with strain, John Keats pounded for the Universe News. "National prejudices tonight are set aflame and the crisis cannot be exaggerated. As yet there is no absolute proof as to whose hand exploded the first fatal shot in the hotel private dining room, and at this writing the death room is closed, under guard, awaiting arrival of high government officials to supervise tomorrow morning's inquest. Mystery is loaned the affair by the invitation sent to Count Garganoff, Rumanian arms tycoon, to attend. This third-party invitation seems to shake the belief of Teuton police officials that Gatreau tried to lure his long-standing political enemy to a private rendezvous where—"

KEATS STOPPED to scrub water from his palms and sympathize with the frightened expression of the British kid whose first assignment had proved a Vesuvius. Stehli, Emmerich and Dubail had already fled for their telegraph offices, the police

having clamped a restriction on local phone service. Shepler
looked up from a stalled typewriter, blurted a scared laugh.

"Bloody, what? Sit here punching this machine with those
Johnnies dead in the next room. It's—it's too big. Got my wind
up a bit—"

Keats grinned sideways. "Never mind, kid, just give Fleet
Street the details; just tell 'em what you saw. They'll write the
stuff."

The boy was sweating. "I say, Mr. Keats. They assigned me to
cover the conference without telling what it was about. Gatreau
was to have—"

"That," Keats growled, "is one of the queer angles. Nobody
knows what it's about." He hunched over his machine; heard
the boy's typewriter going; jabbed the keys furiously, and when
he signed the "30" that marks the end of a news story, and
ripped the copy from the clip, he saw the kid had gone. He sat
a moment in the chair, dragging a finger around his melted
collar. The room was lonely. Underfoot the floor vibrated from
a penetrant droning din, a roar down below as if presses somewhere were running, the news already breaking over the dam.
His eyes moved to the full-length mirror on that door where
he'd almost got it in the neck himself. Queer about that. Devilish
queer. If that dining room beyond was soundproof, and nobody
in the hall could hear the guns going, how could he have caught
whispers in here?

His scrutiny leaped to the transom. That was an answer. Must
have been open a crack, and he hadn't noticed it at the time.

Curious, he started toward the mirroring door, then choked on
an oath and rooted in his tracks, eyeballs magnetized by something on the carpet near the doorsill. A tiny object winkered and
twinkled and cast an elfin shine on a brassy metal cap that had
wedged itself between carpet and wainscoting. Wind snorted
through Keats' nostrils, and he was down on all fours, pawing
frantically at the carpet, nails digging into the woof. "Damn!" A
jeweled cufflink and an exploded shell. Another expelled shell

farther along the wainscot. A third that had been heel-smashed into the carpet weave. A fourth that had rolled to hide against the overflowing waste-basket.

Muscles worked on his jaws when he sprang to examine this little handful of finds under the table light.

"Christmas! Thirty-eights! But they weren't there when I knelt listening at that door, and—"

MICE-FEET RAN down his spine. They couldn't have been kicked under the door where the sill fitted tight, and—his mouth jarred open—Gatreau's bullets were thirty-twos and Von Speer's Lüger nine millimeter.

"Fired in here. On this side. Somebody with a thirty-eight. But you wouldn't stand here to shoot through the windows. If the transom—"

He gulped; squinted at the cufflink. Where'd that fit in? Blue-white fire, the diamond looked genuine. People didn't throw away diamond cufflinks, they lost them by accident, in a hurry. Someone had stood by this locked dining room door, shooting thirty-eights and losing a diamond cufflink. He turned the link in his fingers. Lord! The underside was monogrammed.

"*V.G.!*" Initialed in Old English, letters twined together in the gold as plain as day. Or as dark as night, when your head was spinning like a squirrel cage. What would Victor Gatreau's cufflink be doing in here when he was dead next door? Or was that "V" the Teutonic symbol for "P"? The "G" could be capital "E" in Teuton character.

"*P.E.!*" Paul Emmerich! Winking perspiration, Keats glared at the curlicued monogram. Those letters might be Swedish script for that matter. Or the Old English "G" a fancy "S" the way it was tangled with the "V." Blinded by this acrostic, Keats could have kicked the cacographer who invented monograms into a plain old-fashioned 10-point Caslon type. But it must be *V.G.*, and suddenly a name crawled under Keats' scalp and turned him cold.

"Vasil Garganoff!" If he didn't know that rheumatic old

ruffian was down there in Transylvania in a wheelchair and
nobody could get into this police-guarded suite—He stuffed
shells and cufflink into his vest and darted for his suitcase. Snapping the lock, he started backwards in new alarm. Shirts, shorts,
toilet articles spilled in a jumble across his shoes; wildly he
clawed through the mess of laundry, but the knife trademarked
with its Imperial Russian eagle wasn't there.

"Gone!" He glared around the bedroom, panting. "And you'd
have to own a press card to get in here and cop the thing. It was
one of *them!*"

Headlines could wait. Alexanderplatz police headquarters
first, if the biggest news spot in creation had to hang.

A stunning noise slapped his face as he darted from the suite
to the mezzanine. On the stairway men brawled, yelled, struggling against a fence of police. The lobby boomed.

The hotel quaked to the roar. The din was a blast that carried
John Keats through close-packed, fighting shoulders, a forest
of upflung arms, like a chip down a cyclone. It seemed an hour
before he could tunnel the mob; get through the lobby doors
into a night of swirling, black rain. *"Herren,"* the echo chased
him down the quaggy terrace, "this means war."

He halted for breath, glad of the water that struck his face.
Plaza, park, city had vanished in the cloudburst; he could see
but a single taxi anchored halfway down the block. He started
for the misty red tail-light on a long-legged run; and he was
passing that between-buildings alley when the thing hit him.
The hat was torn from his head as if by lightning. *Zzzzzzzp!* A
lethal croon in the rain. Even as he pitched around he recognized that sound. Last time he'd heard it had been that morning
on a sun-washed mountain road in Rumania.

The bullet that sang it this time ripped off his hat and left a
band of molten fire blazed across his scalp. Shock threw him
belly-whacker against a guttering brick wall. Rebounding, he
made a quarter turn, had a flashing glimpse of hotel windows,
yellow rectangles floating high in the storm; and two stories up,

silhouetted phantom black on an orange blind, the distorted shadow of an arm and a hand clutching a long-barreled pistol. The shadow streaked away, and in dimming consciousness John Keats saw it had been in a window of that bedroom assigned to the press.

His hand made a subconscious fumble for the automatic on his hip. *"Herren,"* an echo came from somewhere, "this will mean war!"

Keats' legs buckled; he slid down the wall and hit pavement. As far as he was concerned, the war had already started.

CHAPTER IV

EMMERICH

THE AIR OF the Café Guste, ordinarily a wholesome admixture of pigs' hocks and woolens and tobacco smoke and beer, had altered to an apprehension. Nobody shouted. Nobody slammed the door. Even "Gussie" himself, five feet tall and as many in circumference, two hundred good-natured pounds behind a spotless apron, moved nervously lightfoot with his stein-crowded tray aloft, pausing anxiously to catch a comment or answer a customer in low tones. Back of the mahogany bar with its glistening mirror, rows of stubby kegs, shelves of painted stone mugs with their silver roofs, Gussie shook his head at the foaming spigots and rolled uneasy glances at the coalscuttle helmet hanging over the cashbox. He didn't like this, *nein*. Not with the wife in the hospital having what certainly ought to be twins. *Ach*, and when he had just finished payment on the new piano for Frieda to take the lessons. It looked bad. Bad. Men running in the Telegraf office across the street. And talking, here, voices so low.

Talk was all right when it was loud. The favored clientele familiar to the Café Guste came here to talk as much as eat. From the great newspaper offices across the block they came; from the *Tageblatt, Abendpost, Zeitung*. From the International Bureau, too. You could tell the editors by the severe eyes of their spectacles (there was one with a face first cousin to the moose-head under the eaves) and the pressmen by the greasy overalls, and the young reporters who liked to throw dice, and the foreign correspondents by their accents. Talk was noisy and arguments voluminous over the red-and-white checkered tables. Inflation and horse racing. Elections and railroad wrecks and murders. The Café Guste knew the headlines before the world knew them.

And sometimes things that were not in the news—like the night Schnitzler's Work Troopers marched in and shot old Peter Schleuvag who had edited a Socialist daily under Ebert. Shot him right at the bar, and Gussie had smashed a bottle over one ruffian's head. Schnitzler, himself, had come next day to apologize, and the ruffians had been dismissed from his service. Dying on his feet, old Peter Schleuvag had faced the mob. "I am glad to die under a roof that once sheltered the immortal Goethe—"

Gussie, himself, had never read the poetry of Goethe, but he could read the faces of men, and tonight they filled him with foreboding. The nervous face of the Esperenchman whispering to the Swiss at a corner table. The Swedish gentleman who had joined them, and now sat lighting cigarettes one after another and throwing them away as if they were fire-crackers. Unmindful of the rain, young lads from newspaper offices hurried in and out and in again, exclaiming over latest editions. Steins stood at elbows, forgotten. Outside the soapy windows newsboys were calling. *Himmel.* And here was Paul Emmerich coming in from the downpour, wet clothes pasted black to his tall frame, eyes downcast under the dripping brim of his hat. How pale he was. Never had Gussie seen his friend so white. His pink fingers bustled to fill a stein which he slid across the bar with quick solicitude.

"For you, Paul."

EMMERICH'S SHOES squelched water into the sawdust. Tucking a folded newspaper into a wet pocket, he leaned on the bar, lit a cigarette, smiling across the match at the damp *moon* of Gussie's countenance.

"Wie besinden Sie sich?" His eyes appeared to ignore the smoke-befogged buzz about him, kindly on the stout host

"Shepler!" Keats howled.

behind the beer-taps. "How goes it, Gussie? Everything good with the wife, I hope. What is the latest from Frau Guste?"

Gussie polished his double chins with the hem of his apron. "The hospital at eight o'clock said it was good. I should hear any minute."

"And Fräulein Frieda? The piano lessons?"

"Such a musician, and only thirteen. You must come some time and hear her play, Paul." Stomach and cheeks pouted pridefully, then the blue eyes clouded. "Paul! Wet to the skin, you are, and cold—"

"It is nothing. The rain is like hot soup and will be good for the farmers." He accepted the foaming mug with a thankful nod.

"But nothing to eat," he directed. "I've got to get going." But then, instead of drinking, he stared at the painted stein moody-eyed. "Gussie, do you remember that night outside of Ypres when we sat up to our hips in mud and the rain was coming like tonight? A couple of Scotchmen with a machine gun were giving us the devil—"

"Do I remember? Those men in ladies' skirts. Shot the corporal's stripes right off my sleeve, they did—"

"Werhat das Schiefspulver erfunden? You wanted to know. You asked me, do you remember? I would like myself to know who invented gunpowder."

"Gunpowder!" Gussie considered the word with concern. His eyes puckered at the helmet over the cash box, and he put a hand on his friend's sleeve. "What is it about, Paul? What is happening? Those murders this evening at the Metropole. I have not seen such an uproar here since the Haarmann case."

It was the quiet voices, the quick low voices over the tables that made the uproar. When a mechanical piano started suddenly with the melody of "Am Springbrunnen" somebody called quietly, "Shut the damned thing off." The music stopped with a jerk. Low conversation, rapid gutturals filled the smoky warmth under the fans.

Emmerich caught his hand shaking on the mug, and he quickly put it down. Nothing, he told Gussie, was liable to happen. The killing of two important statesmen was bad news, but there were always good men to take the helm. And had Gussie by any chance seen an Esperenchman, tall, with a limp, scar on his cheek, in the Café Guste tonight? Might have come in with a Swiss?

BEFORE GUSSIE could reply, a hand on Emmerich's arm pulled him around. His slow smile disguised apprehension suddenly quickened.

"Raoul! I was just asking for you."

Dubail snapped out a hand. "We saw you come in, Paul. Stehli and Nielsen and I—we wondered where you were."

The Swiss pushed forward. "Paul, what's up? What's new?"

Nielsen drawled, "I do wish your police wouldn't shut up like mousetraps. I can't get a thing from the Alexanderplatz."

"I got off my story an hour ago," Dubail exclaimed. "Then I ducked in here out of the sauce. Stehli came in, and Nielsen just got here before you did."

Emmerich lit a cigarette with studied deliberation. "Any of you chaps been back to the Metropole?"

"Mon Dieu!" Dubail growled. "I would just as soon keep out of there. That is why I came here from the telegraph office."

Stehli said over his pipe, "I am somewhat of Dubail's mind. Do they expect us to sleep in that bedroom next door to the dead all night?"

"What's happened at the hotel?" Nielsen's head came forward.

"I went back there from the *Tageblatt* office. The editors wanted a story on that waiter who served the dinner. Couldn't locate the fellow"—Emmerich narrowed his eyes—"and there's hell to pay in the lobby. Those drunken brewers." His glance met Dubail's. "I am surprised you did not go back there, Raoul."

"I am waiting a telegram from the *Etoile* editors. It will come to the Telegraf across the street, so I thought I would pick it up here. What do you suppose became of the English boy?"

"His paper owns a branch office across town," Nielsen suggested. "The Russian girl was late, and will have a time getting a wire to Moscow. The American was smart. They lease a cable for their special flashes. He could take his time writing his story."

"Where do you suppose Keats is? Usually he comes here. His story will be in New York before mine is in Lucerne."

Dubail turned to the Swiss. "But if I had suspected such a story to break from this cursed conference, I too would have leased a wire. I do not like this affair, my friends. Tomorrow's inquest will tell. Perhaps the police will back down on their hasty conclusions." He raised his eyebrows at Emmerich.

"No," Emmerich dissented. "Police Chief Von Guhle does not

make decisions without certainty. His standing as a criminologist cannot be challenged. I covered police court for years and have never heard him at fault. But it is my opinion the Esperench minister must have gone insane—"

Nielsen asked, "Do you think war will come from this?"

"War!" Anton Stehli flung up an arm. "There was never any end to the last war, do you know that? You cannot end wars by signing a sheet of foolscap. As for Teutony, this country has been at war ever since the republic collapsed and Schnitzler came to power. War is a state of mind. This country has that state of mind. The fighting psychology. Propaganda everywhere. Such as that." He stabbed a finger at a black-lettered placard fastened above the bar mirror. The slogan read: "Only the wicked cannot bring themselves to love August Schnitzler."

"Propaganda!" Stehli iterated fiercely, gesturing his pipe. "That is the first gun in any war. What nonsense. Bah! Am I a wicked man? But I do not love August Schnitzler!"

A CHAIR scraped the floor behind the fulminating Swiss. Commotion. A broad-shouldered man, heavy-jowled, beady eyes glaring under an inflammatory shelf of forehead, surged up in the smoke. He wore the ink-smudged overalls of a press hand; and his muscled arms, shirt sleeves rolled back, flexed upward like the arms of a wrestler. His face was contorted, darkly grotesque. His thick voice bassoed at Stehli.

"Jew! Who dares speak of *Der Meister* with such insolence—"

The Swiss lifted his shoulders calmly; removed pipe from lips without concern. Smoke swam through his bushy mustache. "I do."

The man booted his chair aside. "You hook-nosed old rat—"

"Just a minute." Wheeling swiftly, Emmerich stepped toward the press hand. "These gentlemen are friends of mine," he instructed crisply. "I am Paul Emmerich of the *Tageblatt*. I do not know you. Sit down."

The man sat down.

"Stehli," Emmerich advised in English, "I know how you feel

about these things, but just now it might be wise to be careful. Mob spirit, you know what that is. The riot at the hotel was pretty bad. And I meant to tell you"—he included the others with a guarded gesture—"things are off to a serious start. I don't know why the government has shut down on all longdistance telephone service, but the long lines are all *verboten*. The editors are on their toes waiting to hear word from the High Command. Somebody, nobody knows where the report came from and it's not been verified, started the rumor that Esperance has called a special session in their War Office—"

Dubail's black eyes went luminous. *"Sacré!* I cannot believe."

"It came through to our editorial office," Emmerich insisted, "and there are some damned queer—well, unexplainable aspects to the Hotel Metropole tragedy." His glance traveled the faces grouped about him. *"Ja,* and once a rumor starts, there is no stoppage of the thing. Teutony may proclaim *Kriegsgefahrzustand,* or 'condition-of-danger-of-war.' I'd advise you chaps to cash all travelers' checks as soon as you can. And here's something straight from the inside. *Der Meister* is on his way to the capital from the south, coming by special plane."

A little bomb of smoke burst from Stehli's lips. "Schnitzler himself is coming!"

"Bones of Queen Christina, that is a tip!" Nielsen stabbed his monocle into a kindled eye. "Schnitzler rushing back from his vacation, eh? I'll shoot a wire to the S.P. at once; and then I've got to get back to our mourgish hostelry and try to dig up that xanthorous public stenographer out of some traveling salesman's room." He flirted a hand, swooping himself for the door. "This begins to look like something. See you later—"

"Morbleu!" Dubail jammed on his hat. "I must wire the *Etoile* Service. A thousand thanks, Paul, for the news."

Stehli had followed Nielsen for the telegraph office. Through the rain-curtained window Emmerich could see them as two shadows crossing the stormy gulf of the street. He made a restraining gesture, half controlled, toward Dubail's retreating back.

"Raoul!"

The other swung about with a limp. Something in Emmerich's expression brought a startled lift to Dubail's mobile eyebrows. "What is it, Paul?"

But Emmerich was merely smiling, extending a hand. "Nothing, my friend. It is eleven o'clock; I only wanted to say I would not be here if you came back from the Telegraf. I shall go out home for a while. If I do not see you—why—*Auf Wiedersehen.*"

Dubail's slim hand gripped with comradely pressure, "Remember me, Paul, to that charming mother of yours. *Au revoir.*"

THERE ARE few private houses in the Teutonic capital, but some distance beyond the outlying apartment districts the Carlottenburgstrasse quiets into an old-fashioned avenue patrolled by ancient elms and fronted by the hedgerows, formal gardens and arched iron gateways of venerable estates.

Standing proudly back from the road, the Emmerich mansion overlooked a secluded slope, flower beds on one side, willow pond on the other. From the front hedge one could not discern a need of repair, tile patched on roof and gable, the top floor shuttered dark, panes broken from the cupola. One could not see patient mending in the lace window curtains, or the garden, homely with cabbage and potato, at the mansion's back.

Paul Emmerich dismissed his cab at the gate, and swung on foot up the weedy gravel drive. The rain had quit at the moment of his leaving the Café Guste, and now the night drained and steamed. Clouds hung in green tatters on the pale shoulder of a drowned midsummer moon. Moonlight lay blue on the untrimmed lawn, silver on the dripping twigs of the elms. There was warmth in the smell of drenched grass. A frog cleared its throat in the willow pond where once Paul had raced sailboats with his brother Wolff—

His mouth set in a harsh downward curve. Wolff was gone,

no use calling up memories. No use remembering anything. A lot of things he'd have to forget this night. His hand slid down over the folded newspaper in his pocket, fingers closing on a heavy blunt object secreted in this wrapping. Thank Heaven they hadn't noticed the bulging pocket at the Café Guste!

He muttered *"Gott!"* throatily, and, nearing the house, was sorry to discover light in the curtains of the library and a lamp-shine in the window of his mother's room upstairs. Going quietly into the vestibule, he spoke a subdued greeting to Schnapps, the brown velvet Dachshund, then straightened his shoulders with an effort and turned into the library.

At the far end of the book-walled room his father sat under the mellow aura of a tasseled reading lamp, feet in carpet slippers, meerschaum in teeth, ashes down the front of his flower-patterned smoking jacket, engrossed in writing. Hearing his son's entry, Balduin Emmerich brushed aside his pad, gripped a stout cane and reared from the shabby armchair.

"Paul! I have been hoping you would come." His voice was gruff, virile. No wincing from the neuritis that had troubled him lately. One read intolerance for wincers in the leonine head, the underthrust of the jaw, dominant brows, the level demand of steely eyes. Seventy years had not dimmed the gleam of those eyes; he looked forty-five, hardly ten birthdays beyond his son. A Junker. A Teuton of the Old School.

STRAIN THICKENED Paul Emmerich's speech. "Father, I—I've just come from the *Tageblatt* office. Something happened tonight—"

The heavy man drove his cane into the rug. *"Ja!* At the Hotel Metropole. That swine of an Esperench minister killed our Iron Premier—"

"You know, then?"

"It was announced over the radio. Your Uncle Gottlieb was here and we were playing chess. A special announcement over DRX. Your uncle left at once for General Headquarters at the

War Department, saying he might return later and would wish to see you. They telephoned for him."

"G.H.Q. put in a hurry call for Uncle Gottlieb?" Paul lit a cigarette, hiding worried eyes. "Do you like the sound of that?"

His father's face smoldered, blazed. *"Aber,* I can tell you something you may like the sound of! You know my lawyers were about to put me through bankruptcy; your mother and I were on the verge of losing this house!"

Color recurred and faded in Paul's cheek bones. He had known of nothing else for the past twelvemonth. His father storming home from the factory, pacing the floor, bursting into impassioned rages at the morning mail. His mother, silent as always, moving about the old rooms with that expression of resignation in her eyes. Paul had a way of turning pale under emotion.

"Well," his father exclaimed triumphantly, "I am not to go bankrupt, *nein!* Not half an hour after Uncle Gottlieb left the house, the phone rang again. Listen! My factories go under government subsidy tomorrow morning. They are taking every bit of stock, all the material that has been idle in my warehouses for the last ten years!" His voice rang down the room. "Fifty thousand leather belts at once. Five hundred thousand leather straps! Every scrap of leather will go the first thing in the morning. Government order!"

Paul flung himself into a chair and watched his father's face, shading his gaze with a white hand. Herr Emmerich might otherwise have noticed a strange light under his son's lowered lids.

"The Emmerich Leather Company is saved!" Balduin Emmerich thundered. "That is not all. I had scarcely put down the phone when Herr Borger called from his brokerage office. He asked for you! *Ja,* he wanted to buy all those Central Chemical bonds your Aunt Elizabeth left you—"

"I know," Paul said expressionlessly. "He phoned me while

I was at the *Tageblatt,* just before ten o'clock. Offered me four *marks* a share."

"And he called here to offer you thirty a share!" Paul's father cried. "Seemed beside himself with anxiety to buy them, too. Thirty a share for those chemical bonds that last week were not worth a *guilder.* You will be rich, Paul! Rich!"

"You are elated, father?"

"Elated? Emmerich Leather saved from bankruptcy. My son suddenly rich. My house saved, no more of these tradesmen who are not fit to wipe their boots at the door making insolent demands of your mother and me. All this at one stroke, and you ask me if I am elated!"

Paul Emmerich said in a monotone, "Buying leather. Buying chemicals. Calling Uncle Gottlieb. No doubt you are aware of what must lie behind this unusual turn of events—"

"Shades of Friederich Wilhelm," his father exploded. "We are suddenly rescued from miserable poverty, and you sit there in that wet dinner suit white as a drowned cat. I could never understand you, Paul."

He countered in quick resentment, "You might be pale yourself, father, if you did the job I had to do tonight. That dirty assignment—"

"What assignment, Paul?" His mother's quiet voice in the doorway brought him out of his chair.

INSTANTLY HIS features warmed to a smile and he hurried to take her by the hands; forced a laugh, pretending to admire her faded lavender dress, with its high lace collar and old-fashioned sleeves. She was small and stately, her face delicately lined under silvered hair, and she was not fooled by his chuckle. "Paul, you are ill—"

"Never better in my life, *Mutterchen.*"

"Running about in the rain. You saw that dreadful business at the Metropole—"

He patted her hands. "It was not exactly a cheerful evening. But that is the reporter's job. Father has told you his good news?"

She nodded, watching his eyes.

"I am glad," he said firmly. "Now, then, don't you worry about that Metropole affair. I believe the Esperench minister went insane—"

"The radio announcement," Herr Emmerich boomed, "claimed the Esperenchman deliberately started shooting at Baron Von Speer, after inviting him to that private dining room and making sure nobody would come in. *Ja!* A plan to assassinate our strongest man under Schnitzler. I tell you, and I have always said, the dirty Esperenchmen are scoundrels to the last man—"

Paul reminded, "You enjoyed meeting Raoul Dubail, father."

"The newspaper fellow? He is not typical. You yourself said he appreciated the Teutons. *Gott sei dank!* our country is in a position of strength and must not take these criminal acts from the Quai d'Orsay any more. I say Esperance will pay for this crime. Pay through the nose!"

Balduin Emmerich shook a fist over his head.

"Too long we have been ground under heel by those dogs across the Rhine. We lost the war twenty years ago, and honorably signed for peace. But they kept at us, those Allies. Spurred on by that accursed Esperance. Was it not enough that we were beaten? *Nein,* but they had to starve us, undermine our finances, ring us in with steel, surround us like a land of criminals. Now they have murdered our Premier! But this time, maybe, we hit back!"

His massive voice grew in the lamplight, sentences punctuated by furious thumpings of the cane. "Despite her Allies of today, Esperance is secretly hated by every country. You think the United States would aid her after she cheated the Americans of their loans? England will sit quiet, too, and *Herr Gott!* she had better not interfere this time, or London will be blown to a heap of bricks.

"Soviet Russia will not help Esperance. To invade us she would have to cross Poland, and Moscow dare not move with

Japan on her tail. Italy will not help, now that the Duce has gone to his heavenly reward—whatever that might be—and the Italians lack a leader.* For all her famous alliances, Esperance may find herself alone in combat and have to fight even for once!"

"Please, Balduin," Paul's mother soothed. "You are so excited tonight. Your heart—"

HERR EMMERICH stamped the floor. "This is the best thing in the world for my heart; *ja,* it is! I say it is high time we had a reckoning with those murderous Esperench, and every good Teuton in the empire feels the same way."

He stabbed his cane at a map of Europe enshrined above the library desk; this was a never-tiring tirade for Balduin Emmerich. "Esperance! Alone she sits across the Rhine, thumb to nose, whiplash in fist. But *Der Tag* will come yet. Thank the good God for a strong man like August Schnitzler—"

Paul said quietly, "Only a short time ago you did not think so highly of August Schnitzler—"

"The murder of our Premier," his father boomed, "is an attack on our country. A nation's honor is above party politics. If Schnitzler is strong enough to defend our honor, I stand behind him with all my heart!" He struck the map with his stick. "We must move quickly, so! This time we go through Switzerland. We go around that beautiful wall of forts the Esperench have built between Belgium and Alsace. Ho-ho! While our bombing fleet flies straight to the Esperench capital, our army sweeps through Godek Pass in the Swiss Alps!"

"But Godek Pass was given to Helvania after Austria was broken up by the Treaty of 1935," Paul protested. "A move through that mountain corridor would involve us in war with the Kingdom of Helvania!"

Herr Emmerich regarded the blue-bordered Kingdom of Helvania with contempt. "Then we will take Helvania! Swit-

---

* AUTHOR'S NOTE: The story takes place in 1936. The author assumes for fictional purposes, without pretending to prophesy, a hiatus in the Italian Dictatorship.

zerland, Esperance, Helvania, we could smash them overnight, we who stood against the whole world—"

"Balduin, please," Paul's mother begged. "The doctor would not like you to work yourself up like this. The doctor—"

"Bah for the doctor! I am as good as ever. I tell you, I would go myself, if I had the youth."

"Go?" Frau Emmerich looked from husband to son in alarm.

Paul's arm hurried about his mother's shoulder. *"Mutterchen!* No need for all this. Father always talks this way. Nothing will happen."

Herr Emmerich's face veined crimson. He shouted, "But if something does happen it will happen fast. Air transports and motor trucks are not the slow infantry of twenty years ago. We went through Belgium last time and were stopped within twelve miles of the Esperench capital. This trip we go through Switzerland and do not stop!" His cane was a sword lashing the lamplight. "The whole world helped Esperance the last time, and we lost. This time nobody helps them—and we do not lose!"

Cracking into a throttled cough, his voice choked in his throat and he stumbled backwards, cheeks blown, eyes smudged, cane shaking for support. Paul's gasp was echoed by his mother's frightened cry, but Herr Emmerich waved them off, body struggling in inward fury. Normal color returned to his face as he found his chair, where he sat in sullen abeyance and opened one furious eye to glare witheringly at the knees that had betrayed him.

"I envy you, Paul," he panted after a little. "If I do not see the day for the Fatherland, it may come for you."

THEY HAD not heard the big car wheeling up the drive. In the vestibule the Dachshund barked; then rapid steps in the hall brought a visitor into the library. A stocky man who bowed, yanked off gauntlets and spiked helmet, came down the room with a faint clinkle of body harness, the gray skirts of his military field coat rustling at the calves of polished boots. Above the chesty buckles and tabs of a ranking general his shaved head was rigid, features saturnine, unsmiling, eyes directed at Paul.

"Gottlieb!" Paul's mother held up a cautioning hand. "Balduin has just suffered an attack—"

The general gave his sister a curt nod. "Hello, Pauline." A solicitous grimace at his brother-in-law. "Too much excitement, eh? A little quieter you should stay. But I think Balduin may not be the only one to suffer an attack." He swung at Paul. "Report has come that Esperance has cancelled all military furloughs and started a secret mobilization. And Schnitzler has declared condition-of-danger-of-war!"

Balduin Emmerich sat up fiercely. *"Kreigsgefahrzustand!"*

The general nodded sternly; shot back his cuff to inspect his wrist dial. "I have only a minute to speak with Paul. I must hurry."

Paul's lips had whitened. He began, "I'd like to thank you, Uncle Gottlieb. What you did to help father. The government order for leather—"

"The least I could do. Also those Chemical bonds of yours, Paul; I would hang on to them. They will go higher." He rested a hand on his nephew's shoulder, clipping out: "And for your distinguished service in the last war, Paul, I have seen to it that your rating in the Reserve Officers' Korps was tonight advanced to major. In case of war you will serve on my general staff. If I step beyond regulations to tell these developments, it is only because an extraordinary national emergency has arisen and I would save red tape. An aide will arrive within the hour to advise any further procedure. You will please be prepared for any exigency, and I suggest you retire at once for a few minutes' sleep," His hand snapped to his temple. *"Gute Nacht,* Major Emmerich."

Emergency! Staff appointment! Mechanically Paul Emmerich steeled himself to attention. The salute shadowed pallor in his face. *"Gute Nacht,* Herr General." Dumbly he saw his uncle go down the long room, bow himself out; heard the big car go roaring out of the drive.

His father's excited voice: "A major! *Mein Gott,* he has ranked our Paul a major. And prepare for active duty! It is the day, Paul! Your chance at last!"

Balduin Emmerich's eyes were blue fire in the lampshine. Paul listened without hearing his father's words; then walked silently from the library, following the sound of his mother's footsteps. He knew she would wait for him on the stairway landing; wait tight-lipped under the dim portraits of those unfriendly ancestors who looked down from the upper hall gallery like so many windowed ghosts. Great-grandfather Wasserman with his pitchfork whiskers and unforgiving eyes that had aimed the gun-sights with Blücher at Waterloo. Great-uncle Moritz who had died at Gravelotte. Stern old Grandfather Emmerich who had fallen before the cannon at Sedan. Uncle Wilhelm and Uncle Helmuth, grim-jawed, frowning, long-buried lieutenants under the muds of the Kameroon. And Wolff—the brother whose novel lay unfinished in the library desk and whose life lay unfinished, ashes somewhere beyond the Marne.

"PAUL." HIS mother's voice put a bur in his throat. Gently he caught and held her hand in the brown darkness.

"Paul—you will go?"

"You would not want it otherwise, Mother. The Fatherland—"

"I know." Her tone was leaden.

He said heavily, "One cannot put self above country, Mother."

"I am very tired, Paul. When the order comes for you, I will be in my room."

"Nein, do not take it so hard, *kleine Mutterchen.* They have only declared a national emergency. Surely the Esperench government will recall their rash move. We are not going to have this war."

"I will be waiting in my room, Paul."

"But, Mother—"

"When the order comes—you will stop at my door to say good-by?"

Dumbly he nodded. She released her fingers from his hand, stood on tiptoe to press her cheek against his, then moved silently through the upper hall dusk to her door.

Closing the door of his own room, jabbing angrily for the lamp-switch, Paul Emmerich stood white with clenched teeth while light blurred on his eyes and his lashes stung. A china clock on his bureau struck *ding-ding-ding* on a foolish little chime twelve times. He dragged a trembling wrist across his mouth, and watched the panel above the bureau where a tiny spider was valiantly pulling a mercurial thread between a Heidelberg rapier and the varnished splinter of an airplane propeller. Wolff's Fokker had burned at ten thousand—

Emmerich's hand dropped woodenly to his pocket, touched the weighty package under the cloth, galvanized. *"Gott steh uns bei—"*

Whipping about, he locked the door; then stepped to a tall window to throw the shutters wide. Below the window blue willows dreamed gracefully on the banks of the silver pond; the warm breeze stirred his hair with its midnight perfume, and dried the perspiration on his forehead. An oath muttered through his teeth as he dragged the folded newspaper from his coat, tore apart the printed sheets and unwrapped a long-barreled .38 army automatic.

"One cannot," the whisper lay deep in his throat, "put country above everything—"

Gripping the .38 by the barrel, Paul Emmerich cocked back his arm, wound up slowly, let fly. The automatic sighed out of the window and made a black streak through the moonbeams. Soaring in a high, slow arc, the gun flip-flopped twice in mid air, went swish through the upper fronds of a willow, and lit in the center of the pond. A nocturnal splash. Water spouted, rippled, froze flat. A couple of bubbles floated to the surface to mark the spot where the gun was nosing into mud. Then the bubbles drifted away.

CHAPTER II

DANGER OF WAR

CONSTELLATIONS OF A size and brilliance unusual to a night of rain cometed in bat-like orbits about the sky, and when the star-shower faded away, John Keats found himself coming conscious with the headache of a frontiersman who had just been scalped. Must have been lying in the alley here about fifteen minutes.

Keats saw a Reichswehr soldier standing over him.

"Betrunken!" the soldier grunted. "Coming out of it, are you? And a nasty smash you have given yourself on the head for staggering into that wall. The little boy found you before I did, and ran to summon an ambulance. You foreigners! First it is that English boy crazy with liquor climbing a fire escape to the roof of the building next door—"

"A Britisher climbing to the roof?"

"All dressed up in a fine dinner coat, too, clambering around that dirty fire escape in the rear. Ordered him down in a hurry, I did, and he ran like a rabbit."

John Keats had no time for Reichswehr soldiers just then. Butting the surprised man out of the way, he charged into the hotel. His press card opened a channel up the police-fenced staircase, and he darted across the mezzanine to find the Royal Suite guarded by a stoic Reichswehr sentry.

"Press!" Keats rasped. "Has anyone gone into or come out of that bedroom where the newswriters are?"

"Ja. A Russian woman was in there for five or six minutes.

59

After she came out a young Englishman from the London papers went through into the room. Several minutes later Herr Emmerich followed him. He came out. The Englishman is still there."

Keats stepped by the guard and entered the dim corridor, slipping the Colt from his hip pocket as he did. He entered the bedroom. It was unlighted, pitch dark. The bathroom door was closed, but a trickle of light came through the keyhole. That was it—Shepler was in the bathroom.

Stepping across the hall, Keats was suddenly attacked by a whirlwind. A knife slashed his finger, whacked the gun from his hand. Keats uppercutted blindly, heard the knife clatter to the floor as his fist landed. Claws raked the side of his face and he threw himself blindly forward. His shins banged on a wooden cot, tripping him into a hurly-burly of sheets and blankets. A blanket whipped over his face. Batting it away, Keats could grasp only empty blackness.

He found the table lamp, switched it on. The room was empty!

Springing to the bathroom door, Keats kicked it open, breaking the panel. On the floor, in a pool of blood, lay a man.

"Shepler!" Keats howled.

ONE WOULD expect the fellow to quit playing 'possum, to scramble upright and start the shooting. But Philip Shepler refused to move. When Keats pounced into the bathroom to turn the body over with sick hands, the curly boyish head lolled as if broken at the neck. The arms flopped. John Keats found his fingers smeared vermilion. He stared in an agony of disbelief at the three raw bullet-holes punched in a row across Shepler's ribs. The silk gym shirt was cherry-color.

Keats wet a towel at the tub, bathed the gray forehead. "Shepler!"

Eyelids fluttered in the pinched, unyouthful face. "I'm—hurt—"

"Who did it? *When?*"

"Don't know—" The young Englishman's eyes were glassy.

*"Come on!
What are you
waiting for?"
Keats growled.*

"I—came back from—newspaper office—going to shave—" His lips struggled on the whisper. "Walked into bathroom—bedroom light went—out—"

"Who was in the bedroom, Shepler? Who turned it out?"

"Didn't—see anybody. Lights just—went. I turned around—saw gun flash. Flame—in dark. Hurt my—chest—"

Keats gasped.

"For God's sake hang on!" The lad's face was hollowed in the

cheeks, lead-color, dropping perspiration. Keats was gentle with
the towel. "Stick with it, kid. Can you hear me? I'll get a doctor
right away—" He groaned at the futility of trying to stem blood
on the riddled gym shirt. "We'll get him for you, kid! Whoever
did this—quick, tell me! Were you on that roof across the court
tonight? The next building?"

"Yeh—roof—" the lad was panting, "I wanted—buy handkerchiefs for—my girl. Going past building—thought I saw
woman—running—side alley. I—followed—up fire escape in
back—think it was—Frantsovna—"

"Frantsovna!" Keats echoed hoarsely. "You saw her?"

"Not sure—but thought maybe—she was after news—peek
into hotel or something. I follow—but soldier in hotel courtyard—call me down—" In spasmodic strength, young Shepler gripped Keats' arm. "Please," he panted. "Don't leave me.
Don't—go away—"

Keats had been striving to fasten a bandage across the punctured ribs; but he heard the whisper trail off into silence, and
when the fingers fell from his sleeve, he saw young Shepler was
dead.

KEATS WONDERED if, somehow, he had shot the lad himself.
No, his Colt had not been fired. The kid had been dying in the
bathroom while he struggled with that unseen knifer in the dark.
Anger flamed. He had scarcely known this youngster, but the
lad's murder was a cruelty beyond reprisal. Shot down in cold
blood like this. Shut in here to die. Keats found himself rinsing
his hands at the washstand, his eyes filmed. Emmerich must
have done this job. The *Tageblatt* reporter. He'd followed Shepler into the bedroom, murdered him ruthlessly.

So much was clear, the events of a nightmare, actions without logical motivation. But the enemy he'd battled in the dark,
the creature who had faded like a banshee at the snap of the
light-switch? This bathroom made the only possible retreat, and
Shepler had been in here alone. Maddened by the impossible,
Keats sprang out into the bedroom for another search. He flung

himself at the dining room door. Locked on the dead. The hall door, too, remained fastened. Windows down and locked. Beds empty above and under. Satchels and kitbags where he'd kicked at them. He pressed his forehead with a fist. Shepler dying in the bathroom. Somebody in here, waiting in the dark with this Russian knife. Somebody who had to be here now, and wasn't.

His knees wanted to shake as he pulled shut and locked the bathroom door. No doctors could help the lad in there now. The cage wanted a Houdini. He jabbed the key into his slashed vest and paced the floor, searching walls, ceiling, furniture, with frightened eyes. What should he do? Houdini wouldn't come. Instead, they would send Homicide Squad Number 1, Commission 17K on Ballistics, Chief of Police Von Guhle with a scientific brain unlikely to accept a ghost story. Police already frenzied by the furies that had been turned loose in the next room.

One thing he knew. He must get out of this wizardish bedroom. He had to get to the Alexanderplatz, and his news story to Universe wasn't telegraphed. Hadn't he started for police headquarters once that night with a collection of .38 shells and a monogrammed cufflink in his pocket? Those shells! His fingers flew into his vest. His mouth hung open as he dug from one pocket to another. They'd been there when he'd raced from the hotel; when he took that clip on the head. He tore at the starched cloth. They weren't there now. Shells, cufflink had disappeared.

In heightened confusion, he recalled the words of the soldier in the court. "The little boy found you before I did, and ran to summon an ambulance—"

KEATS UNLOCKED the hall door, slapped it shut behind him, and wasted no time in making for the mezzanine. The lobby below was livid with a continuous, babbling roar.

He found the sentry at the suite door leaning on his rifle and calmly chewing the tips of his yellow mustache. He had not expected to find the sentry calmly chewing. He shouted because it released his feelings and he had to be heard.

"Did anyone come out of that bedroom? Since I went in there?"

The sentry squinted. "No, *mein herr.* Nobody came out."

People were behaving like maniacs at the foot of the staircase, gesturing and bellowing, cheering, pushing, snapping their fingers, saluting; but they saw the eyes under his hatbrim, the jut of his scarred jaw, and stepped out of his way. Something had happened to these brewers, these goose-footed officers, but he had no time for questions about it. "Schnitzler!" a mouth bawled into his ear. *"Der Meister* is coming to the capital!" He nodded as if it meant something. Rotating through the whirl, caroming between a gilt sofa and a fat army officer, he barged for the terrace doors. Outside he was surprised to find the night clean-washed, airy after the downpour.

There was his man. The apple-cheeked Reichswehr soldier peering out of the side court. Shadowy against the wall where Keats had fallen. He shouted; and the soldier came at him menacingly.

"That is you, *ja?* My station is by the courtyard or I would have chased you for a clubbing. You dare strike a soldier of the—"

"Hold it!" Keats snarled. He displayed his press card.

Confronted by a seal of authority, the guard was obsequious.

"I did not know, *mein herr*—"

Keats was stern.

"Never mind that! What became of the little boy you said found me against the wall?"

"The child, *ja?* But he ran off in terror to call an ambulance. He was leaning over you in the rain, trying to hoist you by an arm, the little fellow." The trooper pointed up the terrace. "Did he not run into the hotel?"

"Where did he come from? Who was he with?"

"Why, he said he was walking behind you when you reeled—"

"For God's sake," Keats shook out, "what did he look like? You are certain it was a child?"

An emphatic head-nodding.

"But a little one," the soldier stammered, "no bigger than six years old, I should say, and wearing a white sailor suit. I could not see him well for the downpour, but his hair was yellow in the rain—"

Keats interrupted with fury, "We have got to find that child, you understand? Somebody had him trailing me. I've been robbed!"

The soldier's face paled, fatuous in alarm. *"Himmel!* He was going through your pockets? But he gave me your name, *mein herr,* the same as on your press card. I thought you were his father. He said he was your son!"

"My son!" Keats echoed this lunacy with jaws unhinged. The Russian knife in his coat was not enough. His alibi needed the evidence of those .38 shells and that cufflink. What fiendish plot had flung a six-year-old child into this screeching jabber-wok of hiding murder and death? A kid, tutored by someone to trail and rob him, to claim his body in that alley under pretense of being his son! Had Emmerich ever mentioned a little boy? Frantsovna?

"You wish I should enter the hotel with you?" the soldier was mumbling.

Keats stared at that haunted upper window. What were police doing in that drawing room with a red lantern? If they visited the bedroom—That wasn't a red lantern, either. The window filled with the glow. The light grew. Now the soldier was staring. Another window caught the reflection. The glass was scarlet. There was a faint, blanketed *thump* as if an engine somewhere inside the hotel had burst. One of the window panes tinkled and came down to the terrace in a bright shower. A subtle pungence invaded the wind. Doors broke open on the terrace, spilling men.

"Fire!"

Far up the plaza the sirens were wailing again.

JUST HOW he managed to force a path through the boiling current of the mob, John Keats could never remember. Crown hysteria had Roman-candled to insanity. The hotel lobby was a madhouse. Bodies eddied and whirled around him, clawing at his coat, beating at him, hollering. Men twisted together, fell. "Fire!"—"It is a plot!"—"Somebody threw a bomb!"— "The hotel is burning!"—"Stay out of here!" A policeman's billy whizzed past his nose. "Here, you, get back!" He lowered a shoulder and drove himself through to the lobby desk, off-tackle.

Smoke was coiling and winding through the upper air; hot, brown festoons swirling, dissolving, thickening, clinging to chandeliers, weaving in pools against the frescoed ceiling. On the mezzanine, bellboys romped with brass fire extinguishers. He saw the door to the Royal Suite was bright with hot light, and beyond the frame an inner door was crackling like a grate.

A hand dropped on Keats' shoulder. Anton Stehli was standing behind him.

"The suite!" Keats shouted.

Stehli remained in his attitude of detached sadness. "We heard it. Dubail, Nielsen and I. We came in not ten minutes ago from the Telegraf, and were sitting in the public stenographer's booth. It sounded like an incendiary bomb."

"A bomb—"

"To start so violent a blaze. See, the dining room door, there, is split to kindling." The Swiss was shouting, but his expression was that of conversation. Like yelling quietly. His fingers bit into Keats' shoulder. "It is going to be very bad."

"The fire?" Keats yelled.

"No, my friend. The floors are fireproof. It will be confined to those rooms. But why did they burn that dining room, with those two in there? Did you hear the latest at your news bureau? The Teutons may declare condition-of-danger-of-war—"

Keats' hands had begun to tremble uncontrollably.

"Wait!" Stehli pointed. "Dubail and Nielsen are up there now. They will rescue our luggage if they can." He cupped his palms at Keats' head. "Have you seen the young Englishman? He will be lost in this madness!"

"I can't hear you!" Keats shouted back. "Do you know if Paul Emmerich is in the hotel?"

"We left him at the Café Guste some time ago," the answer came through the din. "Terrible things are happening tonight. At the Telegraf I received a wire—my paper has recalled me to Switzerland, at once. I do not like the sound of it. Look—the firemen!"

A SQUAD of helmets charging in from the terrace. Axes gleaming. Hose. Brass nozzles. Loud, stuttering commands. Swimming down from the mezzanine, the smoke curled through the lobby in a biscuit-colored fog. Keats hugged the desk, coughing, and turned to see Stehli's body, caught in the whirl, go bumping off through the crowd. Head of Moses uplifted above the pandemonium of Baal. The brass-hatted police were driving the stampede toward the doors, billies swinging. "Line up there! Line up! Plenty of time!" A tall woman whose peach satin evening gown had been torn off to the waist had caught an ankle in a writhing loop of fireman's hose. Her blond hair twirled around her powdered shoulders like a carnival dancer's. Stehli sprang to catch her as she fell; swung her into his arms and lifted her clear of the stampede.

Keats hooked an arm across his eyes and stumbled for the stairs. An angry fireman barred his way. People were coming down the staircase in a surging cascade.

"John—Keats!"

The cry passed him in the smoke. He spun to glimpse Alexandra Frantsovna swept beyond reach in the outrushing jam. Must have just escaped her room. Her hat, a white toque trimmed with blue braid, was mashed jauntily on one side of her head. She had changed into a traveling suit, brown military trench-coat. She waved a black patent leather traveling case, crying out:

"Look for me outside! Must see you!"

He tried to answer, but the fireman was driving at him with both fists. "One side, foreigner! Back! Back!" Firemen galloped by him, dragging hose. Water was streaking on the mezzanine.

A stream had smashed the burning door, and the dining room beyond was a molten, hissing hole. Vague shadows ran down the staircase in the cindery fog. Nielsen. Dubail. He could see the dry shine of Dubail's teeth, and the gleam of the Swedish correspondent's monocle. Dubail's arms were loaded with typewriters, pieces of luggage. Nielsen staggered with his pigskin kitbag on his shoulder, Keats' suitcase in hand.

Tight-nerved, stiff as if waiting for a blow, Keats hailed them.

"Sacré!" Dubail raced at him. "I wanted to see into that dining room. A furnace! We saved as much luggage as we could—"

Nielsen flung the salvaged suitcase. "Some story, eh? Blew up that dining room! Fire bomb!"

Keats leered sickishly. His head felt airy, faint. Young Shepler's body up there. But they hadn't entered the bathroom. Heartsick, he stumbled after his two companions, across the cleared lobby, into night. The terrace was thronged with firemen and police. The plaza a solid mass of people.

"I've got to find a cab," Keats yelled to Dubail. "I'm going to the Alexanderplatz!"

Dubail hadn't heard him. Cantering along the fringe of the mob, the *Etoile* reporter suddenly shot an arm in the air, pointing above the drift of hats. "Look there! Look at that!"

Men were shouting and trampling, milling about some hub of interest in the street. Keats saw the crowd's eye was not on the hotel, where the blaze was now not apparent from the outside, but attention had switched with that strange wolf-pack instinct toward a new excitement.

Dubail lifted a yell. "Stehli!"

THE SWISS was caught against the fender of a crimson fire truck. His coat had been snatched from his back, and his linen blouse hung in fragments. His face, illuminated by a street lamp, looked swollen and unnatural, and under the tangled thicket of his hair his eyes were bright coals of defiance.

Nielsen blurted an oath at Keats' elbow. "They will kill him!" Even as the Swedish newspaperman spoke a fist pumped out of the crowd and struck the side of Stehli's head. The Swiss could not retaliate. Two hatless young men held his right arm pinned to the fender of the truck. A big sandy man in a black jersey had hold of Stehli's left arm and was turning it around and around in the shoulder socket as if it were some kind of crank.

On the driver's seat of the truck a fireman leaned bare elbows on the polished handrail and looked down with lack of interest. Farther down the curb a policeman directed traffic with no time for this. His brass helmet was aloof, his business conveniently elsewhere. But the girl struggling on the inside wall of the mob was interested, her face white with anger, her arms squirming to evade the clutch of a grinning Work Trooper who held her back. "Swine!" Alexandra Frantsovna was wailing. "Let me go! Take your dirty hands off that man! Leave him alone!"

"Hang the dirty scoundrel!"

"Break the rat's neck!"

"Show the rascal no filthy foreigner can put his arms around a Teuton woman!"

"Dragged her out of the hotel, and her dress half off! Emil and Hans saw her, too! Teach the swine his place!"

Sounds crashed and flooded over Keats' head. Gongs ringing. Auto horns. Cries. Oaths. He saw Alexandra Frantsovna yanked backward. The crowded faces closing in were masks of imbecility. Features scribbled with the fun of hate. Wolves baying for a victim. A final vandalism for this midnight's hecatomb. He heard Nielsen's warning shout, "Don't go into that, Dubail!"

But the lame newswriter's black head was tossing through the swarm, his fists lashing out.

"Let him alone, you swine! Unhand the Swiss! *Mon Dieu,* you cannot torture the man—"

The twisted faces caught and spat out the *"mon Dieu."*

"Here is an Esperenchman for us to play with!"

THE NIGHT took up the roar. Keats felt as if his head would burst. He was fighting blindly, kicking, beating, forcing his way, to Dubail's side where the tumult was wildest. A wide man with the face of an infuriated moose towered over Dubail.

"Frog, we will show you how we treat murderers and assassins! We will show you how we entertain a spy!"

Dubail's head came up. "I am no spy, but an honest citizen of Esperance and a guest of your government like this Swiss whom you have brutally manhandled—"

"Blackguard! Thief! The Esperench assassinated our Premier!"

"I am neither blackguard nor thief," Dubail drew himself up scornfully, speaking to the crowd, "but I am Esperench and proud of the fact. As for this Swiss gentleman, this lady and these colleagues, they are newspaper correspondents like myself, and friends of Herr Paul Emmerich of the *Tageblatt,* who has connections with General Gottlieb von Neumann of your High Command. If our credentials cannot win respect among you, I will tell you something that can. That *salopard* in the black jersey will take his hands off the Swiss or I will put a bullet in his thick skull where he stands—"

"I'm with you, Raoul," Keats promised. He sidled against Dubail with his fingers ready at his hip.

Words muttered in English from the corner of Dubail's twisted mouth. "We must bluff fast. I have somewhere tonight lost my gun—"

The sandy-haired man in the black jersey had dropped Stehli's wrist to leap behind the moose-faced citizen. An ugly, deep-throated hissing issued from the close-packed faces.

"Bash the frog's head for him!"—"The Esperench swine threatens us!"—"Show him how the Fatherland will handle his country the next time!"—"Give it to the foreigners!"—"The American, too!"—"Hell with them!"

Light sped across Keats' vision. *Tang!* The hurled beer mug burst like a shell on Dubail's jaw. Hand covering his mouth, Dubail remained swaying upright, blood pouring on his chin. Somewhere in the jam Alexandra Frantsovna screamed. Colt leveled, John Keats stepped between Dubail and the massive man whose bovine jaw was chewing out oaths. The man's jaw stopped chewing. His eyes dilated at sight of the gun, and he whirled, tried to claw himself backward into the crowd. Bodies surged, piling up like a dark tidal wall gathering to crash over Keats and bury him deep in the street.

His teeth grinned ivory. He could see this antagonist. A human mob. Better than the thing which had wizarded away up there in that bedroom. "Come on! What are you waiting for?" he growled.

It seemed as if the charge was waiting for the only climax that could have stopped it. It came. Down the plaza it whirled like a wind, catching at people on pavements and curbs, sweeping around corners, echoing over treetops and roofs; a yell that thickened to a many-toned roar and filled the city canons with a million echoes.

"Schnitzler has declared condition-of-danger-of-war! Schnitzler has declared condition-of-danger-of-war!"

Another, a wilder outcry roared down the plaza, as if ten thousand paper boys had followed with a final edition.

"Schnitzler just landed at Tempelhof Airdrome! Schnitzler is coming! Schnitzler is coming!" The news was carried above a staccato rataplan of hoofbeats; mounted police racing across the square with the sound of cavalry. "Make way before the Metropole! *Schnitzler kommt!*"

MEN BLEW like leaves before this gale, leaping around corners, tumbling and skipping to go scattering away up the sidewalks. Things were happening too fast for John Keats, right then. Dimly he made out the Russian girl and Dubail hauling Stehli to his feet, the Swiss' face sweaty green, his left arm dangling. A red and black taxicab wheeling past the fire cart, slowing at the curb; Nielsen's face hollering from the cab window.

"Inside, all of you! This man will take us!"

The cab driver's blue eyes were kindly under a rag of cap. "Step in quickly, *herren*, I will gladly assist. I saw it all, *ja*. The Hebrew was only helping the lady out of the hotel—"

Nielsen and Dubail propped the fainting Stehli between them on the rear seat. Suitcases, typewriters, the Swede's kitbag, John Keats and the Russian girl tangled together in what little space remained. The cabby honking, juggling the hack for an opening in traffic. His anxious visage screwed around in the driver's window.

"Where to, *herren?*"

Nielsen's monocle glared through the strap-handle of a suitcase. "Take us to the North Station!"

"Gladly, *mein herr!*"

"No," Keats bawled. "Drop me at the Alexanderplatz Police—"

"Impossible," the Swedish correspondent cried. "Police won't see you, Keats. I've been there twice tonight. Threw me out." His voice bit through a fanfare of motor horns. "And Teutony has just declared danger-of-war! With this national emergency they'll throw a *Razzia* around the hotel. Arrest us all to stop the bombing story."

Dubail cried, "I must get to Esperance—"

"We can just about make that one-thirty train," Nielsen yelled. "The European Express—"

John Keats thrust an aching head through the driver's window. "North Station. We've got ten minutes—"

The cab screeched around a turn, piling him against Alexandra Frantsovna's huddled form. Luggage swarmed around them. A moment the girl's cheek was pressed against his, marble cold. Her stifled voice barely brushed his ear. "On the train—must talk to you without fail—"

"Right."

CHAPTER VI

EUROPEAN EXPRESS!

THE WAGONS-LITS, THE Pullmans of Europe, boast a number of advantages over the American sleeping car. Constructed on Continental lines, the European sleeper, first class, has a narrow corridor running the length of the car on one side; instead of curtained berths, doors open off the passage into private compartments; the traveler may occupy a compartment to himself, bed, table, washstand, window giving view to fleeing countryside.

To nullify these comforts one suffers a suspicion that seventy miles an hour is too fast for a system engineered without automatic block signals; the locomotive shrieks four times where the American hogger blows once; the train must stop at any of a dozen cow pastures or frontiers for any of a dozen complications. A bull astride the rails. Teuton police ferreting for an anarchist. Bomb-scare on a mountain trestle. Inspection of baggage, tickets, visas, permits of entry, passports. Europe builds fine roads, then clogs them with red tape.

There were train guards. Captains. Police guards. Railroad officers with Francis Joseph sidewhiskers. A division chief. Two officers of the Reichswehr. They threw the sliding doors of the compartments and stamped in. Tickets. Visas. Permits. Passports.

John Keats leaned against the window in Stehli's compartment, calming bruised nerves with a pipe, watching Dubail massage the Swiss newspaperman's sprained arm, listening in pretended indifference to their talk. Plenty of time for his chat with Frantsovna, and he needed a breathing spell, a chance to think his way back through this Witch's Sabbath, time to sort the hand and choose his game.

One thing was certain; the attempts on his own life and poor Shepler's murder tied up somewhere with the violent end of Von Speer and Gatreau in that dinner-hour camarilla. Hard to think when your ears were deaf from the sound of all hell popping. Europe teetering on the lip of a volcano.

Propped on his swaying bunk, Stehli was gesturing a quarter-filled whisky glass at his companions, his face furrowed, dejected. The Swiss was not lamenting any personal injury.

"I tell you, this is the beginning of the end. For all of us. The Teutons declaring danger-of-war. That Metropole shooting was the spark, and they have fanned it to a torch. The haystack waits."

DUBAIL DID not think so. "We cannot afford a war, *mon vieux.*"

"Money? There is always money for the guns to shoot. Not enough for honest debts, but plenty for the melting into howitzers."

"The man will not be so ready to march again," Dubail said, doggedly optimistic. "They will not go."

"And I was just telling you, the new crop is raised. See how they have supported the dictators and buried democracy, learned the old catch-words and invented newer and more violent ones. Our youth has been weaned on a rifle bullet. Already our school books are calling the World War the war of 1914–1918. One-third of the world population of today cannot remember the Armistice. And how could they? Not when its memory is allowed but two measly minutes a year."

"But," Dubail said over his glass, "there are mature minds who do remember. The older generation—"

"Bah! It is we old ones who have failed the young. The World War soldiers who suffered—for the most part they are dead. The maimed are imprisoned in hidden hospitals; they make nice

cane-bottom chairs but they do not make polite table conversation. Blinded, dismembered, they are studiously forgotten.
The lucky who came out unscathed are the biggest liars of all.
They do not like to speak about the War, no. Their silence is a
falsehood. Youth sees them as heroic veterans from the romance
of the past—"

"Eh bien." Dubail stared through his knees at the vibrating
floor. "Where is an answer, my friend? Peaceful men like you are
victims for the mob. See how they treated you tonight. It is hard
to love an enemy, hardest when you see him harming a friend.
If I had found my gun—"

"No, no, Dubail! That is not the answer—"

"Perhaps not, but the only answer a bloody *lourdaud* like that
scoundrel in the black jersey can understand." He stood up,
punching his fists into his pockets. *"Enfin,* I would like to know
what became of my gun."

"You lost a gun?" Keats put in, with masked interest.

The Esperenchman scowled, "It was in that curst hotel
bedroom. Under the pillow on my cot. *Peste!* I dash up there
during the hotel fire, make a hasty grab for the pistol, it is not
there. What is more, the bed was in a fine uproar."

THE COMPARTMENT door slid open with an oily creak.
Thick-lensed spectacles, comedy sidewhiskers framed themselves in the opening. Scanning the compartment, the myopic
spectacles finally settled a suspicious glance on John Keats.

"You are the American correspondent, *Herr Keats?"*

Keats bit the pipe-stem in his teeth, steeling himself for fresh
disaster. So the Teuton police octopus had put out a feeler at last.
"What can I do for you? I'm John Keats."

The whisker-garnished face squinted in the rattling doorway.
"A message for you, *mein herr.* The Fräulein in Compartment
Seven would like you to call at her door."

His grin masked relief.

"My thanks, and I will come directly."

"Romance?" Dubail smiled, after the official had departed.

Keats scowled in spurious annoyance. "Hardly. I promised the woman I'd give her some details on the Von Speer-Gatreau fracas."

Dubail joined him at the door. "Myself, I am that tired I feel as if I had been flogged. It will necessitate drinking myself to sleep. You are all right, Stehli? Then I bid you good night, *messieurs.*"

Keats watched the Esperenchman rocking down the corridor to his door at the far end of the car; then, closing Stehli's door with a "See you in the restaurant car for breakfast," in a lively tone he by no means echoed from the heart, he hurried up the forward end of the passage, hunting Number Seven.

When Alexandra Frantsovna answered his knock he wrenched the door open, swung into her compartment, closed the panel swiftly. She stood at once from her seat near the window, reaching out to give him both hands.

"Bolt the door," she said in a low voice.

He slid the clasp; swung to face her, yanking off his hat. Her face looked drawn, pale, lipstick on her mouth unnaturally carmine. She had not altered the costume in which she had escaped the hotel fire, traveling suit, military trench-coat belted tightly man-fashion, white and blue toque tilted soldierly on her head. Her portable typewriter sat on the folding table, a sheet of manuscript paper untouched in the machine.

"You were going to tell me something—" he began uncertainly.

"Yes."

"And I wanted to see you," he told her, sitting stiffly on the bed. "Stehli—the Swiss—asked me to thank you for trying to help him in that street fight."

"You've been hurt!" she cried. "Your head is cut."

"A scratch. I fell down."

"Let me bandage it for you, John-Keats." Her eyes had

widened, deep blue with alarm. "Ointment. In my traveling case—"

He waved her off brusquely. "It's nothing. Let's come to the point, Frantsovna. What'd you mean, saying you didn't think the minister of Esperance killed the Premier of Teutony?"

SHE CHOSE a cigarette from her case, and returned to her seat at the partly opened window. A dark gale wailed faintly through the cinder-screen, stirring the coppery ringlets about her ears. There was a sudden concussion in the night, a thundering that shook the car, a cinnamon glow in the dark, the drumming tumult of a passing express. Smoke blew in gauzy wisps through the screen. The girl waited tight-lipped for the uproar to diminish. *Whooo*—the night screamed *whooo—whooo—whoooeeee*—

Then, "John-Keats, I am almost certain Gatreau did not shoot Von Speer. I dared not say so in my newspaper dispatch—the police censors would have arrested me. But it is true."

Exhaustion betrayed his guard, and suddenly he was savagely angry, leaping up with face suffused, snatching the Russian girl's wrist, yanking her to her feet. He was shaking her.

"What's the game, Frantsovna? I've had enough of these whispers and hinted secrets. Out with the story. What," he snarled, "were you doing on that roof across from that hotel bedroom tonight? Don't lie to me. The British kid told me he saw you there—"

She listened gravely to this indictment, unresisting in his clutch. "If you will release me, please, I was about to tell you."

He dropped her wrists sullenly. "So you admit you were on that roof just before the shooting?"

"I am not admitting, John-Keats, I am telling."

"Out with it, then!"

"Please sit down. You do not need to threaten me like this."

Her calmness baffled his temper. No good blowing up like a paranoiac. Daily he reseated himself on the bed. Above the chanting of the rails, the sewing-machine echo of the cars, her voice came low, vibrant.

"Directly after you escorted Mr. Nielsen into the hotel, tonight—you remember, he had just arrived—I was paged in the lobby. An *Izvestia* editor calling from our branch office on the phone. He wanted photographs of the two statesmen at conference, and was going to send a photographer. The Teuton police, it seems, had forbidden photographs. However, the editor asked me to scurry around the hotel to discover a place where such pictures might be taken."

"So you ducked around the next building and climbed to the roof, is that it?"

"That," she nodded, "is it. I located a fire escape at the back, and walked over the roof hunting a location for our camera man."

"I see. And the best station for your camera man was exactly across from the windows of the bedroom occupied by the press."

"No," she ignored his caustic implication, "I was not spying into your windows, John-Keats. I saw them, yes. And I saw you run to the sill and stare out. But I was hidden behind a chimney across from the windows of the dining room, you see. I was looking in at the two who sat at table."

"And who else was on that roof over there with you?"

Her expression was bewildered. "Was somebody else?"

IT WAS on his tongue to tell her about the knife-throwing episode, but her next declaration sat him bolt upright in astonishment.

"But I was alone on the roof, and looking into that dining room. I could see but little, for the shades were lowered; but I had a clear picture of the table, Gatreau at one end, Von Speer at the other, apparently engaged in conversation. The view was cut off, you comprehend; I could see their arms, their hands gesturing and thumping, but I could not see their heads, nor did I have a full view of the dining room."

She paused to listen to the hammering undertone of the

trucks. "Then all at once," she resumed, "from where I was hiding, I saw *you* at the windows of the next room, the bedroom. You appeared suddenly in the frame and stared out. Fearing you would see me, perhaps raise an outcry, I dodged between the chimney-pots and hid."

Good Lord! Then the woman had been over there when the knife was tossed. She'd seen him jump for the sill. He knew he was staring like a fool, and he wanted to take her by the neck and shake the truth out of her, but he could only blurt: "And nobody was on the roof besides you—"

"I didn't see anybody," was her wondering reply. "Did you?"

"I heard you over there," he hedged. "Thought it was a sneak thief, or something. Go on! Where'd you go from there?"

"Why, I saw you lean out of the window and look down into the court. Then you pulled down the bedroom shades. After that you must have left the suite, for I saw the lights in the bedchamber go out. I crept back to the chimney from where I could see into the dining room. I was wondering how a camera might manage some sort of picture with one of those new periscope lenses or something and then—I don't know why I was looking at them"—her fingers were twisting nervously in her lap, her eyes widened, blue, enigmatic—"I don't know why I was looking at them, but I was watching the hands of Baron Von Speer, and I saw red drops begin to fall on them, as if someone had thrown from over his shoulder a glass of claret. It was amazing. Drop, drop, drop. His fingers clawed across the table cloth and he knocked over the goblet at his elbow. Nothing of his head or body could I see but only that little strip between window-sash and sill, his elbows and waist. He seemed twisting, sagging in his chair. Then his hand dropped to his belt, yanked out his pistol. It—his hand was dripping red."

"You didn't hear the shots?" Keats cried.

"Not a sound. It was twenty feet across the court. The windows were all down. It was like a silent picture on colored film. There was a spurt of fire from the Teuton Premier's gun. Once! Flash!"

"Gatreau! What was *he* doing?"

"And that is just it," the girl whispered. "At first the Esperench minister's hands were resting on his napkin. Then he stood up, clutching at the edge of the table, body twisted at the middle as if looking at someone behind him. I could see no more of the room. Only the two at table. Von Speer's red fist on that gun of his, and Gatreau standing upright. Then he fell across the table, face among the dishes. *And there was no gun at that time in the Esperench Minister's hand!*"

KEATS' VISION blurred. The compartment dimmed and swam. Only the girl's whitened face stood clear in the foreground. He could hear his words going, metallic as the flying click of the car-wheels. "You're trying to tell me Von Speer was shot to sponge, and Victor Gatreau didn't do it? The Esperenchman fell across the table without any gun?"

"It is what I saw."

"Why didn't you tell that to the police?"

Alexandra Frantsovna said quietly, "Because I did not trust the Teuton police. I am from a Communist country. I would have been arrested for espionage; There are other reasons, John-Keats. I was—stunned. At once I knew another party must be in that dining room. I fled across the roof to the fire escape. I would phone the Soviet embassy for them to give the alarm. On the fire escape I was halted. It was that English boy, that young journalist, Shepler. He must have tried to follow me. A soldier in the court had seen him, and was—how do you say?—bawling him up. The boy ran down into the court. I waited for the soldier to go away, and hurried down around to the back street and into a side entrance of the hotel. I could hardly think."

She swayed against the window, caught off her hat and shook her hair. "What should I do? I ran straight into that Swedish newspaperman, Nielsen. He took me by an arm and said I must have a drink with him on the terrace. I went out to the table, thinking I must talk with somebody, I must talk with you, John-Keats—"

"Why me?"

Her hand trembled on his sleeve. "Do you not see? I am hardly known to those others. You have seen me before. Perhaps you I could trust. An American, not involved in this Chinese box that is Europe. But—"

"Then you knew the statesmen were murdered while you sat there with us at the table!"

"Only I had no chance to talk with you. A moment later the news was out. We rush up to the dining room. And there it is, the two men are dead, and I see a pistol is, after all, in the Esperench Minister's hand!"

"So you must have been mistaken the first time," he rapped.

"Mistaken! Never!" She stood away from him, white-lipped. "Never was I mistaken. From the roof I saw Gatreau fall without a gun. In the dining room there is a pistol in his hand. Do you understand it, then? Someone, after I was gone from the roof, entered the room of death and planted that pistol!"

Keats' face was gray and sweating. Whisky, his scalp-wound, the lateness of the hour had put dagger edges on his nerves. The whir of the wheels speeding them down the night was like the sound of his aching brain. He groped to his feet and braced himself, unsteadily confronting the girl.

"Just why are you telling this yarn to me?"

"I told you before. You are an American. Of a reputation. I had to tell somebody, and you—I felt I could trust you. Don't you see? The others are Europeans, opinionated, suspicious, perhaps—guilty."

"Guilty?"

"Involved in this murder plot," she whispered fiercely. "To kill Von Speer and Gatreau. To embroil Europe. Oh, can't you understand how big, how terrible this is? Listen! After the police dismissed us from that dining room, I fled to my own room and wrote a plausible story to Moscow. Then, instead of going to the *Izvestia* bureau, I rushed to the Soviet embassy. Naturally the buildings were closed, so late at night. I could arouse no one.

John-Keats, I was desperate. I am not known in the Teutonic capital. I hurried back to the Metropole, hoping to find you. They told me all the correspondents had left. I had to see into that dining room again, but the sentry refused me admittance. But I went into your bedroom and saw what I wanted."

A STRING of empty box cars made a booming on a siding. "What did you see?" Keats blared.

"That door into the dining room—with a transom! Cannot you understand what I am trying to say? The dining room was under close guard. On the outside. But anyone in the bedroom could have opened that transom and fired into the dining room; killed Von Speer and Gatreau. It must have been after you switched off the light. You and Nielsen left the room together?"

"Yes."

"Then anyone with a press card could have sneaked into the bedroom."

Anyone with a press card! It shocked him mentally alert. Nielsen had gone wandering in the lobby to seek a stenographer. Emmerich, inside somewhere after cigarettes. Stehli? There were rear entrances to the hotel by which the Swiss could have dodged in unobserved, gained the press room and down before Keats threaded the lobby to the terrace. Even Dubail, deserted at table, could have entered the hotel, taken elevator to mezzanine, ducked into the suite and out again—and there were those missing .38 shells and that cufflink ground into the carpet near that between-rooms door.

"Frantsovna! For God's sake, if you suspect anybody—"

She said in alto desperation, "But there are so many motives! What were the statesmen discussing? Were they killed to hide a government scandal? Did the Teutons wish both men out of the way? It would not be the first time Schnitzler's party executed a high official. Suppose Von Speer was plotting a government overthrow with Esperench help? In that case—"

"Emmerich?"

"I do not accuse," the girl denied. "I merely try to discover the motive. Also there is Anton Stehli. You recall him saying he would rather see those statesmen dead than have them start another war?"

"But that shooting was exactly the thing to start a war—"

"What if the man was turned in the mind? Off-balance. Remember, a son of Stehli's was accidentally killed in the last war. Suppose he has brooded. In his mind he blames the diplomats. Such revenges are not unknown. And there is Raoul Dubail of the *Etoile* Service—"

"Would he kill Gatreau, one of his own countrymen?"

"I do not know." Alexandra Frantsovna's voice was close to tears. "I only try to weed out the ones who could have been in that bedroom. Nielsen, too. He was in the hotel. The young English journalist is the only one who could not, because he was on that fire escape—"

Her voice broke, as if the telling of her secret had released overwrought nerves, and hiding her face in slim hands, she began to cry silently. John Keats watched this feminine performance in a misery of consternation. The abracadabra of the past twenty-four hows had almost robbed his capacity for thought, and the Russian girl's disclosure had scattered the jigsaw forty ways. He couldn't stand there gawking, either. They were going places at seventy miles an hour, and things were doing. The world, wound up too tightly, had broken its governor. He could see the night flying past the window. Events running wild in the dark. Every second counting. If he could but lift a palm and holler, "Stop!" for time out to think.

"Here!" He balanced the whisky bottle on the table. "Take this—"

She looked up gratefully, brushing a copper-gold strand from her forehead with the back of a hand. Despite the tears, there was undeniable charm to the smooth oval of her face. Something devilish attractive about these foreign women; She was saying in that throaty accent, "I am so sorry. And I am—frightened—"

"You," he ordered gruffly, "turn in. I mean, get some sleep.

Lots of time before we reach the Rhine, and meanwhile keep
your story under your hat until I can figure out what to do with
it Don't tell anybody, see? It's dynamite and wants some damned
careful handling. I don't mind saying I've got a couple of sticks
in my own pocket. I think Gatreau and Von Speer knew about
it, and that's why they were knocked off. Somebody's trying to
fire the stuff. That's the one we've got to get, and we've got to
get him quick—"

PACING THE floor didn't help. Neither did soaking his head
under the faucet. Smoking cigarettes, he stood at his compartment window and stared at rushing night. Six minutes of four.
Five minutes of four. Damn that hogger in the cab, he'd race
them all to hell before he could gather his wits.

Nielsen! Completely slipped his mind. The Swede had wanted
to see him. Something urgent. Man had been waiting for him
all this time; had something to tell him.

With swift, quiet strides John Keats got himself to the Swedish correspondent's door. But his knuckles never contacted the
panel with their intended knock. As his fist moved upward to
rap the wood something lumpish struck the inside of the door,
bump! sodden as a thrown cabbage. The door jarred perceptibly
under the blow, and at the same moment the Wagon-Lit slewed
on curving rails, pitching Keats off balance across the passage.

He was back like a snapped spring, ears stiff to listen above
the hammering gallop of the wheels. Things were doing behind
Door Five. *Sock* and *whack!* Grunting. A quick scuffle of shoes.
Stifled gasps. Nielsen's voice exploding muffled Scandinavian,
then queerly pleading, whining words Keats couldn't understand. A second voice, pixie-thin, womanish, screeling a parroty
gibberish of anger in a tongue foreign yet oddly familiar to Keats'
hearing. There was a choked-off moan; the faint tinkle of bursting glass. *Sluff!* A heavy object dropped on wood.

"Nielsen! Kurt Nielsen!" Yelling like a Choctaw, Keats struck
the door, recoiled, struck harder. Catamaran. Wood bulged

under his slamming shoulder, but the inner bolts held. "Nielsen—are you all right?"

WITHOUT AWAITING an answer—none came—he assaulted the door with his gun-butt, hammering, pounding. Splinters flew. Bolts groaned, cracked loose. Prying at the frame for leverage, he succeeded in jamming the gun barrel between door and sill. A wrench, the report of a snapping hasp, and the door slid crashing in its grooves; unable to check himself, Keats stumbled inward. Instantly he was crouched, gun leveled to shoot. Then the automatic froze with the blue veins in his hand.

The compartment had been in darkness, but the bilious illumination from the corridor entered the gloom in sooty yellow shafts to dimly penetrate a haze of cindery smoke. Wind struck at Keats' face, ruffling his uplifted hair. Floor, walls, bunk, ceiling, wash stand, window—his eyes sped around the compartment, taking in a scene of furious disorder, the overturned typewriter, manuscript scattered everywhere, a toilet case spilling its contents in the wash basin, Nielsen's big pigskin bag kicked into a corner, clothing askew on the luggage rack, evidence of terrific conflict.

In the center of the floor, body twisted in the folds of his silk black and gold lounging robe, knees drawn up, arms outflung, Nielsen lay on his back with his mouth open in a posture of sleeping nightmare. Even in slumber his features were contorted with terror, a mask of fright, stained from chin to forehead a glistening wine-color, a grass-green bruise the size of a toadstool swelled above one closed eye, and in his wheat-colored pompadour a shimmering tiara of shattered glass. His head lay toward the window, his slipper-toes pointing at Keats; the neck of the bottle that had given him that facial made a jagged gleam against the side wall. A stertorous snoring gurgled from his throat; and John Keats gained his side at a leap.

Kurt Nielsen was not dead; but where was the enemy who had knocked him out? Someone had been in this compartment not fifty seconds before; someone with a strangely foreign voice;

someone who had smashed a full bottle of Hulstkamp's over the Scandinavian's crown. Keats explored the empty corners with astounded eyes. The window was open and the cinder screen gone from the sash, admitting a seventy-mile-an-hour smoke barrage.

Cursing, Keats threw himself at the sill, thrust head and shoulders out into the whistling darkness. Cinders pelted his face. Far rearward down the swaying black wall of cars that dwindled in perspective glimmered the trailing green comet of the tail light. Forward, bending a curve, the bonfire-yellow smear of the engine-cab, the swinging white spear of the head-light tunneling through dark, the cinnamon spray of the stack. *Whooo—whooo—whoooeeee*—No man alive would have gone out of that window.

But for himself and the unconscious Nielsen, there was no man visible in the Swede's compartment, nor any visible place for a man to hide. Lips parted on soundless profanity, John Keats dropped to his knees beside the recumbent body and began a frantic first aid on the contused forehead. He saw faint color return to the grassy eyelids, the lips stirred on a sigh, life came into one outsprawled arm. As Keats strained to lift the man to a sitting posture, Nielsen's right fist came unclenched and a little rag of torn paper scurried from his cataleptic clutch.

Keats snatched the scrap from the floor; held it lip to the light. He felt his lungs go empty, all feeling rush from his fingers. That crumpled scrap of ricepaper had been torn from a book. The scrap was gilt-edged. Page 63 in the upper corner. Only a single line of print along the raggedy edge, but the aborted sentence of diminutive black letters lithographed themselves with a smash on his brain:

So Foul A Sky Cannot Be Cleared Without A—

Good God! He could complete that sentence of Shake-speare's from memory. "Without a storm!" And clouds had ridden like horsemen across the city's skyline. They'd been sitting on the Metropole terrace. Word had just come of the shooting. Gilt-edged book! Frantsovna!

Pearls of sweat stood on his face as he tucked the bit of paper into his dressing robe and began to shake Nielsen by the shoulders. "Nielsen! Nielsen! It's Keats! Who was in here—"

IN THE midst of all this chaos, John Keats knew he didn't want to hear any name, to listen to the name of this vanished assailant. Somehow he had closed the corridor door and snapped on the overhead light; voices were making an angry chattering somewhere up the passage. In his extremity, he wrestled the tall man to his feet, clutched him upright as one might hold an inebriate, shook him until his jaw rattled. Incoherent Scandinavian words mumbled from Nielsen's loose mouth, and for a moment his half opened eyes stared at Keats without recognition. Then abruptly he shocked fully awake, and grabbed Keats by the arms.

"You!"

"Who went out of that window?" Keats husked thickly. "Tell me quick who it was—"

The man fumbled dazedly at his swollen temple. "Where— where did you say it—it went?"

"Who was it, Nielsen! For God's sake—"

"Why," the Swede's pale eyes were misty with bewilderment, "I swear to God, I—I don't know. By Heaven, Keats," his voice quickened in agitation, "I—I was waiting in here for *you!* Did you hear the fight?"

"Hell! I broke in the door and found you knocked cold. Someone was in here, and—"

Nielsen blurted, "Of course there was! I tell you, I don't know who the devil—listen, I was waiting for you to come. You had said you'd be back. I know—I was going to ask you about Dubail!"

"Dubail?" Keats had to gulp.

Nielsen wet his lips, supporting himself with a shaky hand. "The *Etoile* correspondent, yes! I was going to ask you how well you knew the fellow. Check up on him—because of the Metropole shooting—Von Speer and Gatreau—"

"Lord!" Keats groaned, "how does Dubail figure in that—"

"I want to know," the injured man panted. "That's why I'm leaving that news story cold to get to Esperance. You know there was something fishy about that Metropole affair and so do I. Outside job. I can't explain, but—suppose a man hated Gatreau, planned to murder him, shot him in that dining room? Well, he'd have to kill Von Speer, too—"

"What do you mean?" Keats whispered tensely.

"Only this," Nielsen twisted out. "Raoul Dubail has hated Gatreau for years. Always wrote articles against him. Once they had a fistfight outside the Chamber of Deputies. Dubail told another newspaperman he would get Gatreau some time if it was his last act. Seven years ago. I remembered the talk it created among the profession. Going to ask you about it tonight—if you knew. I was waiting in here; there was a knock at the door; I thought you'd come—"

He dragged a wrist across his wine-drenched face. "I was writing there by the window, and called, 'Come in and shut the door,' and didn't look up from the typewriter. Next second, just after the door closed, the lights were out. Fellow must have pushed the switch, and I heard the door lock, too, I jumped around—something hit me in the face. The devil was strangling me." Nielsen put his hands to his throat, and fear grew in his eyes. "I thought it was *you,* by Heaven! Didn't know what the devil it was all about—in the dark."

"You didn't see—"

"Blind as a bat, I tell you." He mashed a handkerchief to his sick mouth. "Lord, I'm all in from that blow. Things were flying in the dark—fists, glass, seemed to wear a cape—I thought he—it—struck me with a book—"

KEATS SPECULATED, "Whoever it was jumped out of the window," and hoped the nausea in his head wouldn't prevent his reaching the corridor door, where fists had started an imperious knocking. A heavy basso demanded, "What's going on in there, Number Five?"

Pallor crawled under the stickiness on the Swede's face. His nostrils fluttered. "Don't tell anything," he whispered, "Fellow's gone. I'll wire police next station to hunt along tracks. Your word of honor about Dubail." The knocking loudened sharply. Nielsen's eyes flicked at the door. "Gut the light. Tell them it was delirium tremens. Anything. I'll see you later. We must talk. Esperance—meet there—"

Keats assented, "Right," and, darkening the compartment, slid the door and lounged out into the passage. He pulled the door, put his fists in his pockets to hide their agitation, and found himself genially fabricating to a pair of frowsy-eyed train guards. This was nothing to concern them. Passenger behind Door Five had just suffered, and quite recovered from, a violent spasm of D.Ts. Routed from the forward car by the disturbance, the guards (dead ringers for Tweedle Dee and Tweedle Dum) lifted suspicious railroad lanterns at Keats' face, but didn't fail to light up the banknotes ready in his hand. Keats lied with skill, managing arrogance. In his own country he was a physician of repute. The gentleman in Compartment Five would best be left alone to sleep it off. Had anyone in the car been aroused by this unfortunate incident?

The guards winked. Drunken tourists were not a novelty to European trains. They wanted to get forward to the mail coach where the train captain was telling about the excitements at the capital.

"No, *Herr Doktor,* no one else is disturbed. There are only the foreign journalists aboard this car; few people traveling tonight. Both the Swiss in Compartment Two and the Esperenchman in One were asleep just now when we examined their doors. Only one other passenger in the car. That Russian woman in Number Seven—"

Keats' heart missed a beat. "Those vestibule doors," he put the question casually, "are never open?"

"Not while the train is moving, *Herr Doktor.* Both ends are locked, with guards on the other side. If you wish to get through you merely ring the call bell. A porter will come. Call us if we may be of further assistance. Let us hope Number Five will be all right. Thank you a thousand. Good night."

John Keats did not watch them depart. John Keats was staring down the corridor like a blind man, eyes riveted on Door Seven. Door Seven had opened; and Alexandra Frantsovna was framed in the swaying dimness, a picture in black lace negligee, her copper-glinting hair loosed in a shimmering shawl about ivory shoulders, the pale oval of her face glowing with dark-eyed alarm. John Keats forced his legs to maneuver him up the passage toward his own compartment; but he whirled too quickly as her voice called him around.

She looked at him steadily. "John-Keats. Everything is all right?"

"Never better."

But he could have enjoyed the D.Ts. himself when he shut himself behind his door. He fastened the bolt elaborately; fumbled out his automatic and placed it alongside the pillow of his bed. Nerves twittering like a thousand sparrows, he dropped his head beside the unlimbered gun. Seventy miles an hour the European Express flogged on its way to the Rhine. The pert radium face of his wrist dial smirked 4.34. Grayish pallor seeped across the window pane. *Whooo—whoooeeeeeeee—*

And this infernal car had been locked at each vestibule. Only passengers aboard were the foreign correspondents, and all were there. That scrap of paper from the Russian girl's book—in Nielsen's fingers! Who in the name of sanity had gone out of Nielsen's window?

Strength, memory, panic, reason flowed out of John Keats' body into nameless ether. He was asleep.

CHAPTER VII

ESPERANCE!

THE GREAT SPIRED building on the corner of Boulevard St. Martin and Avenue Jacques overshadows the Parc and the avenue and the tallest plane trees, and rises like a portent against the sky. It is a portent; nightly you may read its pronouncements of good or evil written in moving letters of fire against the stars. Its windows never sleep. Its doors, elevators, telephones are constantly alert. It is tall; so tall its lofty steeple can peer across Esperance, across Europe to the farthest meridian; not thirty stories high, but one thousand stories a day. Taller than the topmost gargoyle of Notre Dame, but it is not a cathedral. If a microscope could not discover the name of God legible on one of its myriad frosted doors, then only a blind man could fail to discern the legend, *"European Headquarters Universe News,"* and on the tallest and frostiest door the legend, "Major Asprin."

On this afternoon of blue and gold summer, Major Asprin's eyeballs were as frost-bitten as the glass on his office door. Major Asprin was mad. When he pushed little buttons on his desk, small-boned men three offices away jumped as if stabbed, and scuttled to Major Asprin's door and moaned, "No, Major Asprin, he hasn't come in yet."

Major Asprin squalled into three telephones at once, flung the receiver from a fourth, rumpled his necktie and bawled at his secretary.

"We can't locate him anywhere, sir."

"Call the railroad station. Phone the hotels. Get a detec-

tive. Don't stand there like a popeyed catfish. Any word from
Teutony?"

"Sorry, sir, the phone service to the Teutonic capital has been
cut off," he was told.

Major Asprin's stubbed fingers pounded like drumsticks. His
pearl-spatted shoes stamped. Major Asprin wasn't a major—
save the title represented a commission in the army of the unem-
ployed (six months a year on his private yacht)—but he could
grow every bit as empurpled and muster twice the rage.

"Find him, do you hear me? He's in the country. Bring that
crackpotted drunken scoundrel to me if it takes the Republican Guard. Look at that." The major's pointing finger shook.
"Look at that, I say!"

The secretary looked and fled the room. "That" was a stack of
rival newspapers on the major's desk. Papers from the four ends
of Europe. Rome, Amsterdam, Helsingfors. The Copenhagen
Aftenbladet. Belgrade *Universul*. The *Times* and the *Temps* and
the *Dernier Cri*. Five telephones rang in concert. Major Asprin
grabbed an armful of receivers and struck the stack of newspapers a wrathful blow, scattering the floor with scareheads.
Headlines in twenty languages shouted silently from the carpet,
drowning the major's squalls in his own very pink ears.

> Von Speer and Gatreau Dead In Teutony!
> Esperench Minister Slays Teuton Premier!
> Europe Rocked By Duel In Hotel Metropole!
> Teutons, Esperench Reported Mobilizing!
> Swiss Frontier Reported Closed! Allies Alarmed. No Word
> From Helvania!
> Esperance Denies Responsibility. Accuses Teutony. Schnit-
> zler Declares Danger-of-War!
> England Aloof In Crisis. London Out Of It, Says Church-
> wood. Would Appeal to League. Situation Alarming!
> Esperance Fears Air Attack, Cholera Germs. Border Forts
> Prepared. Stocks Go Down as Bourse In Panic—

"No," a voice yammered through the receiver at the major's

ear. "No news, Major Asprin. And we've held up the two o'clock editions and America is calling by transatlantic wire every minute. No news at all."

"Fake it! Copy it! Steal the *Etoile* leads! Lovable Christmas!" veins threatened to uproot on the major's forehead, "every other sheet in the world has it by this time, and Universe News without a line!"

He threw the telephones, saw the headline "Bourse in Panic," and rushed to the glass-globed stock-ticker in the corner with an apoplectic squawk. Jets of white tape spurted between his thumbs, more headlines, the story unreeling in cryptic Egyptian numerologies and high-signs. Continental Furniture was ruined. De Lesseps Paper at 6. Metro Underground off 20 points. Amsterdam Dairy at 3. Atlantique shipping dropped from 90 to 7½. The major screamed at these symbols, but he'd been smart about a few things, thank God. Siberian Nickel was up 19. Rubber jumping four points a tick. Gobell Dynamite going 130—140—145. Madrid Metallic was 185. Hertha Gun Works 200. Look at Emmerich Leather of Teutony. And Central Chemicals—

MAJOR ASPRIN made crazy sounds and phone calls. Brokers on the wire. Buy five hundred Hertha Gun, two hundred Gobell Dynamite, Central Chemicals, Emmerich Leather—

"Sorry, major, we'll try. If you'd let us know at opening time this morning when you got the tip on the shooting—"

"Tip on the shooting?" The major would strangle immediately.

"And Universe News is off fifteen points," the phone said dryly, "did you know? Rumor started your syndicate was closing when your papers didn't come out with an extra on the Metropole affair last night—"

The major bawled among the telephones.

A radio cunningly concealed in a panel beside his chair began to shout in a British accent:

"England is calling over Station GBS. Special news release

from London! With war momentarily certain on the Continent, Parliament convened this noon to decree Great Britain shall have no part in any conflict unless Powers in question submit their difficulties to League arbitration. McRamsey makes clear any precipitate hostilities will find England on the sidelines, voting for neutrality a hundred to one. Word from Washington brings certainty America will pursue a 'hands off' policy. Here's news from Moscow. In lieu of a Japanese threat, the Soviet Government cannot promise aid to Esperance in event of European war. From Rome. Engaged with hostilities in Abyssinia, Italy declared neutrality.

"Special dispatch from London *Observer!* As no word has come from *Observer* correspondent, Philip Shepler, covering last night's conference in Teutony, fear is expressed that the young journalist may have died in the Metropole fire. Meanwhile the whole world listens to an ominous silence from Teutony.

"Switzerland is moving troops into Godek Pass. With every reason to fear invasion, the Kingdom of Helvania proclaims strict neutrality, and Europe is wondering what Helvania's Queen will do if—"

The telephone rang. "Local editors calling, Major Asprin. All papers asking for Helvanian news."

The telephone rang. "America on the wire, Major Asprin. New York papers begging information on Helvania."

The telephone rang. "Our London bureau calling, Major Asprin. Want to know why we missed the Metropole shooting scoop."

Major Asprin, owner and operator of the Universe News Agency, the Universe News reputation and the Universe News Building on the corner of Boulevard St. Martin and Avenue Jacques, tore the desk phone clear from the wires with a scream. Pushbuttons rang like doorbells. Nine doors opened at once.

"No, Major Asprin, I'm sorry, but he isn't in yet!"

"Find him," the major trumpeted. "Find that son of a seacook's baboon and bring him straight to me. He got off the train this morning; the station guards saw him. Get him here. I don't care where he is or what he's doing. Arrest him! Kill him! Chloroform him! But get him here!" Major Asprin cooked a lobster-color in his chair. "I want John Keats!"

THE SCREAM charged out of the office and trailed down marble halls. The name of John Keats echoed down stairways and elevator shafts. It caromed into rooms where tired men glared from under green eye-shades and into rooms where lino-types clattered and into rooms where typewriters banged and into caverns twelve stories down where giant Hoe & Co. presses poured mechanical Niagaras of paper over the falls.

It echoed into the oak-paneled conference room one floor up, the room where Anton Stehli, senior Swiss correspondent, was sitting, arm in sling, on a stone window ledge, conjuring bird-like clucks in his throat, and scratching with his free hand the white tail feathers of an inquisitive pigeon.

On the leather lounge in the corner Alexandra Frantsovna waited in studied calm, smart in a white flannel jacket with puff sleeves and low-heeled sport shoes. Might have just run in after a doubles in tennis, but for the latest edition of *Pravda* tucked in her lap and the anxious way her eyes kept watching the door. Then when her eyes left the door they followed the march of Kurt Nielsen who passed back and forth across the line of windows. Under his pulled-down Panama brim, his face was unemotional, but his restless movements betrayed a growing impatience. He turned his wrist to mark the minute on his thin strap-watch. He lit and crushed out another cigarette. He poked his blackthorn stick along the carpet design. He whirled at the windows to stare down on the moving labyrinth of the boulevard. He barked at Stehli and Frantsovna, "Now where do you think that American is?" and without waiting for an answer, began to hum nervously the "Valse Triste."

And the summons echoed finally into the semi-darkness of the room exactly under the major's frosty-doored office. The morgue. The newspaper morgue where the dead were regimented not on marble slabs, but in neatly classified catacombs of time-stained newspaper clippings, dusty past-histories spread out to dry. Where the dead were not quite expired as yet, but their obituaries waited in readiness to beat their funerals down the street.

THE TWO men whispering at a littered table might have been consulting morticians, but were not. One was lank and Yankee, smelled of spearmint gum. The other was thickset and white under the eyes and breathed of whisky as his hands pawed through a box of filed newspaper clippings.

"Beats hell," the one with the chewing gum observed. "I get there to Athens and photograph a pageant—can you beat it?—and miss the swellest pictures of the year. Then I break my neck to get back here by plane, and the Big Boss gives me hell for not being in Teutony, where I wasn't sent. And is he sore up there? A boil. But you was tellin' me how that guy vanishes out the train window last night and the Russian girl stands in her door. So what?"

"I fell asleep in my compartment, I tell you. Never woke up till the train stopped at the frontier. I got hold of Nielsen, then, and told him to sit tight until we could get the crowd together and have a little talk. That's what we are going to have in about five minutes."

"How's your head now?"

"The medico gave me an anti-tetanus injection at the station. What makes it worse, though, is thinking about that business on the train. You know those Teuton inspections. I tell you, the guards know everybody aboard, and if a passenger jumped out of Nielsen's window they'd check it soon enough."

"Well, there it was. Everybody accounted for at the frontier. Nobody was missing."

"Yeah," the gaunt man said, hen-scratching in his hair, "if I didn't hear it from you I wouldn't take it. Here. Here's another file of names under *G.* You better hurry it. The correspondents are up in the Big Boss's conference room where you asked me to sneak 'em, and if Sour Puss finds out you're here in the building he'll blow out a fuse. Listen. That Russian dame looks the nuts. Swiss has his arm done up. The Squarehead reporter seemed to have ants in his socks, but them other two don't look like killers. This fella Dubail from the *Etoile,* he ain't come yet."

"It's not quite four, is it?"

"It's five after, now. Hell," droned the gangly man, "is popping around here. If I can help—"

"Never mind!" His companion was suddenly sorting a sheaf of news clippings in excited fingers. He looked up, electrified. "I've got it! Here—'Victor Yvon Césaire Gatreau—Born 1871 in Limoges—Student military engineering, highest honors at Ecole Polytechnique—Abandoned engineering to study Law—Brilliant record in Esperench Peter-Paul trials—At age of thirty elected Chamber of Deputies—Admitted Academy four years later—Made Minister of Public Instruction—Minister of Finance—Awarded Legion of Honor—Ambassador to Rumania—Took Portfolio of Foreign Affairs under President Villerand, 1934—Married Countess of Tardeau who died heart trouble at ceremony—remained single man thereafter— favors government lottery—advocates Soviet alliance—stirring anti-Schnitzler policy—principal in many duels—' Here's the one, Crazy! Get this!"

The printed columns crackled in his fingers as he read, " 'December Third, 1929. It is common talk on the boulevards today that the two gentlemen seen meeting in a certain spot at dawn yesterday in the Bois de Boulogne were none other than Victor Gatreau, eminent Republican from the Chamber, and M. Raoul Dubail, former Air Corps ace recently recognized for his trenchant editorials and sorties in the field of journalism. He did not fare so well, however, on the field of honor, as it is reported the experienced Gatreau, veteran of many such meetings, struck his young challenger in the cheek at the first exchange of shots. Seconds stopped the duel. It is rumored the engagement was fomented by certain attacks on Gatreau written by the daring journalist. Another source refers the matter to rivalry over the hand of a certain countess recently seen in the company of both. A witness declares Dubail as saying he has by no means received satisfaction in the case, but our inquiring reporter is inclined to think the young gentleman lucky, as a broken heart is seldom so fatal as a punctured one—'"

The gangly man took the gum from his mouth. "Say! I guess this fella Nielsen had the right dope on him, at that."

Hinges squeaked in the dimness. A face tinctured by a green eye-shade poked itself through the door at room's end. The man's eyes were worried, and he pointed a blue pencil at the ceiling.

"Say, you guys, I can't keep it quiet any longer you're down here. You should hear the one-man riot goin' on upstairs. The Big Shot is having a hemorrhage."

"I'll go right up," John Keats promised quietly, "and he'll bleed to death."

But he wasn't worried about the Big Boss as he steered his way out of the morgue with Crazy Hooper at heel. He was remembering the terrace of the Hotel Metropole (last night, or a thousand and one nights ago?) and Emmerich turning at the table with his face gone the color of bone. "Von Speer and Gatreau are finished. Locked in that room up there—they have shot each other to death." And the only movement at that table was Dubail's hand jerking to touch his cheek. Touching that scar the way he had touched it again on the train out of Teutony when Stehli had mentioned forgiveness.

KEATS MOVED down the room with a "Close that door, Crazy, and stand by," over his shoulder. Alexandra Frantsovna stood up from the leather lounge and watched him, attentive, inquiring. Nielsen stopped humming to scowl at Crazy Hooper, the camera man. Anton Stehli stood back from the opened window. At the Swiss correspondent's quick movement, a score of pigeons which had congregated on the sill took flight.

Keats could see the white birds scatter across the blue upper air, join in flight formation, then circle down over the avenue elms like a handful of paper bits tossed from the roof. From

*There was a sound like the
ending of a world.*

the eminence of that twelfth-floor window the city spread in panorama, Rue and Faubourg, Place and Parc, rooftops and chimneys and spires and brassy-green domes in a distillation of afternoon sunshine. There were the twin spires of Notre Dame, and on a far escarpment the white façade of Sacre Coeur, cleanly above a smudge of rookeries.

John Keats paused at the window; looked down. Despite the shrill-tongued tidings of news merchants, the intersection of Boulevard St. Martin and Avenue Jacques was going about its business. Traffic placidly unwinding at the corners. Lads with tennis rackets chatting at the entrance of the Metro. Workmen on their bicycles. A sailor with a red pompom on his nautical hat emerging from one of those "corner lavatories" to the salacious glee of tourist Americans. The pavements droned in the sun. Habitués sipped their *cointreau* in sidewalk cafés and shrugged. Were there not always headlines? Surely the bête Teutons would calm down. And some superannuated *gigolo* was taking leave of a matronly lady in a svelt Renault sedan, to the amusement of a moustachioed gendarme and an apple vendor, while a nice old gentleman in a béret was puttering around the Cupid-and-Virtue fountain; marble Virtue pouring water over Cupid's head in mid-square. Keats swung back to the room, and his voice was casual. "I'm glad to see you've come. Let me introduce Mr. Hooper. We can talk in front of him. Where's Dubail?"

"Must we wait for him?" Alexandra Frantsovna cried. "My office is sending me tonight to Helvania, and I haven't much time. John-Keats, what is happening?"

"And I, too, must leave at once," Stehli declared.

Keats said, "We can't go on without Dubail."

"And that British lad, Shepler?" Nielsen demanded. "Did you get in touch with him, Keats?"

"He's out of it. Dubail's the man we want right now."

STEHLI'S GRIZZLED features were mystified. "Raoul Dubail told me he was coming. I ran into him in front of the *Etoile* building an hour ago. On second thought, he might be a few minutes late. Busy at his writing, he said, and also he wanted to stop at his home to visit his father."

"Fifteen minutes late, he is." Nielsen's eyes looked knowingly into Keats'. "Perhaps our Raoul will find it expedient *not* to meet with us here."

"But why have you asked us to meet you here?" the Russian girl asked.

And then before Keats could frame an adequate response, the door burst open at Crazy's back, and a stout figure in the primary stages of an apoplectic stroke charged into the room and rushed at Keats with his fists sawing the air above his bald spot.

"Yes!" he screeched. "Why have you asked anybody to meet you here, you condemned rapscallion of a nameless son! My conference room! *My* conference room! Up here for a crap game, I suppose. Well, you can gather up these friends of yours and get them out of here as fast as hell, you addle-pated drunken dunce, but before you go I just want to tell you—"

"Major," John Keats said stiffly, "this is Alexandra Frantsovna of *Izvestia*—"

"Of wha-a-a-at?"

"And Kurt Nielsen of the Scandinavian Press—"

"Rival newspaper men!"

"And Anton Stehli of the Swiss Star Syndicate—"

"*Rival* newspaper people! Well, my God! Well, I am damned! You low-life reporter, you! You miserable sleep-walking bungler! You let me down on the biggest break since the Armistice, and then dare—dare to bring a string of rival newspaper men into my offices! Get out!" The Major clawed his collar, rocking on his heels in paroxysmal fury. "Get out!" he shouted the philippic at Keats, concluding with a salute of twenty-one oaths. "And don't ever let me see that double crossing mug of yours in my building again. And before you go, I'm going to tell you—"

"I'm going to tell you to shut up," Keats snarled, "and ask you to get out of here, yourself."

"Wha—wha-a-a—" Palsy overcame the Major's tongue. His abnormally protuberant eyes threatened to unsocket themselves from his head. He clutched at the table to stabilize legs taken with vertigo. "*Me* shut up! You tell *me!* You butter-fingered fool, don't you know you let the greatest story since Lindbergh's flight slip through our hands? You've ruined the reputation of my press service? You! Put Universe News off twenty points on the market! Every other paper but us got that spread! You missed it! Not a line! And when I want a man to send to Helvania this afternoon, where are you? Asleep at the switch! Under some table. Bed, more likely! No news from Teutony! Nobody to send to Helvania! You fall down on me like that! You dare! By heaven on high, I'm going to tell you—"

"Going to tell me I'm fired," John Keats said, brushing the Universe News owner out of his path; charging at the telephone-stand to grab up phone and catalog, "and I'm going to tell you I resign. You liver-faced old tycoon, you're throwing a catfit because you didn't learn about the Von Speer-Gatreau shooting in time to put in an order for munition stocks on the Exchange. I don't suppose I can throw you out of here because it happens to be your building, but I'll be triple damned if you can throw *me* out until I use this telephone—'Allo, Central! *Vite!* Give me *Elysée* 1-2-4-9—"

AT HIS back the irate Major Asprin continued to flaw the atmosphere with the voice of condemnation. He could glimpse a happy grin on Crazy Hooper.

A nosey voice twangled out of the telephone, "Office of the *Etoile* Service. *Bon joooor!*"

"Raoul Dubail's wire, please!"

"Raoul Dubail is not in the building, *m'sieu,* but left word he may be called at his home, the Pâtisserie of the Four Little Pigs on Rue Jacob—"

Damn! Another minute, and the Major would burst like an inflated bullfrog. Keats' fingers raged through the phone book. There was the place. Pâtisserie of the Four Little Pigs. 44 Rue Jacob. *Litré,* 2-0-6-0. Keats called the number of the pastry shop, pressing the mouthpiece to his lips and cupping a hand to his ear to blot out Major Asprin's quickened vituperations. The receiver sputtered in that exasperating way of Continental telephones, then the connection went through and a distorted voice spoke from the receiver. " 'Allo. It is Raoul Dubail who speaks."

"Dubail!" Keats was forced to shout. "This is Keats—John Keats. We're all waiting for you at the—"

Whang! The shout gurgled out in Keats' mouth and for a minute he regarded the desk-phone in astonishment. Had a membrane snapped in the mechanism of the receiver, or had the eardrum burst in his head? The tiny explosion from the receiver rang and buzzed in his ear. He clasped the phone to his head again, and recoiled in astonishment at the sound. *Slam!* A second explosion, a far-away but sharply defined concussion, as if a pistol had been fired into the mouthpiece at the other end of the line. The electric echo seemed to vibrate the phone in his fist. *Pop! Fizz!* The line had gone haywire. The receiver at his ear crackled like a broken radio; seemed to scream and wail an unintelligible jargon of syllables amidst a clatter not unlike breaking crockery.

"Dubail!" In consternation Keats pounded the hook with his finger. "'Allo! 'Allo! Dubail!"

Pang! That time everyone in the room heard the sound from the phone, recorded so distinctly it might have been somewhere in the building underneath, or a mile-away report in the sky outside. Instantly the telephone went dead. Frantically John Keats worked the hook. *Clickety-clickety-click.* No answer. Even Central was gone. Moisture came on his forehead as he carefully adjusted the receiver on the prong, returned the phone to its stand, turned to stare at the people across the room.

"Did you hear that?"

"The devil!" came from Nielsen. The Swede screwed the monocle into a glassy eye. "It sounded like a shot—"

"I could hear it in this corner," Alexandra Frantsovna cried.

A melting fear lay under John Keats' belt. His mind was racing again, trying to achieve a mental picture of what had happened at *Litré* 2-0-6-0.

"I had Dubail on that wire! Then that crack. The phone's gone dead—"

"It did sound as if a gun had been fired," Stehli seconded.

"Three times," Keats blurted. "Right near the phone. Sounded as if he fell over, I tell you. Listen! I'm going straight to Dubail's house and find out what hap—"

CRASH! HIS words were blotted in mid speech by a sound like the ending of a world. It wasn't in the telephone that time. It seemed to come from the daylight, a blast straight out of the atmosphere, an atomic detonation that tore the sunshine to shards directly under the conference-room windows. That sound smashed every window in the oak-paneled room. Its violence shook walls and floor. Major Asprin recoiled across the carpet as if kicked by an invisible mule. Crazy Hooper was uprooted, thrown backwards against the door. In that deafening instant

Nielsen went plunging around the table; blood spurted from Anton Stehli's nose; Alexandra Frantsovna screamed amazement, staring wide-eyed at the sun-filled windows where the glass had vanished.

Beyond those windows the sky was blue, cloudless porcelain; and John Keats was too stunned to move. That appalling aërial report had erased the last brain from his head. He could feel his nose beginning to bleed. He could feel the Universe News Building shuddering underfoot as if gripped by a seismic shocking. The silence after that terrific smash was the quietude of death. An awful cavity of hush, like a hole in the blue and gold afternoon.

Then the cavity of hush began to fill with little sounds. The sounds grew and grew, like the voice of dead leaves beating through the forest before a storm. A confusion of sounds, like rain after a thunderclap. In the blue above the city there was no sign; no fracture in the azure overhead. The babel uprose from the street. Everywhere glass was smashing with the noise of a million breaking goblets. In the golden daylight cascades of shattered window-panes showered past the twelfth floor, raining down from floors above.

A thousand auto horns were honking in the street. The day had a million tongues; the babel mounting to a chorus, a singsong, a vast many-voiced wailing that ascended heavenward from the canyon of the boulevard like a chanting from Dante's Pit. *"Ah la la!"*—*"Aidez-moi!"*—*"Ah, Sacré Dieu! Sacré nom de Dieu!"* A piercing shriek crescendo through vocal bedlam. *"Yaaaaahaaahaaa—"*

JOHN KEATS discovered he had reached the window without any apparent volition of his own, and was leaning from the frame where the pane had been, looking down.

A twenty-foot, ragged-rimmed excavation had ripped open the intersection of Boulevard St. Martin and Avenue Jacques, and around this yawning crater an ever-thickening crowd of pedestrians boiled and screamed. Glass lay ankle-deep on the pavements. An astonishing rubbish, a mixture of men's hats, wagon wheels, automobile fenders, brickbats and powdered cement strewed the adjacent gutters. The excavation steamed, smoked. Water from a broken main geysered forty feet in the air, wetting the crowd. Those in front shrieked to get away from the crater, and those behind jammed forward to see. Whistles shrilled as a squad of gendarmes helter-skeltered around a corner, swinging their white clubs. Sirens were coming.

But the ambulances would not be in time. Too late for the three newsboys who hung on the lip of the excavation like a single bundle of scarlet rags. Too late for the spitcurl-moustachioed gendarme who sprawled face up on the paving stones with a bite of apple in his mouth. Nor could any ambulance succor the aged fruit vendor sitting upright amidst the wreckage and kindling of his pushcart, or the contorted remains of two workmen tangled with the contorted remains of their bicycles.

And the nice old gentleman was struggling at the base of the Cupid-and-Virtue statue like a wingless beetle trying to rise. Water in the fountain had ceased. No more sweetness and light from Virtue's inexhaustible pitcher. A man's shoe had plugged the mouth of the marble pitcher; and the nice old gentleman in the béret could not rise from the sidewalk below because his feet were blown off.

TRANSFIXED IN that twelfth story window above this carnage, John Keats lifted his gaze to the sky. Not a sign in the blue, but a dentist's drill had started in the atmosphere, a menacing *zmmmmmmmmm* that increased in volume like the coming of an invisible express train. He heard Alexandra Frantsovna's scream of warning. Nielsen's ejaculated oath. Stehli and Crazy Hooper cursing at the next sill. And before he could move a muscle, the lightning had struck again.

But the projectiles you hear coming aren't the ones to be feared; it was not a near hit. And this time he had seen it. Perhaps a mile off in the sky a blade of light had stabbed the blue. No more than a mercurial, rainbow-colored flash with a

thunder-peal in its wake. Ten blocks westward the afternoon
split open with a second heathenish roar. The sound pierced his
head like a sword, and he glared in something close to terror
at the distant roofline where the green dome of a building had
burst like a shattered light bulb.

A great funnel of rubbish geysered darkly against the sun.
Stucco fragments, kindling, blocks of cement, steel girders
doubled like hairpins, shards of plaster and bits of iron rose
skyward like a flock of terrified crows. You could hear things
falling in the streets, another shower of window glass, a third
zooming invisible express train—*Crash!*—the sky to the south-
ward was black with another explosion.

It seemed to John Keats as if the city's skyline was altering,
breaking up, crumbling to pieces, then, under his eyes. Light
flashed where the Tower had stood, a single lick of white fire
that blinded the day; and when he looked again the colossal
landmark had burst like a splintered cane. A fourth explosion
lit on the panorama about Sacre Coeur. And now the sky was
alive with those criss-crossing rainbow flashes, street after street
was crashing, the anthills of the city boomed and banged, from
every visible quarter of the metropolis great spouts of smoke
began to spurt. A sulphurous haze rolled in the sunshine, black
smoke, white smoke, escaping steam, a stench of chemicals. A
deafening, terrifying undertone came up from below. Bellow-
ings, caterwaulings, long-drawn screams, the shrieks of human
distress mingled with a mechanical uproar of bells, steam whistles, sirens, motor horns, fire gongs. And *smash, smash, smash!*

Once, in a forgotten boyhood, John Keats had heard a cata-
clysm. The Black Tom explosion in the early days of the World
War. Again at Charlevaux when a barrage of 370s was giving the
Leathernecks hell. But in this roaring eruption those remembered detonations would have been the plinks of mandolins in
a collapsing iron foundry. He sprang around from the window
with the last spot of color washed from his face. Surprisingly,
that oak-paneled room was still there, swimming in fine yellow

dust. Surprisingly, Alexandra Frantsovna was posed at the table, even lighting a cigarette.

He found time to like her for that. Outside the world was bursting to pieces; inside the room was ringing with the crash of the Final Day, that fatheaded Major Asprin was capering in terror with his fingers stuffed in his mouth; Anton Stehli, Nielsen, Crazy Hooper, he, himself, were shouting fear, but the Russian girl was facing it with a smoke. Her hands, he saw, were trembling; and her eyes glowed behind the flare of her tiny lighter, but something about her was steel.

"DO YOU think the building will fall?" The sound of her voice coming level through the din of Vulcan brought a babel of coherent yells from the others.

"My building!" That was the Major's scream. John Keats stared at the wretched man in disgust. His glance sought Kurt Nielsen, as if the Swedish correspondent might somehow confirm what was going on. No use trying to run from this tempest, and Nielsen was slowly picking his way toward the door, a queer Chinese expression on his face, half fear, half contemptuous of fear. Whatever admiration Keats might have conceived for the Scandinavian's conduct under fire, gave way to a feeling of anger at the words he shouted across the room.

"I'm going to find my press bureau! Do you realize they're blowing this city off the map! I'll get this story through if it's the last thing goes to press."

"Story?" Keats bawled. "Nielsen! Wait!"

Stehli came stumbling from the windows. "But the planes?" he screamed. "Where are the bombing planes?"

Nielsen turned to lash his blackthorn stick through the dusty air. "Don't be a fool, Anton, those are not bombing planes," he shouted. "They're aërial torpedoes. It's the first time in history they've ever been used to reduce a city. If you want to get that story to your syndicate you'd better find the telegraph before all the wires are down. My God, what a scoop! Aërial torpedoes!"

The Swede's shouting was drowned in a storm of crashings

that shook a fresh tremor through the building. Major Asprin parted his coat tails and fled. An unaccountable anger prickled the skin on Keats' forehead, his eyes misted, his jaw shut in a clamp. News stories. Buildings. Aërial torpedoes. But there was an old man lying in the street out there with his feet shot away. Citizens were dying like cattle. A girl, here, calm enough to smoke a cigarette. God help him, he had something to do in this Armageddon, and even that deity wasn't going to stop him.

"Get out of my way!" he shouted at the room. Somehow he had flung his hands at Frantsovna to grip her by the shoulders. He was shaking her; shouting down at her upturned face. "Wait for me in this building, can you hear me? Safer inside than on the street! I'll be back and take you to your hotel. You're staying at the Savoy?"

Odd how clearly he could hear her. "Savoy. Rue Invalides—"

"Don't try to get there alone. Wait till I'm back."

Her eyes levelled up at him from the calm of her face. "Take me with you, John-Keats. Where are you going?"

"Crazy," he yelled at the jabbering camera man, "look after Miss Frantsovna for me. Take her down to the ground floor. Safer there. And wait. I'm going after Raoul Dubail—"

Nielsen and Stehli were shadows vanishing through the door. A delicate bronze smoke swam through the windows and fogged the room. Keats, Frantsovna and Crazy raced for the corridor. Charging from the conference room they collided with a little man in shirtsleeves, a wireless operator who turned a putty-colored face up at Keats, opened a mouth of gold teeth, and howled.

"*C'est le fin du monde!*" the man screeched. "From the Alps word has come. The Boche are on the march. *C'est la guerre!*"

In the roaring city outside a million mouths were echoing the cry. "*C'est la guerre! C'est la guerre!*"

CHAPTER VIII

WAR!

SHERMAN, THE INARTICULATE, said war was hell, and merely praised with faint damnation. Something heroic might be said for the charge of a cavalry squadron riding hell for leather down a shot-torn battlefield to the tune of Hollywood bugles and storybook battle cries, pennons flying and sabres flashing, but nothing could be said for these shattered faubourgs, this charnel of private homes where citizens were scattered on their doorsteps, where priests fled from door to door with hopeless spiritual first aid, where the afternoon sunlight was sprinkled with the smudge of flying building materials and singing fragments of steel.

That side street was Inferno. The avenue beyond was Inferno. The street beyond that. Compared with this thunder and lightning, this smiting comet of death that had struck the metropolis, the Civil War was a sham battle fought by elves in a glade with wooden swords. Here was no hand to hand engagement with the Reaper. No cavalry sword could cut down those droning, unseen monsters that fell from the twilight like the brands of Thor to smash the foundations of a city block.

High in the blue a pair of tri-motored scouting planes armed with light artillery, manned by the finest motors and the stoutest pilots Esperance could supply, cruised in circles of futility. Beneath them their capital fell to pieces like a city of A-B-C blocks. Houses crumpled in the sun. Parks founted in the air. Keats craned his neck to look at the war planes. Quixotic men gone up to do battle. A pair of sparrows rising against an attack of hawks.

But the artillery planes had nothing to shoot at. The horizon was without a target. The hawks were mercurial lances of light that passed under them with a roar and detonated on house-tops a mile below. There was an alley at the end of the street where one of the monsters had come to earth and, for some reason uncalculated by the inventors, had failed to go off. Its only damage was a five foot hole in the paving, and a little crowd of raving citizens had braved extermination in the open to cluster around the thing. Keats paused to study the engine. A new device from the workshops of Mars. Death gone modernistic. The crowd regarded the dud with expressions of hate and high terror, as well it might. "Made in Teutony"—the sender's address was plain for any who were left to read. Men pointed trembly fingers and squeaked. *Ah, mon Dieu!* Why had not Esperance invented this wonder? But the Teutons had the jump on them again.

Keats, staring at the invention, chilled. Nothing but a flying shell, its construction a horror of simplicity, the last word from some secret machine-shop beyond the Rhine. A 42-centimeter projectile, perhaps a ton of explosive in a beautifully polished case, not unlike a submarine torpedo given wings. Powered by twin propellers, an electric motor in its base, it was probably steered by directional gyro; its nose was deep in the pavement, one metal wing was crumpled, but its propellers were still spinning with a menacing buzz. Good God! They could launch these flying sharks from some hidden field and they would rocket across the sky at four hundred miles an hour to drop, at the command of wireless, anywhere in the world.

THE SKY above the city was alive with these atrocious gimcracks. One, two, three—they were roosting on the heights of Montmartre. The Montmartre skyline had come loose and was bumping along the ground. Colored flame-balls flashed, roared, bounced across those distant roofs. Keats pulled his belt tighter on an empty stomach; backed away from the sinister promise unexploded in the street. Shelter? Nothing was secure from these Big Bertha shells with wings. Aërial torpedoes! Against such engines as that, yesterday's military science was obsolete as chain mail.

Sickened, half blinded, cold to the marrow with fear, Keats spun from that object and ran on. A city boomed and fell about his heels. Buildings swayed before his eyes and came down like towers of sand. He saw the front open from an office skyscraper like the front of a dollhouse, revealing a honeycomb of rooms where astonished typists sat paralyzed at their desks. There was the Church of St. Pierre le Pauvre, its spire like a jagged bottle with the neck sheared away, doors jammed with a yowling crowd.

The End had come. Time to put on your gas mask and remember God. How did that grand piano get there in the middle of Rue Danou? Who drove that omnibus intended for "Place St. Germaine" through the plate glass window of that beauty parlor? Keats sprinted down what was once an avenue and thought of a storm in Hell. A corner where a boy in velvet knickerbockers lay broken in the dust with a hoop still quivering in his hand. An old woman pilloried on a rail fence, her skirts splattered with egg-yolk, a basket of shells on her arm. A cocker spaniel somersaulting across the pavement, yipping as it twisted its head to snap at a broken back. A girl in a white pinafore thrown like a discarded doll against a rubbish barrel.

He groaned aloud at every turn. What malevolent demon could be served by the death of children, the agony of lop-eared spaniels? Zmmmm—*Crash!* Zmmmm—*Crash!* and two statesmen dead at a dinner table were ending the world. Keats hung in a ruptured doorway to let a herd of fire trucks race by. The *pompiers* hung like monkeys on their engines, screeching from maddened faces. *"Citoyens! Aux armes!"*—throwing packages from hampers strapped to their carts. Keats picked up one of the canvas bundles. A gas mask. He tucked it into a palsied elbow, plunged around a corner, charged through a panicky swarm of women pouring from the gilt doors of a cinema. The women wore gas masks and looked like miniature elephants in performing clothes escaped from a show. Their goggle eyes glowed terror, and sounds came from their rubber snouts. *Crash!* That was somewhere on the next block. The women wheeled like frightened antelopes, bolted in another direction.

KEATS TOOK the middle of the road, keeping clear of the buildings which might momentarily bury him in blocks of concrete. The entire city seemed to be coming down. Crash upon crash. From Montmartre to Montparnasse the smokes of a thousand conflagrations chimneyed skyward to join a mammoth, bulging thundercloud that fattened in the sky to obscure the sun. Napoleonic avenues smothered in blowing fogs. In the parks and shrub-flowered public gardens the dead were piling like cordwood. He fled through the Tuileries with an arm shielding his eyes, pointing his course for a cliff of ferroconcrete palaces that marked a bend of the river. But in this awful tempest one's destination was uncertain. One sighted a landmark; then, suddenly it was gone. One looked around, and the place just passed was not there.

Somewhere in the Aceldama he passed the entrance to a Metro. The subway was alive. An inhuman, conglomerated stew of people clawed, elbowed, fought, kicked in an effort to get underground. In the glow of that deadly twilight the faces of men and women seemed to boil. A gendarme's club struck at him as he stopped to look.

John Keats never knew how he found a hotel that afternoon. How he fought his way through those scribbled city cañons and boiling streets, through stampeding crowds and howling traffic jams and rolling forest fires to stand finally, battered and shaken, in a courtyard furnished with peaceful tea-tables and potted yew trees. The rococo façade of the famous hotel was singularly undisturbed in the midst of hurricane. One could imagine Voltaire lounging in the court uncovered goblet in fingers, watching civilization go down with an epigram and a leer. Otherwise the hotel was unoccupied. A cat was a lost soul calling for help under a grating. The curtained windows were empty, and from where he hung on the gate John Keats could see the foyer was echoing and deserted. The guests had gone away. His boots ran up a path of tile set in mosaic, and he pulled a bell. No *concierge* could have heard that jingle above the tempest; for that reason no *concierge* appeared.

THE LOBBY was desolate. Chairs and divans unoccupied, a sideboard set with untouched *apéritifs,* somebody's steamer trunk abandoned at the door of a stalled elevator. Shaking off a shiver, he dodged across the foyer to the desk where Madam should have been presiding over her books. Madam had gone, leaving her knitting. The key-rack behind the desk was deserted. A buzzer droned in the telephone switchboard. Keats shouted because any man would want company in a hotel with that racket blowing outside. His voice brought nothing but a shower of concrete fragments that crashed like hail among the tables of the court. A mile across the city another roof had blown.

He swung himself lightly across Madam's desk; snatched the hotel register. When he found the name he wanted "Alexandra Frantsovna—Moscow," penned in a woman's handwriting, he had only to jump for the key-rack and find her number. No moment for etiquette, he told himself with a snarl, as he unlocked and entered the Russian girl's second-floor room. Damnation! As if it had known he would come for it, the little gilt-edged volume of Shakespeare was lying on the pillow of her bed. Reading it to improve her English, she had said. Her remembered words brought a sardonic and hollow mirth to his mouth. Who in God's name read Shakespeare to improve his English? And then for some unaccountable reason his hand must hesitate in touching the Russian girl's book. His mind recoiled. But a jarring, metallic blast, a convulsion of earth and sky beyond the window curtains, prompted his intent. The room shuddered underfoot, rattled its doors, was engloomed with smoke and a stench of calcined earth.

He plucked a scrap of paper from his vest, smoothed it in quivering fingers. Then he grabbed the book from the pillow, and stood in a haze of dust-particles, fanning the pages of the volume in his hand. A little map of plaster broke from the ceiling. Pictures were dropping from the walls. He hurried to the windows for the little light that was left. Page 64. Damn! Page 64 was intact, but—

"God! It *did* come from her book—" The upper edge of Page 63 had been ripped away. Perspiration drenched his collar as he fumbled with the numbered scrap in his fingers that bore the printed line, *So Foul A Sky Cannot Be Cleared Without A—* It worked. The jagged under edge of the scrap fit perfectly into the mutilated top of that torn page. The last word of the sentence was reëstablished. So *Foul A Sky Cannot Be Cleared Without A Storm!*

THE STORM had come but the sky, right then, hadn't cleared for John Keats. The darkness in his mind congealed to midnight. No denying this evidence; he had known it for a certainty the minute he discovered that scrap of paper in Nielsen's unconscious hand. How could the girl's book have been in the Swede's compartment on that limited? How, unless she was in there with it? Why had she attacked the Swede, then, and how the living hell did she return to her own compartment in that mile-a-minute sleeping car?

A city was exploding in his ears, but his brain pinwheeled with a puzzle more maddening than the demolition of a metropolis. Jigsaw pieces formed, fell apart, tried to reform in his mind. Frantsovna! She must have escaped Nielsen's compartment by crawling through the window, swinging along the outside of the car. Impossible! The train had been flying. But how was the fade-away accomplished? Unbounded nerve in the girl, the way she'd lit that cigarette with the shells coming down.

And it was Nielsen who'd seen her arrested as a spy in Spain. "Kissed the judge and got off." The Swede had seen her. Had she tried to kill him because he knew too much? Killed Shepler for the same reason? Then admitting her presence on the roof across the court because she knew he, Keats, had spotted her there and she had to tell him something? Lord in heaven, and the girl had confessed a hatred for Von Speer, too—

Keats shouted at the ceiling. Closing the book on this deadly chapter, he crammed it deep in his pocket, raced from the room. On the stairs of that echoing, boom-rocked hotel, he stopped to drag breath and summon the last of his wits. Frantsovna! His eyes were like darkness in pits. Only one other name could enter his mind. Somewhere, in that cauldron of a city under an eclipsed sunset, he had to locate the Pâtisserie of the Four Little Pigs, had to find Raoul Dubail!

THE METROPOLIS had fallen to ashes and the day with it. City and sky together were afire. Aërial torpedoes had stopped coming, but their echoes persisted. While the night sky burned, the city slopped over on its broken foundations. A loosened cathedral spire crashing on the upturned faces of worshipers. A landslide of rookeries pouring down a river bank. Shell-shocked, fear-maddened, suffocated, the populace raved at the threat of nightfall. That delicate mechanism which holds a million humans to the paths of their obscure destinies had lost its trolley. The paths were buried in mortar. Police turned into bandits and surgeons into cut-throats. Brother fought brother, and women and children, as usual, were last.

Somewhere in that race across Inferno, John Keats was crossing a bridge. A crazy tide of craft crawled the waters below. It was a river of molasses, a waterway of strawberry jam. Morning there'd been fishermen angling minnows, sleek motor launches, excursion steamers, barges bright with vegetables. Delicate in suspension, the bridge had been a model of civic architecture, white concrete set with a graceful patrol of light-poles. Now it was a span of rubbish, precarious over a shrieking fleet of junks. The river was like blood. Its bridge a cross-ladder of bones. The body of a naked man, his yellow hide spattered a harlequin red, dangled in the wind under a lamp post. Keats was forced to sprint beneath the hanging toes. A square of cardboard was pinned to the lynched one's stomach by a breadknife. The dead man's fair mustache and the printed words on the cardboard told his story. He was not for rent.

"Boche," the sign said. *"Spy."*

Not far from this impromptu gallows stood a woman who might have been the man's wife. A fair-haired toddler clung tugging at her skirts in an attempt to move her away. She would not move away. Swollen eyes in a convulsed face blazed at John Keats. "Hans was not a spy! He was born in the Saar, but he was not a spy! We had come to visit the city—"

Behind the woman an Esperenchman in black cloak and broad-brimmed hat, an artist with a canvas landscape hugged under arm, leaned on the pitted bridge rail and contemplated this drama of modern civilization without sympathy. As Keats stumbled forward, the painter pointed a thumb at the hanged.

"Rengardez! There is one to even the score—"

"Rue Jacob!" Keats flung at the man. "You know a place called the Pâtisserie of the Four Little Pigs?"

The face under the broadbrim grimaced. *"Rive Gauche.* Two hours ago the Rue Jacob was just beyond that statue of Napoleon. The statue of Napoleon is not there any more. The Rue Jacob? Who can tell?"

KEATS DISCOVERED the street sign by the bonfire glow of a burning book stall. A narrow lane crowded with a carnival of light and the sounds of Roman Holiday, just beyond the bridge.

Smoke billowed in the lane dense as a London fog. Keats found himself jammed in a mob that had collected around an overturned Renault sedan. Wheels to the sky, the car was a ludicrous catafalque with a mummified object peering upside down through its cracked windshield.

An aged Esperench woman, bent over a staff like Mother Goose, turned her shriveled face at Keats. "Can you see, *m'sieu?"* pointing the staff, standing back to let him pass, "it is the wife of President Villerand, they say. *Pardieu!* And she had just come out of the pastry shop yonder. They say it was the first explosion in the city. The pastry shop was—"

"Pastry shop," Keats demanded. "Where? Show me!"

Her shrunken hand steered him across the curb. *Voilà!* The Pâtisserie of the Four Little Pigs. Noted for the finest pastries in the city. But regard it now. Of the shop there seemed little left but its sign. The store front was not there. A smoldering stack of kindling, matchwood composed of shelves, furniture, plaster, baked goods, grocery cans under the hole where a roof had been.

The old woman cupped hands at her mouth that Keats might hear. "I saw it all, *m'sieu*. I, Grandma Gilette. From the house across the street where I sit in the window. God was good to me. My house was not harmed. But the noise, *m'sieu*. Like the thunder of God."

Hand to sick mouth, Keats staggered back from what was left of that doorway. From that charred inner room where a telephone was visible, overturned on a table, and a man's body lay flattened amidst a scatter of tarts, *croissons*, eclairs, jellycake.

"Raoul Dubail!" The cry broke from his lips.

The old woman shook her head. *"Non,* that is not Raoul."

"Who—who is it, then?"

"His old father, *m'sieu*. You seek Raoul Dubail? But he has gone. I, Grandma Gilette, saw him go. I saw it all. He had returned this day from afar to visit his old father, the baker. Young master Dubail and his father, the Blessed God have pity, they were my neighbors—"

"Raoul Dubail!" Keats yelled. "Where did he go?"

"I am telling you, *m'sieu*," the granny cackled. "I saw him enter the shop, embrace his parent. *Oui.* But a moment later he walked to where you see the telephone. Then—*pouf!* I, who watched, saw the store front blast away as if struck by cannon. You are a friend of his, *m'sieu?*"

"Yes," Keats panted. "Yes. I want to know where he went!"

"M'sieu, it seemed an hour, a year before the smoke and noise cleared away. And then, when I could see and hear, the Pâtisserie

of the Four Little Pigs was in ruins. And Raoul Dubail came rushing through these ruins with a face of blood. His father! His father! *Ah, la la,* but the sound of the young gentleman's cries, *m'sieu.* His father, as you see, had been killed before his very eyes. Raoul Dubail shook his fists above his head. *'Aux armes!'* he was screaming. 'The Boche have done this to me. God strike Teutony for this thing. I go to join the Air Corps! I go to fight them all!' And then, *m'sieu,* he ran down the street like a crazy man, and a dozen citizens ran with him. Raoul Dubail has gone—"

"**YEAH,**" **A** chewing-tobacco spoke up behind John Keats, "the guy's gone, all right, as I found out half an hour ago. Went somewhere to join the Air Corps, a guy was telling me. Secret flyin' base somewhere."

Keats whirled at this loose-jointed shadow which had detached itself from the crowd around the Renault.

"Crazy Hooper!" Keats bellowed.

"That's me. I come here an hour ago lockin' for you. You said you was comin' here, an' when you didn't show up after a while I—"

"Frantsovna! Didn't I tell you to hold onto that woman—"

"What," the camera man grunted, "do you mean, woman? Wildcat's the word for that dame. Lookit this scratch on my kisser, can you see it? You'd been gone an hour when she decided to take it on the lam—"

"My God! She's got away—"

"Listen, it's time we all got away. Everybody's doing it. We was waitin' there in the Universe Building, the dame and me, when one of these police cars tore up the boulevard. Gang of gendarmes jumps out and starts scattering into all the buildings around that's left standing. Gendarme runs in at us and starts hollerin' through a megaphone. Spread the word to beat it. A plague was comin', he said. Teutons were gonna send torpedoes at midnight loaded with cholera germs. Bacteria stuff."

"Cholera! Good God!"

"That's what the gendarmes was yellin'. All citizens to get

A white dove fluttered down to Stehli's shoulder.

outa town. Three roads would be open to the coast, a couple of routes to Belgium and there's a highway open for automobiles to Switzerland. Well," Crazy hurried to say, "the Russian girl made a dive for the exit. 'I'm taking that road through Switzerland. Tell John-Keats to follow. Tell him I'm after the greatest news story he ever heard of.' Something like that. She hadda get to the Alps before the roads was blocked.

"I tried to stop her. *Zing!* she blew outa my hands. Next thing she's in a big blue automobile—"

Veins stood on John Keats' forehead. "How'd you get across, town, Crazy?"

The camera man imitated a chuckle. "Took the first car I c'd lay hands on. A big Minerva. You shoulda seen me climb traffic to get here. But there's a fender an' one headlamp left. Yeah, I took the Major's car."

KEATS WIPED slime from his forehead, staring. He flung a hand to his pocket, yanked out a book. "Listen, Crazy. I got this. From her room at the Savoy. It's—" His mouth gagged. That was no ordinary volume of Shakespeare's plays. His fingers must

have jarred a hidden spring. Alexandra Frantsovna's little gilt-
edged volume snapped like a rat trap, flew open. Shakespeare's
plays were not all there. From "Two Gentlemen of Verona" to
"Henry VIII" the plays were intact. From "Troilus and Cressida"
to "Othello" the subject matter was missing, the pages gutted
to form a hollow rectangular shell. Nesting in that secret hide-
away was a snub-nosed Russian automatic and a shining clip
of .38 caliber shells.

Keats shut the book with a whispery oath, jammed it into his
coat. His face was lavender as he stormed at Crazy. "You saw
that? Get going! They won't let us out of the airport. Get the car!
We'll catch that woman if we have to steal God's own chariot
to do it in. News story she's after? I'll show her some news! The
rottenest story you ever heard! Come on!"

THE DAIRY farm of André Chibou, and André Chibou,
himself, had retired at the customary twilight hour in the
customary twilight peace.

Situated in that slumberous valley between Bois Chaperon
Vert and Chuseville, two hundred miles and at least two hundred
years from the capital, the dairy farm, like André, was as fixed
in its ways as the ambient hills in rural landscape. Sundown on
those snowy border peaks that marked the roof of Switzerland.
To bed.

André, careful man, did not own a car. The old gray mare
was fast enough for him. He did not own a radio. His interest
stopped with the borders of his farm, bounded on the east by the
main line railroad, on the west by a parallel turnpike, metal and
concrete highways curving together towards the Alps.

At three o'clock that afternoon the limited to Lake Geneva
had streaked along the rails, and André had watched it go with
a hand-wave. Around four o'clock a group of American girls in
knickers (those mad Americans!) had bicycled up the road on
their way to Bern. The day proceeded to wane in blues, pinks and
golds. Black and white kine kneeling in emerald clover. Chick-
ens at roost in the fruited barns. Larks wheeling above the yellow

millet. Come 7 P.M., André saw no reason why he should not go to roost, too. But his wife turned on the stairs to declare she kept hearing thunder somewhere in the air, and he'd better see to the calves. The old woman, of course, was imagining things again. Thunder, nonsense. On this ripe summer evening with the dusk as clear and fragrant as Moselle?

He quarreled mildly with the old woman about this, slipped out of his cowboots, put on his nightcap and grunted into bed. He was dreaming cheerily that he'd just cheated Pierre Tulacque at the horse fair by trading him a mule for a full-blooded Percheron stallion, when a cry from his wife yanked him awake and upright in bed.

"André! What is that which is that?"

"What is that which is what?"

"In the barn yard. An automobile. I heard it turn in. There have been many fast cars on the road. Suddenly it stopped, this one."

André must grumble out of the eiderdown, stub across the room, open the shutters. Warm moonlight, almost as bright as day, silvered countryside and roadway without. A long, dust-grayed roadster had parked under the poplar, and its driver was boldly drawing water at the well, slopping it into a steaming radiator. As André blinked from the window a number of motors flashed by in the moonlight. He called at the stranger who had stopped.

"A fellow who but wished to water his car," he complained to his wife when the intruder had gone. "Looked like a Norwegian, perhaps. These foreigners! Wanted to know if I had seen a Swiss go by, a Swiss with his arm in a sling, probably in a taxicab. When I told him certainly not, he thanked me with a curse and flung himself into his car and drove like the devil away. One of these dirty tourists with a big yellow bag on the seat beside him—"

"But you noticed many other cars on the road also?"

"There should be a law against it. Do people never sleep any more? It is almost ten by the clock."

"André, was that thunder in the sky?"

No sound. More like a fluttering of the air. "Nonsense. Go to sleep, Mathilde. Do not wake me up again."

BUT THE cuckoo clock was hooting twelve when she woke him again. It was unprecedented. At that hour someone was knocking at the door. André Chibou glared cautiously, then indignantly from the upper window. A blue touring car in his dooryard, and a slip of a woman in a khaki trench-coat calling up at him. Did he have a telephone here? No? Then had he seen a roadster driven by a Swedish gentleman, a man with a big yellow kitbag? Had such a car, such a man gone by? *Sapristi,* was his dairy farm an information bureau? Then, the woman asked, was she on the direct route to Switzerland?

André Chibou told her she was. He could have told her another direct route she was on, a girl like that driving around unchaperoned at so godless an hour. The young foreign woman whisked her car back onto the road and flashed away. Name of a name! Look at the automobiles. André knuckled his eyelids, bade his wife get out of bed to witness.

Ventre bleu! was there a redness in the sky toward Switzerland? Maybe far-away heat lightning. But in the barn a rooster crowed. Regard the hour! Only midnight. And there was a train pounding up the railroad track for the Alps, headlight rushing up the metals, a full-lunged whistle on the curve. Never had there been a midnight express like that. André Chibou craned his neck out into the moonlight, eyes like saucers under the silly tassel of his nightcap. *"Sacré nom de Dieu!"*

And then it came. Pouring down the turnpike out of the north. Slam-banging down the railroad. Roaring past the farm of André Chibou like two runaway rivers that had burst their dams somewhere in the night and were obligingly keeping to the edges of his pastures, going by his house on two sides. The turnpike, familiar to creaking wains and leisurely hay carts, began to grumble, rumble with the sound of a coming avalanche. The railroad came alive with a steaming, clanging rush. Twin streams pouring themselves toward Switzerland. The Army of Esperance! Mother of God! The Army!

By railroad and parallel turnpike two earth-shaking, smoking clouds boiled down the valley, horizontal columns of dust in the wine-clear moonshine. On the highroad came a squadron of motorcycles with wailing police sirens, an advance guard clearing civilian traffic to one side. Then a sixty-mile-an-hour fleet of staff cars. Motors and officers gray with dust. In the open tonneaus a glimpse of scarlet-topped *képis* and oak-leafed collars.

Next a dizzy file of army lorries, private cars, taxicabs, vans, trucks, automobiles of every description packed to the doors with powder-blue infantry. *Ziff,* the cars went by. *Ziff, ziff, ziff!* Tires singing on concrete. *"En Suisse!"* Hoarse yells above the continuous roar of gas engines. *"En Suisse!"*

THEN THE cavalry. Squadron after squadron. Lancers with machine guns instead of spears. Dragoons; horsehair plumes blowing above their shining helmets. Mounted *Chasseurs d'Afrique,* picturesque in scarlet and blue. A company of Algerian *Spahis,* white turbans streaming in a thundering processional, crimson cloaks bannering. More staff cars. More regular cavalry. Then an interval filled with motor ambulances. Car after car marked with the Red Cross. After that a company of motorized Engineers. Followed by light artillery, battery after battery of *suixante-quinze,* clattering, clanging limbers, muzzles a-gleam in the dust, their gunners clinging for dear life to the skidding caissons. Horse-drawn rapid-fire guns. Mule-drawn ammunition carts. The jangle of chain and harness dying into a great *thud-thud-thud* of hobnailed boots. Now the men were coming. Miles of swinging shoulders, jogging heads. A torrent of feet on the road.

And the railroad parallel with the concrete pike. Shaking with the roar of flying trains. Locomotive following locomotive. Cattle cars jammed with men. Box cars jammed with men. *Quarante hommes—huit chevaux! Quarante hommes—huit chevaux!* Then the artillery trains. One after another at five minute intervals. Great railroad guns long as three ordinary flatcars, their muzzles shrouded in tarpaulin. Anti-aircraft guns on special carriages. Naval cannon.

THE VALLEY trembled. Soot from the railroad joined dust from the turnpike; under a stifling, varicolored, rolling blanket of coal smoke, gasoline fumes, dust, a thousand smells of sweat and cinders and leather, an amalgam of sounds that came from both sides, the dairy farm of André Chibou was engulfed. André himself was engulfed. At three o'clock of that moon-washed night every pullet was gone from his barn, every cow from his pasture, every cabbage from his patch, every drop from his well. Midway between two running rivers of steel, André stood at his farm yard gate with more worthless checks from the "War Office Supply Department" in his corduroy jeans than Stavisky ever passed in a lifetime of frauds. André's wife was getting back at the government by selling wine to thirsty faces at a dollar a bottle. And at exactly five minutes after three a dirt-plastered Minerva limousine came hooting and rocking along the line of marchers to stop with a scream of brakes at André's door.

Two grease-blackened men in civilian clothes sprang from the driver's seat. An American flag fluttered on the car's radiator cap (that had been Crazy Hooper's idea) and Papa Chibou read the legend *Diplomatic Party—League of Nations Government—Mission Extraordinaire* painted in bold letters on the doors (John Keats' idea for getting through).

The two grease-blackened men were hardly off the running boards when a staff car sirened up behind them and a chubby colonel of infantry darted forward. But Crazy Hooper only grunted a mouthful of chocolate "no spik Esperench" and pointed at John Keats, and John Keats only held up an American passport and pointed at the writing on the car.

The colonel of infantry then shrugged and turned to buy a

cup of wine from André's wife. After all, he was but a colonel of infantry, was it up to him to stop two Yankees on the road? The pair must be official or they could not have come up from behind. If they were not all right let the General Staff apprehend them up ahead.

For the hundredth time since midnight, John Keats drew a heady breath of relief. God knew how they'd gotten this far, but the magic had worked again. It seemed a thousand hours since he'd left the capital with Crazy. A million miles the Minerva had battled its way forward through this endless parade of men. The chant of those running feet was forever established in his head. The look of those nameless, unnumbered faces.

Every road south-east of the capital had been a river of soldiers, thickening from a thousand railway terminals, side roads and lanes, deeper and deeper with men as they neared the Swiss border. Summoned by radio, by telephone, by rocket signals, by a hundred modern Paul Reveres, Esperance was moving in the night.

KEATS PULLED himself together with a start, motioned Crazy back to the car, and hurried at André Chibou.

"Listen, *mon père,* did you see by any chance a blue touring car go by in the early part of the night? A motor car driven by a Russian girl?"

André Chibou scraped and bowed. Not every night he was selling wine to army officers and consulted by League of Nations diplomats. "There were many cars tonight, *m'sieu.* Early before the coming of the army. A lady, one dressed in a sort of trench-coat stopped here, but—"

"Reddish haired foreigner? Gray eyes? A hat," Keats shouted, "not unlike a little white chimney braided with blue piping?"

"The same, *m'sieu,* and she drove away with much speed—"

"Good!" John Keats tossed a handful of francs at the rustic and leaped at the car. Hand on the door he paused, listened, turned his face skyward with an exclamation. A new sound had started in the night. A vast, insistent drone that loudened

as it wept up over the horizon behind the running army, pene-
trated the valley's thunder, shook the stars. Next minute the
very constellations were eclipsed as if by a heaven-high passage
of locusts, a nocturnal migration of countless birds. Out of the
south they came, headed north-eastward, an orbit of comets
streaking as the crow flies for the Rhine. The tumult of an earthly
army corps was obscured by that sound. The heavens were darkened, blotted out. A black torrent rushed across the face of the
summer moon. Planes! Battle planes and giant bombers. Aërial
battleships convoyed by aërial destroyers. Dreadnaughts of the
stratosphere motored with a dozen engines, armed with .75
cannon. Weird helicopters. Observation and pursuit hawks.
Mailed seaplanes from the coast. Buzzing auto-gyros, tiny
one-man hornets, giant fifty-man cruisers. For an incredible
moment the entire firmament was swallowed.

Then they were gone.

Keats found the chubby colonel at his elbow. Tears streamed
on the man's uplifted face. "The air fleet of Esperance!" he
cried. "In an hour every ship we have will be above the capital
of Teutony. The Boche will see—"

Planes over Teutony. Reprisal!

"Crazy! Get going! She's still up ahead!"

The dynamite was blowing. Too late to stop catastrophe, but
he'd find the hand that had fired the fuse, if it was the last thing
he lived to do.

CHAPTER IX

GODEK PASS

AT THAT MOMENT when André said good-by to the
"League of Nations Government" officials (and so passed out
of the story), a lurching Esperench taxicab was screeching to a
halt in an Alpine village some ninety miles away.

"Name of a pig!" the driver snarled at his passenger, his voice
muffled by one of those dirty scarfs that European taxi men are
liable to wear, "never have I made such a drive. The fare is four
thousand francs."

Grease-smeared to his hair, clad in an ash can topcoat, the
cabby looked a pirate, shifty-eyed, unable to stare his passenger
in the face. The rumpled passenger made no protest. In shapeless clothes, scraps of paper sticking from every pocket, he was
not unlike a scarecrow, himself, a dummy losing its stuffing. His
sling-bandaged arm impeded a reach for the wallet, and the
cabby's anxiety to get away openly increased.

"If I were you," he muttered at his fare, "I'd get out of here,
home or no home." Then, without waiting for the money, the
taxi fled.

Anton Stehli stayed. He did not seem to realize the car had
gone. Leaning on the doorsill of his cottage, he looked about
him. His eyes were strangely untroubled. The village was still
here. He said, "I'm home," and mused gravely at this cobblestone
street precarious on the mountain where the first chill of the
snowcaps began. Little stone cottages with pottery roofs. Dr.
Marcel's *Kurhaus*, white walls and red tile, where the nervous

127

old ladies came for the springwater cure. Randoval's Inn, favorite resort of the winter skiing parties. Church, town clock, market place, pump. It was a clean little place, a village for quaint mountaineers in Alpine hats, for china-toy sheep, for yodeling and accordion playing and soundless sleeps in deep feather beds. But the little pottery-roofed cottages were empty. The nervous old ladies, the guests of the inn had gone away. Instead of the tinkle of cowbells or the genial call of the watch, the high altitude quiet was smashed into a thousand rolling echoes, a titanic thunderstorm toiled and flamed on the slopes a mile below.

Standing alone in that upper calm, one commanded such a view as God might have if He stood on a step of heaven to scan the Pits. Stehli waited in the cool of the stars, and below him raged the Damnation. Where an electric railway had branched like a compass, westward to Esperance, south to Lucerne, northward to Teutony, the indigo night was being blasted away in eruptions of dazzling fire. The thunder of an avalanche echoed like the crashing of peaks down the pass. Continuous electricity above a boiling blanket of cloud that hung from valley rim to valley rim in the appearance of lower weather. But the storm was no work of climatic change. That lightning, Stehli knew, was the flame of Switzerland's naval guns, and the sound was Switzerland falling.

FAR DOWN the valley the forts of the Confederation were making their final stand. Furnace-hot gun pits cracking in their beds of Alpine rock. Rolling lines of shattered cannoneers. The White Cross of Switzerland had long since been shot away; against the enemy coming, Arnold von Winkelried could have done as much with an arrow; the little republic's naval guns were dogs barking at the legs of a mastodon. Where the great divide opened eastward, its lower walls lay in a sea of darkness. That way was Helvania; from the looks of her outpost mountains the little kingdom remained asleep. Where the divide narrowed westward the sky was a sullen flame; the war dogs of Esperance had joined the fray. Too late for Switzerland, though. Old Stehli told himself he was just in time. But then, instead of going into his cottage for shelter, he took the path hurrying to the courtyard in the rear. Crossed a low-walled garden of sunflowers and Alpine shrubs to a stand of dove cotes and rustic birdhouses pyramided in corbie-steps at the garden's back.

One after another the startled birds took wing as the Swiss moved from cote to cote, thumping, calling, opening the little cuckoo-clock doors. Anton Stehli was holding a white pigeon in his blunt, typewriter-gnarled hands when a gray-green motor car suddenly appeared on the high road like a rocket shot from the stormclouds below. Brakes screamed as the car turned into the village main street, halted before Stehli's cottage. Stehli ran from the courtyard to see what had happened, and what had happened was a be-spectacled young man in an elephant-colored greatcoat and bowl-shaped iron helmet, leaping from the car to chalk a Teuton numeral on Anton Stehli's door. From door to door the glassy-eyed man scampered with his arithmetic, the gray-green car dashed on toward the market place—then the thing came.

It was gray. It came up the mountain at sixty miles an hour like a reversed river of lava, chugging, smashing, clawing its way uphill, chewing the face from meadow, pasture and culvert, eating up the flank of the valley like an enormous skybound glacier. The company of Swiss *Chasseurs* and mounted Alpine riflemen, suddenly sprouted from hidden entrenchments below the village, was swept away like glass before a firehose. A pyrotechnic scroll of green fire swept like surf over the trenches where the Swiss troops had been. In that single breath trenches and men were immolated. The Juggernaut came on.

FIRST A wave of iron caterpillars. Snub-nosed tanks manned by driver and gunner, the gunner in a turret operating a nozzle of liquid fire. Crashing over meadow and haystack, flattening stone walls, crushing every boulder, shrub, stick, fence-post in the way. Then a herd of giant tanks, trooping like dinosaurs on the heels of their young. Great trapezoidal mammoths with swinging heads and trampling centipede feet, pulverizing the wreckage.

An astounding company of monsters followed the wake of the tank corps. Scavengers. Anton Stehli was reminded of insects magnified gigantic by an opium dream. Great iron measuring worms. Huge steel grasshoppers. Nodding mechanical mantas that hissed and spat and dug and scraped at the mutilated landscape. There were machines that levelled the wreckage, colossal steamrollers. Machines that swept the earth with spinning wire brushes. Caterpillar steam-shovels that would pause to scoop up mouthfuls of rubbish and hurl it aside. Machines with enormous noses that resembled vacuum cleaners, inhalers to suction up shell fragments, human fragments, refuse. Machines that sprayed the air with purifying chemicals and spread the ground with white lime.

Tank corps and clean-up squad roared up the mountainside, smashing opposition, clearing the path, unrolling a road where no road had been before, and the hosts of Vulcan followed. At the edge of the village the giants stopped to draw back in formation; the army came through. An armada of armored cars, painted in that *feldgrauen* camouflage that melted into a streaking blur before the eye; the flash, flash, flash of light on their gun-barrels racing through the village like the passing of shells. Then the motorized camions, giant heavy artillery on ten-wheeled trucks, siege guns half a block long dragged by thunderous twenty-caterpillar teams hitched tandem to each piece. Then the light artillery, mobile, every piece motorized, the latest in science from the shops of Essen. Guns for gas, for shrapnel, for projectiles that exploded clouds of bacteria, muzzles fuming from their recent assault, their gun crews leaning from the turrets naked and black to the waist. Followed by lumbering truck-loads of ammunition, shells that smashed, shells that dug, shells that poisoned earth and sky and water.

Behind these flying gun-batteries came the thousand and one departments to each unit. The trucks of the quartermaster corps, the signal fleet—radio, telephone, searchlight equipment—

motorized field kitchens, hospitals on wheels, ambulance after ambulance. Then the anti-aircraft batteries, the Army Topographical Sections, a fleet of motorcycles with machine-guns mounted on sidecars, trucks to unreel barbed wire at full speed, trucks labeled "Sanitary Corps," trucks labeled "G.H.Q." No circus ever moved with such precision. No traffic ever traveled at so diabolical a pace.

AS THE first armored car raced through, a squad of traffic officials on motorcycles had appeared in the village square, directing this mechanized onslaught with winking searchlights and colored semaphore signals. There was no hitch, no stalling, no wrong turning or going off the road. Behind every gun battery an automobile of officers had slewed into a side lane, the majors, colonels, lieutenants and their aides piling out like firemen and occupying the cottages without bothering to knock. By the time the batteries were gone, the troops were coming through.

First the machine gunners, twenty to a truck, gray-green men in jaunty forage caps, singing and bawling, features sweat-plastered, mouths squalling victorious song. "Glory—and love to the men of old—" To the radiator of each truck was fastened a flag flying the Trefoil Insignia and on the side of each was painted the legend, *Gott Mit Uns.*

Then the men with machine-gun rifles, crack marksmen of the Reichswehr, faces expressionless under bucket helmets. Truck after truck of these sharpshooters; followed by load upon load of Work Troopers in khaki, youngsters equipped at last with Mausers in place of shovels; and finally the regulars, the gray-green Reichswehr Infantry in gray-green lorries; their coalscuttle helmets going by in torrents, the lorries roaring two abreast in a never-ending stream. Never had there been such an invasion, and never such an army. Not a single man on foot. Not a cavalry patrol. Instead of the old fashioned rifles of World War days, their arms were the latest of modern design firing smokeless powder and a cartridge that did not flash. Saw-tooth bayonets. On the breast of each soldier the newest in gas equipment, masks for every conceivable chemical and emergency. On each belt a machine-gun pistol capable of twin rapid-fire discharges of ten bullets a second.

Against the monster Goliath-machines of the tank corps, against the technicians who drove those mechanical behemoths, against this mechanized army of racing armored cars and truck-loads of man power, the disorganized taxi-driven *poilus,* the gaudy cavalry and blistered foot soldiers of Esperance would have no more chance than had the roofs of their capital against the aërial torpedoes.

ALREADY THE Swiss Republic was paralyzed, her borders swept into history. The mountains themselves trembled under the blow. In that Alpine village through which the Teutonic hydra was advancing, the cottages were crumbling from nothing more than the sound of wheels. Infantry and more infantry, gray-green, endless in flood. Baggage vans. Little barber shops on wheels. Operating rooms on wheels. Garages on wheels. Whizzing car loads of solid rubber tires for replacements. Tank trucks of gasoline, each with a score of pumps for thirsty motors. Tank trucks of water for the men. Great motor sprinklers to vanquish the dust. A truck labeled "Propaganda" drawing aside in the public square, boys leaping from its rear step to plaster the village walls with showcards. *Switzerland Surrender!—Teuton-land eüber alles!—Teutony was betrayed! Schnitzler comes to bring peace!—We promise you Switzerland will be Free!*

"Free for what," Anton Stehli snarled under his breath. "Free for the Teutons."

Stunned to an image by the passing Moloch, suffocated in dust and blue petrol fumes, he could only hug the door of his cottage; could not draw his eyes from the thing. Time stopped. The sun must be rising in Helvania, but the clock in Switzerland had lost its hands. Imagination quit. In that limitless period from darkness to morning a half million men, every one a twin in discipline, dress, almost in facial expression, must have been transported from the north to the south side of an Alpine pass.

An entire division of Swiss infantry, an entire chain of Swiss forts had been whisked to oblivion, smashed up, cremated, threshed like wheat in those awful mowing machines, turned to dust and blown away.

And now the conquering rulers arrived. Long columns of gray-green limousines. Goggle-helmeted chauffeurs driving the masters of Armageddon in balloon-tired cars as smooth as cats, *Generalstabsoffiziers* in their spike-topped field helmets, their buckles, beltings and tabs, lounging in steel-lined luxury behind windows of shatterproof glass. Pullman-type trailers, gas-and-bulletproof, in which the brigadiers, the scientists, the be-spectacled and be-monocled generals-of-division sat at tables over reports and maps. Armored sedans filled with artillery generals working over decimals, corps commanders, electrical wizards, high-ranks of every description. Each car was convoyed by a cordon of motorcycles, liaison officers, and in every car was a radio telephone.

So this was the culmination of effort from Franklin, Marconi, Steinmetz. Wireless telephones in armored automobiles to direct the movements of tanks and cannon. McCormick had invented the way toward a Grim Reaper; the fruits of Roger Bacon were smokeless shells; Hippocrates' last chapter a projectile of bacteria; the final concept of Christianity as written on that banner above one of the Reichswehr lorries—*A Mighty Fortress Is Our God!*

ANTON STEHLI turned from that parade of staff cars with an oath in the prongs of his mustache. It was then he discovered another occupant of his doorstep, another who watched this Martian review.

"Nielsen—"

"I say, Stehli—I was wondering when you'd look around."

Sitting on his upended kitbag, the Swedish correspondent was jotting industriously on a little writing-pad. Swinging to his feet, he fitted monocle to eye with a practised twist, and flirted a motoring glove at the scene. "Jove! I got through in my car just before they came. Hid it behind the *kurhaus* and came up here behind you to watch." He shouted above din, "Gad, man, what a story! Last survivor, and all that. By heaven, you must be the last Swiss alive in the place. Standing on your doorstep, don't y'know, and watching the invaders go by. By God, and with a dove in your hand—"

Stehli's eyes dulled at Nielsen's enthusiasm. "Story?"

The Swede made a gesture of sympathy. "Of course. It is hard on you, old man. But the Heinies seem to be going right through. Gad, they've done it again. Circled the Esperench forts along the Rhine and caught 'em off guard, *via* the Swiss Alps." He shouted through cupped hands. "You're safe enough here, by the looks. They won't bother a non-combatant. Me, I'm on my way to Helvania. You wouldn't," he nodded at the cottage door, "have a bottle of wine to spare a fellow? Drove all night, and I'm burning up."

"Of course, Nielsen. Bring in your luggage. Until they rob me of my home, you are my guest."

On the cobbles before the cottage wheels screamed. A jamming of hot brakes. Somewhere far at the head of the parade there was a stoppage. Then the valley became livid with the light of an unnatural western sky; A wild panorama was illumined. The western neck of the divide took flame. Far below the mountain the army of Esperance, in all its hodge podge of futile color, was pouring into the pass. Powder-blue columns of *poilus.* Streams of Blue devils, *Chasseurs,* Legionnaires. Gun batteries and cavalry brilliant in sudden revelation under a fired sky. The dawn that had betrayed them was the flashing of enemy star shells. Their railroad guns were too late. Their scouting planes, caught in a zodiac of shellfire, fell down out of the sky in burning showers. An avalanche of flame rolled down the sides of Godek Pass. Tanks dashed down the mountain flanks like thunderbolts. The snorting, gnawing engines of extermination followed. The gray-green armored cars, firing as they charged. A lava of men and guns engulfed the slopes of the divide.

In that livid explosion of daylight, Stehli saw a racing cater-pillar dragon catch an advance patrol of Esperench lancers. Horses and men burst asunder in a scarlet crash. Truckloads of gray-green machine gunners poured through the breach. An answering barrage of *soixante-quinze* shrapnel rattled off the Teuton tanks like so much hail. Under a clanging, thundering, mulcting bombardment of shells, the Esperench advance was smothered. *Poilus* and *Chasseurs,* gaudy Colonials and charging lancers melted away. Switzerland stood handcuffed. Esperance was burning at the stake.

GENERAL OF DIVISION, Gottlieb von Neumann, lowered Zeiss binoculars, turned from the shatterproof observation window of his car to grin at the officer beside him. Parked on an elevation screened by spruce, the staff car allowed an unobstructed view of battle lines below. The general's astrin-gent features were bright with disciplined enthusiasm. His eyes were points of flint sharpening the face under its monkish pall of clipped hair.

"They're beaten. They cannot last an other hour. Observe the fine work of those tanks among that brigade of *poilus. Himmel!* our infantry will have nothing to do. Stand this way, my boy, the view is magnificent."

"Thank you, Herr General."

"Watch the havoc of our liquid fire. Different than the last war, eh, my boy?"

"Ja, Herr General."

But Paul Emmerich remained standing as he was, motion-less, eyes fixed on nothingness in the smoke, face a pale carving, gray, masking nausea against that Roman Holiday below and hiding repugnance for the older man at his elbow. *Grüss Gott!* how could his uncle watch this carnage with the pleasure of a patrician at a gladiatorial show? Studying as calmly as a connois-seur might observe painted cavalry on a canvas by Messonier. The reds pleased the old man who didn't like pastels?

Paul Emmerich secretly shivered. In the valley men were

dying in droves. No more to Uncle Gottlieb than the death of
flies on paper. Yet he had seen this saturnine man sit up half the
night with a sick hunting dog. It was not his fault. This was the
old school and war a game. Esperench and Teutons, once in
soldier suits, were not bleeding, agonized individuals, but chess-
pieces, numbers in a game. These mountains were a problem in
higher mathematics, and pain had no part in the arithmetic.

"Battery Ten Start Firing Position X-A-Y. Hold Steady Fire
370s on Point 19." He could hear his uncle's voice snappering at
the telephone mouthpiece that was strapped like a phone girl's
instrument on his chest. Ear-phones on his head were catching
numbers from the ether. "Crossfire Z to A on Elevation Sixteen."

Crossfire Z to A on Elevation 16. The niceties of code. How
much neater than shouting, "Turn those blow torches on the
Spahis trapped on that hill and cook them alive." Emmerich bit
his underlip, turning away. Mustn't let the old man see his face.
Especially when the general had relaxed into calling him "my
boy." A breach of etiquette almost beyond the rules. Uncle must
be pleased. In half an hour Esperance would be cremated, and
in this secure and furbished motorcar another victory recorded
to his uncle's undying credit; another Iron Cross for the fami-
ly's trophy case.

"Major Emmerich!"

PAUL TURNED in guilt. Von Neumann had put aside his
phone to watch him sharply. Had those steely eyeballs pene-
trated his thoughts? But the general merely put a hand with
friendly pressure on his nephew's shoulder and, sure none of the
staff in the car's forward end was looking, said, "You are tired,
Paul. All of us need sleep badly. Very soon you will go off duty."

"I am all right, sir."

"Nein." The general frowned. "I know. You take it too hard,
my boy. I am sorry about what happened to your father."

Paul nodded silently. His father. He had almost forgotten
that irony. His mind listlessly moved backward to that library
scene—two nights ago, or centuries?—when the word had come.

In the fierce excitement, the glory of his son's leave-taking, Balduin Emmerich had died. Sudden riches and a call to the colors had been too much for Herr Emmerich's patriotic heart. Paul had left him there among his books, left his mother standing, face in white hands—

"As for your mother," the general whispered hurriedly, "it is true the Esperench air fleet bombed the city. The report, I fear, cannot be denied. But the city was well prepared, and I am certain she would be safely taken to the gas cellars and bombproofs.

"What is more, our anti-aircraft shot the swine fleet to pieces."

He snapped his fingers, spun, recited numbers into the phone. In the fore part of the car a tele-type machine was chattering. A half dozen officers, their faces under shaved heads solemn as Buddhist priests, hunched around the operator. The man at the instrument was translating code messages in the voice of a jubilant radio announcer.

The tele-type was not unlike a news reel in constant communication with distant events. Soviet troops were marching in the Far East. Great Britain was remaining neutral. America had protested the shelling of Esperance without declaration of war. Italy was busy with Abyssinia. G.H.Q. reported Swiss army in general retreat and Confederation making overtures for surrender.

"Esperench capital evacuated, all industrial centers paralyzed, all Rhine forts in state of demolition. Esperench government reported rioting, troops at point of mutiny, all front line arms in full retreat'—

"Second G.H.Q. report—no sign mobilization in Helvania—"

THE TELE-TYPE signed off with a rattle of code. Staff officers made sounds of approval. Helmets nodded enthusiasm. Schnitzler had succeeded in localizing the conflict. Nothing could stop Teutony now. A general of the Chemical Corps flushed exultantly. It was the threat of bacteria bombs that had broken the Esperench morale.

High priests of war, they crowded to the lookout windows and periscopes, clucking and chuckling, congratulating themselves on their stratagems. This steel-lined armored motor-Pullman, was like a club filled with stodgy members suddenly animated by a rise on the exchange. Paul Emmerich watched the valley below with conviction of its unreality. Impossible men were dying in that lower sea of flame. The walls of the car were as proof against that conflict's thunder as the generals were proofed against compassion. Not a shell-crash was audible. The car was air-cooled. Only the constant tremor of the steel floor betrayed the travail of the slopes below.

He lowered the binoculars, suddenly summoned to action by his radio phone. Voices barked. Generals wrote feverishly. General von Neumann was working at a set of switchboard dials, an automatic map sprinkled with colored bulbs that twinkled in the topography like stars. One pushed a button in this secure car and a brigade of motorcycle Uhlans five miles away charged into action. One jotted a calculation, spoke to a phone, and a siege gun behind a mountain peak destroyed a train of boxcars beyond the horizon.

Paul Emmerich saw his uncle, his uncle's staff generals, this steel car with its water coolers and leather arm chairs and manifold mechanisms as a whirring, clicking, soulless, meaningless heart to a gigantic robot built for nothing but death. Himself a cog, a comptometer, an automaton without mind for anything but obedience to the wheels behind. A curious rebellion was in him. He stood at an instrument reciting decimals that sent other men out to die and kill, unable to stop his own voice but his mind was a picture of a hotel room where two men sat dead at a dining table, and an American newspaper man grinned nervously against a wall.

A sudden silence in the headquarters car caught him staring like a skull. Everything seemed to have stopped at once. He turned to learn the meaning of this dislocation in the heart of the machinery, and saw the tele-type operator, tense, white-lipped, spectacles winking, lean up from his stalled instrument. The man's teeth shone.

"It has come! Esperance has surrendered. Hostilities to cease in the sector of Godek Pass at once—"

IT WAS over. Any minute the Swiss would forward their surrender at this news. Incredibly the Teutons had won. Less than fifty hours advance, hardly four hours of actual combat, and the armies of Esperance had been smashed. Paul Emmerich got his tired legs out of the staff car, stood on a grassy Alpine knoll, and surveyed the scene of victory with a spinning head. Far down the divide the thunder was retreating in a salvo of echoes; daylight was coming.

In the crystalline heights above him an Alpine snowcap colored to rose in a canopy of cloudless azure, and a little Swiss village, a nest of storybook cottages and pottery roofs came into view. *Gott!* if he could learn what had happened to his mother back home he could almost celebrate. Thank God the War Lords had had their fling, and the thing was out of their systems. Out of the valley's smoke the armored cars, the tanks, the trucks that had been in action were coming back. "Fatherland—Dear Fatherland!" In the blue upper stillness the voices of the men massed into hymn. Good lads, they'd gotten out of it in time with few casualties, after all. He passed a hand through the ashen streak in his hair, and watched the trucks. The men were cheering. Like himself, they'd come here because they had to; were doing this job because of an ideal.

He sighed and leaned tired shoulders against a cool spruce. A little shrapnel. A big adventure. A few wounded comrades. Fellowship and courage. Maybe Uncle Gottlieb was right. Fatherland bigger than self. Duty above all.

Then his eyes were arrested by a carload that had not been so lucky. He saw the van was moving slowly because of its Red Cross. The driver steered along the road-edge where the pace was leisurely; halted not far from Emmerich to let a motorized battery clatter past. Somewhere within the ambulance a voice of pain was screaming and screaming, and the obbligato was not decent against a fiesta of happy cheers.

The driver was scowling, as Emmerich moved forward inquiringly.

The Red Cross chauffeur saluted, *"Ja,* Herr Major, the man is one of ours. Some Esperench swine with a handful of fire grenades got a few of our boys. This fellow took it pretty bad."

Paul Emmerich walked to the rear of the car; peered in. Upper tiers were loaded with silent, quiescent cripples; but the floor was occupied by a lone man of enormous girth who tossed and shouted and beat about in his strapped-down blankets. In his raving he had ripped the bandage from his side to expose an ulcerous, fly-blown hole, black with scorched blood, ordure and bits of straw, that gaped like a shellhole in a house. The man's pudgy face was repulsive with the sweat of pain.

"Frieda!" he was screaming. *"Ach Gott,* my little girl. My wife! My babies! Frieda! The piano lessons! My wife!"

Then he lifted his head to look at Paul Emmerich, and an animal cry burst from his lips. "It is Paul! The newspaper fellow who sits in staff cars writing with a pen! While I am dying, shot to pieces, gun meat—"

"Gussie!" Paul Emmerich screamed.

"Go away," was the answering wail, "and be damned to you! Not a button out of place on your uniform! Go away, you bloody goose-necked aristocrat swine, and be damned—"

WEARILY PAUL EMMERICH turned from the ambulance to see uproar breaking around the staff car. Something was happening, and he was wanted. But he was too ill at heart to take recognition of the affair until, from a babble of shouts, he caught another familiar name.

Paul Emmerich's face went hard and white, and he ran to the car where a dispatch rider was snapping a hurry-call for General von Neumann. The man's motorcycle which had raced down from the village chugged between his spread legs, and his words were loud with excitement. Something about newspaper writers. A Swede, a Russian woman and a Swiss, in a cottage up there. Swiss, it appeared, was resident of the place. House had been assigned to Field Marshal von Reinmar, commanding all Teuton armies in the field, who had meant to occupy it for private head-quarters. Two rooms in the cottage, and the *Feld-Marshal* had generously allowed the neutral press correspondents to go on with their meal in the front room while the Swiss showed the general to a bedroom in the back.

And there, deliberately, the Swiss had shot Von Reinmar through the head. Coldblooded assassination. Second in command, General von Neumann would investigate. The Swiss, a newspaper man himself, denied murdering the Field Marshal, but the two were alone together when the general was slain. And certain papers discovered on the floor of the room implicated the Kingdom of Helvania.

"He was an internationally known correspondent. His name is Anton Stehli."

CHAPTER X

ANTON STEHLI

MORNING LIGHT SHAFTED in a golden dust through the cottage windows and polished the spiked helmets with a refulgent shine. The faces of generals steamed and glittered. The cottage was not made for generals, and their stern field coats, buckles and clanking side arms marred the room. Furniture had been kicked aside, bric-a-brac dashed from the fireplace mantel to make space for radio and phone apparatus, curtains torn down for more light, a splendidly carved table dragged centerward to play rostrum for the weighty elbows of the judges.

A man had been ruthlessly killed. They lay by thousands in the valley, but that was war. This was different. The dead man was a Field Marshal, and slain by a civilian. It was against the rules. It was murder. The generals were outraged, their foreheads dark with indignation.

As General Gottlieb von Neumann crisply summed up the case: "The murderer may expect no mercy from this drumhead court. We can waste no time in these proceedings. A state of war continues with Switzerland, and our troops occupied this village under rules of warfare. Our army commander was treacherously assassinated by this so-called civilian. Our soldiers must, and will be, protected from such gross violations of military code. Moreover, it becomes obvious the government of a neighboring country is behind this attack."

The general made a sudden swivel in his chair, pointing across the room. "You, there. Your name is Kurt Nielsen? You witnessed the crime, so?"

Nielsen lunged away from the fireplace, hands in pockets. "I did not see it, General," he corrected coolly. "You understand, the Field Marshal's arrival was quite unanticipated. He walked in without announcement, his staff remaining in the street outside. Stehli, Miss Frantsovna (she had arrived but a few minutes before the general, you understand) and I—we were seated at breakfast. You see, we hadn't eaten since—"

"This court is not interested in your personal misadventures."

"Of course. Well, Anton Stehli had offered us the kindest hospitality considering the—er—unusual circumstances. At any rate, he had bestowed my luggage in the back room where I would certainly have enjoyed a nap until the, shall I say, conquering general made his appearance—"

General von Neumann brought his glove down on the table with a mailed-fist crash. "Cut your story short, Herr Nielsen, and leave out the long newspaper adjectives, or we may forget your traveling credentials—"

THE SCANDINAVIAN shrugged coolly. "No need to bullyrag, man. Your staff will do well to deal kindly with representatives of a neutral press association. Don't pull any more Nurse Cavell blunders. Public opinion wins wars, you know. Herr Emmerich, whom I see has translated himself into a major, can tell you the power behind my syndicate."

His monocle turned at Emmerich a reproachful stare. Paul Emmerich stirred unhappily. Why in the name of *Lieber Gott* must he cross the lives of these people at this time?

But his uncle thundered, "Get on with your story, Herr Nielsen!" and the unruffled Swede managed a bow.

"The general stalked into the cottage, as I was telling you. When he saw we were newspaper writers he was, naturally, polite. Didn't wish to intrude. Sorry to disturb us. We might finish our repast. Stehli, as host under compulsion, showed the man into that back room."

"The Swiss led Field Marshal von Reinmar to the room in back?"

"Correct."

"The back room was unoccupied?"

"I suppose. You see, I was dining. Embarrassing situation all around. Miss Frantsovna sat powdering her nose, if you must have details. I walked to the front window to see how the war was going outside. Didn't hear any shot. You couldn't have heard a bomb with the racket going on. Then Stehli gave a yell and came running. I turned and saw the Field Marshal stretched out on the floor of the bedroom, beyond that door."

"What did you do then, Herr Nielsen?"

"Stood with my mouth open, no doubt. I said, 'Why did you do it, Stehli, they'll shoot you for this.' He looked stunned. He said, 'My God, I didn't shoot him. We were alone back there. I don't know where the shot came from.'" Nielsen took a cigarette from a case in his vest and blinked his monocle at Paul Emmerich's stone-featured face. "I say, Emmerich, this is terrible. Somehow I can't believe Stehli shot the man, you know.

"Well," to Von Neumann, "then the Field Marshal's staff rushed in. That's all I know."

The generals glared in silent wrath. General von Neumann barked, "Dismissed!" at Nielsen, and stabbed a thumb at Alexandra Frantsovna who stood in white silence, across the floor. Papers, passport documents crackled under the general's fingers. "You, now. You are Alexandra Frantsovna, war correspondent representing *Izvestia* and the *Pravda* syndicate, U.S.S.R.?"

She said quietly, "I am," looking coldly at Paul Emmerich.

"What are you doing in this occupied territory?"

"Taking the best road across Switzerland to Helvania where my editors are sending me after news. I was not aware I was entering front lines."

"You were unaware that this end of Godek Pass was in a state of war?"

"For that matter," the girl said with a show of anger, "it is my business to be in territory where there is a state of war, and those credential papers also allow me the privilege. Is this a court of frontier examination, a court of news censorship, or a military inquiry?"

THE DIVISION general colored angrily. *"Gott strafe* these newspapers, it is enough to conduct a campaign without having to deal with a pack of idiotic reporters running about in the way. I am going to take authority in my own hands and deport you writers across the border." His eyes blazed. "Undoubtedly you are a pack of spies!"

The girl said quietly, "Moscow might resent such an implication, Herr General, made against a non-combatant Soviet citizen."

"When did you enter Switzerland?" he demanded.

"About four o'clock this morning."

"You came by motor from Esperance?"

"Yes."

"Your passport shows you were, two nights ago, in Teutony."

"Am I on trial for espionage?" Alexandra Frantsovna demanded. "If so, I should like word with the Soviet Embassy in your capital. Since Russia and Teutony are not at war, and I am a neutral citizen—"

Paul Emmerich spoke out in a low tone, "If you will permit me, General von Neumann, I can substantiate that much of Fräulein Frantsovna's story. She, as well as Herr Nielsen and—" he spoke the name with effort, "Herr Stehli were all in the Teutonic capital on the Gatreau-Von Speer story."

"And you might tell old lamp-jaws," Nielsen added in English, "that as long as the battle seems to be over we'd like to find a telegraph somewhere and send our dispatches and get the hell out of here. I'm sorry as the devil for old Anton Stehli, but—"

"Quiet!" General von Neumann roared. "You will be out of here soon enough. Proceed with your story, Fräulein, and be brief."

The Russian girl said steadily, "I drove my car into this village two hours ago, left it in the market place and walked around hunting an *auberge*. Then your soldiers came, but could not molest me when I showed my papers. An officer was kind enough to inform me I could find several newspaper correspondents in this cottage, and I was glad to meet Herr Stehli and Herr Nielsen. On their invitation I joined them at breakfast. Herr Nielsen has accurately described what then occurred."

"You sat eating at table? From where you were seated you could see into the back bedroom?"

"I could not," she said slowly, as if the admission was painful in utterance. "The door was at an angle."

"However," her inquisitor snarled, "you saw the Swiss, the accused, lead Field Marshal von Reinmar into that back room?"

She nodded without speaking.

"You heard the shot, Fräulein?"

"No. I heard nothing." Her gray eyes traveled about the room in helpless appeal. "Herr Stehli ran—ran out as Herr Nielsen has told you. That is all."

"*Sehr gut!*" Von Neumann dismissed the girl with a curt nod. A burly staff officer made notions on a report blank, read them in muffled staccato into his radio phone. General von Neumann coughed to clear his throat. "Now! Bring forward Anton Stehli."

FOR THE first time since that parting in the Café Guste, Paul Emmerich found his eyes meeting Stehli's. Hands trussed behind his back, the Swiss had been held face to wall in a corner between a knot of guards; as his escort prodded him to mid room and he staggered to the table he threw Emmerich a look that was not to be soon forgotten. Fear wasn't in that haggard face. But bewilderment. Reproach. An expression in those blue eyes, too, of defiance for these army priests and all they stood for.

"I did not do it," he said simply; and Paul Emmerich was filled with uneasiness and confusion.

General von Neumann sprang to his feet; leaned across the table. "Address your statements to the court. You are a Jew?"

Stehli's head came up. "I am," pridefully.

"Of Swiss nationality?"

"Yes."

"This is your native village."

"It was my home until the invader robbed it from me."

A medley of oaths, angry foot-scuffings, grunts muttered up from the table of officers. "So," Von Neumann snarled, "you are a patriot."

Stehli replied scornfully, "I am a citizen and a non-combatant. Patriotism breeds chauvinism. Chauvinism breeds generals. Generals breed war. I do not believe in war as an instrument of settling international disputes. I am a pacifist."

"Ha!" Von Neumann stormed. "Glib, aren't you? A coward in the bargain. Refuse to meet an enemy face to face in warfare, but lead him into a trap where you may shoot him in the back."

Paul Emmerich looked at Stehli in dreary apprehension. The man's conduct was unsettling in the face of his guilt. He neither flinched nor cringed. Perspiration glimmered on the wide forehead under a tousled thatch of gray, but his eyes reflected no alarm.

"I did not shoot Von Reinmar. I am no coward. Besides, I have nothing to fear."

"I will give you something to fear," General von Neumann said in a flat, deadly voice. "A wall before a firing squad. You would deny your guilt with your last breath, Jew?"

"I did not kill Field Marshal von Reinmar," said Anton Stehli quietly. "I had no gun."

"You led him into that back room?"

"Rather, he ordered me to take him there."

"You were back there alone?"

"I saw no one but ourselves. The windows were down. The room was fusty, for I bad been away several weeks. I walked to a back window, lowered it a few inches, heard what I thought was a muffled shot. I turned and saw the general falling over backwards.

"Blood streamed from his temple. He struck the floor dead. I do not know where the bullet came from."

Von Neumann grimaced, "But you imply he might have been shot by one of these two correspondents at that time in this front room?"

Stehli turned tired eyes toward Nielsen and the Russian girl posed along the wall. Then he said with firm decision, "They could not have done it. Von Reinmar was out of line with the door. No. I believe them as innocent as myself."

GENERAL VON NEUMANN'S fist crashed the table. "This is enough. *Grüss Gott!* the dirty Swiss would have us believe the Field Marshal shot himself!"

Anton Stehli said harshly, "Let me remind my accusers that to shoot a man one must possess a weapon, specifically a gun… Thirty seconds after this shooting, Von Reinmar's men were in the room. Did they find a gun?"

"Nor will they spend time hunting for one, *nein!* Obviously you carried it in the sling of that bandaged arm and where you disposed of it is your affair; enough for us to know you will never employ it again. Your inconsistent lie of innocence is scarcely supported by the evidence, and," he snatched an envelope from the table, *"this!"*

Grim lines deepened in Stehli's face. "I never saw it before."

"It was found on the floor by the men who picked up Field Marshal von Reinmar's body! Did you see it then?"

"It was not there when first we entered the room," Stehli insisted in a thickening whisper. "That envelope, I thought it must have dropped from the dead man's coat as he fell."

"However, it encloses a letter in some undecipherable code written on the stationery of the War Office of Helvania, addressed to you, sealed with the Helvanian badge. The official seal is enough to implicate that country and," he slammed the envelope on the table, "Field Marshal von Reinmar's name is among the ciphers."

General von Neumann spun at his staff. Helmets nodded in unison. The burly officer was barking furiously into the radio phone. Von Neumann turned back at Stehli. "We convict you, Anton Stehli, of espionage. A Swiss national employed by the Helvanian War Office, hired by that country to assassinate Field Marshal von Reinmar. The court sentences you to be shot immediately as a spy!"

Immediately! There was a shiver in the atmosphere, an indrawing of breath, an ejaculated protest from Nielsen, a quiet sob from Alexandra Frantsovna. But there was no suggestion of a quaver in Anton Stehli's voice.

"I am not a spy."

General von Neumann snorted the deadly accusation through set teeth. "Then what were you doing with all those pigeons?"

PAUL EMMERICH remained where he stood, pulses cold in his wrists, his mind as gray as the uniforms tramping about him. *Gott,* the look on that Stehli's face. He wanted to turn away, to run from the thing. He tried to decode the staccato stuttering of the tele-type machines carrying this message to the power behind the lines. He tried to plug his ears with the snarling of the radio installed in the room where the dead general had sprawled. Why had the Swiss done the thing? A spy, of course. Helvania behind it? *Grüss Gott!* but here was another blow-off. Strange how calmly the man denied everything, too. That look.

Tramp, tramp, tramp. Rifle barrels crossing the window like shadows on a cinema screen. He couldn't help it, and at the command to fire his eyes jerked around in horror at the scene. Against the garden wall, the man stood without a blindfold. Facing the muzzles of those automatic guns, his eyes were blue in the sunshine, his features serene. A breeze from somewhere stirred the tangled mass of his unbowed gray hair; he might have been posing for a photograph. Just before the blast of the rifles a white dove fluttered down and perched on Stehli's shoulder.

The dove's head was shattered, too.

Emmerich stood in cold shock as the windows shuddered, the whole cottage seemed to shudder from that gun-blast; and the echoes were hardly gone when a furious outcry burst in the street before the cottage.

"Stop it, damn you! Let me in there! God—too late—"

Cursing, Paul Emmerich whirled from the windows to the door. Dust boiled in the street where sentries were fighting with a man in civilian clothes, a savage-eyed foreigner who struggled to reach the cottage through a swarm of gun-butts and fists. A Reichswehr whirled in the grip of this maddened individual, blocking the jabs of bayonets.

Emmerich saw a dirt-splashed Minerva limousine flying the American flag was halted at the curb, its front wheels on the sidewalk, and a man he failed to recognize came vaulting from the driver's seat, swinging an iron wrench.

"Hit 'em, Jawn. Teach 'em to touch us diplomats. Knock 'em for a row of Ash Wednesdays!"

"Keats!" Paul Emmerich shouted in the doorway. "The devil!" He bellowed an order to stand the Teuton guardsmen like sticks. Mid street in a roil of brown dust, John Keats bent upright, dragged a torn sleeve across his beaten face, then shouted in recognition.

"Emmerich! Damn it, man, you've just shot an innocent— you've just killed Anton Stehli. I saw it all, Emmerich! These blockheaded guards wouldn't let me get in there to testify."

Paul Emmerich said in a low ferocity, "You! Saw what?"

"Behind this cottage," Keats yelled. "I was up on those bird-houses back there. Didn't know the place was Stehli's home. We parked the car on the next street and I'd climbed atop those pigeon cotes to watch the fighting under the mountain—"

MIST BROKE on Emmerich's face. "*You* were behind this house?"

"I'm telling you, Emmerich, you railroaded him! Stehli didn't kill your general. I could see through the window of that room from where I lay. Stehli walked up to the glass and lowered the window from the top. I could just make out that officer behind him. When Stehli jumped around the officer was already falling. I saw him go down—"

Emmerich thundered, "Impossible. You lie! They were in that room alone by Stehli's own admission. He was a spy. You remember how he always talked with pigeons? *Ja!*"

Keats shook a fist out of the dust. "And I say he didn't shoot that man. I got down from that pigeon house, tried to reach the cottage. These damned Reichswehr men caught me before I could get around front. Gagged me and trotted me off to see the guard corporal I couldn't get loose till Crazy drove up—"

"Anton Stehli," Emmerich snarled, "was alone in that room by his own testimony. The only others in the place were in front. Nielsen and that Russian woman, Frantsovna. They were here. They—"

Keats' throat cracked on an amazed cry. "Nielsen! Frantsovna! Where are they, Emmerich? Where did they go?" His body had doubled in a tensed crouch, chin down, arms away from his sides, as if he were about to launch a flying tackle at the officer in the cottage door. Bewildered, the Reichswehr troopers had backed to the curb in a semicircle, bayonets pointed. "I've got to see them!" John Keats husked at Emmerich. "Nielsen! Frant—"

"They," Emmerich bit out, "left in their cars twenty minutes ago; ordered over the Helvanian border. I do not think you will see them, John Keats." He began a strange, dry-lipped grin. "As for *you*—"

As for John Keats, he went backwards in an acrobatic that carried him to the Minerva's running board, and Crazy Hooper with him. Before the surprised Teuton soldiers could apprehend his intention, the car was off through the sunshine at a roar.

"Get 'em!" John Keats was hollering at his chauffeur. "Straight down Godek Pass to Helvania. Nielsen and Frantsovna! They just left here! Go like hell!"

Crazy Hooper went. Following instructions in spirit as well as letter, he sent the long car screaming around a turn, grazed the flank of a motor transport with a hair-raising figure-eight skid, bumped through a ditch to skirt a cart, and streaked back into open highway heading east.

Emmerich plunged out into the dust and vapors of the street, his nerves unfrazzling in a flood of oaths, booting and clouting at his woodenish men. "Stop that car! After them! Stop those men! Stop them, you fools!" Already the dirty limousine was far down the shoulder of the mountain. Eastward the highway was clean of traffic save for two racing specks where the concrete ribbon thinned to a white, curving string at the Helvanian end of the valley. A green hedge of pines marked the Swiss-Helvanian boundary; and, as Emmerich watched, the two specks at valley bottom disappeared into this border-mark of timber. Then the dusty limousine which had temporarily vanished behind a grassy ridge sprang out into view and diminished in size down the open road. Its American bunting made a bright spot of color against the valley's lilac and the car was a flash in wind.

A Reichswehr corporal whipped a Mannlicher sharpshooter to his shoulder and squinted down the sights at the streaking target.

"No!" Emmerich snapped. "Bring them alive!"

THE CORPORAL ducked his chin agreeably, and the Mannlicher flashed. Dirt squirted up in the weeds near the limousine's zigzagging stern. The marksman scowled, tried again. But the car streaked behind a field of wheat stacks; made a crosscut over a checkerboard of fields and was already half way down the divide. The sniper wasn't living who could have punctured a tire at that pace.

Emmerich cursed and flung up frantic arms. A sergeant puffed on a whistle. Motorcycles came in a roaring squad through the village. Sirens going, pennons flagging, a posse of gray-green machines geared to a hundred an hour soared off down the mountain in scorching pursuit. The highway to

Helvania trailed a chrome plume of dust in the azure sunlight; for a minute Emmerich followed the chase through his Zeiss glasses; then he lowered the binoculars with a gloomy curse and ran into the cottage where the radio was crackling.

Through the window to the garden he saw the firing squad was tramping away, and soldiers were moving along the shot-spattered wall with spades and a weighted stretcher. General von Neumann and staff had clustered under the wall in loud discussion. Their gritty voices droned, indistinct in the blurt and crackle of the radio apparatus. Nervously scrubbing his hands on his handkerchief, Emmerich stamped to the table to take a sheaf of reports from the wireless officer.

The Teutonic capital was sending through a code call for General von Neumann. All military operations in Switzerland had ceased. Schnitzler would be on the air in five minutes with special message. Generals of division stand by for important word from High Command.

"Take these to General von Neumann." He was glad to send the subaltern out to his uncle; glad for a moment alone. *Gott,* what a wretched business. Who could have known that the shooting in the Hotel Metropole could have brought so terrible a consequence. Fifty hours ago he had been a conference reporter for the *Tageblatt*—today he was standing in the house of a friend, become an enemy, a cog in the mightiest death-dealing machine the world had ever known. No personal victory in this pogrom. For him, his world had overturned.

He leaned against the table, aching, trembling; rubbed a wrist across his eyes. This was the price one paid for one's Fatherland. His mother lost, maybe dead among the ruins of the capital—his home city ravaged by the Esperench air fleet in payment for that torpedo bombardment on their own capital. His father dead. His friend Gussie dying in that ambulance in a welter of blood and hate, cursing him at the last. Stehli the Swiss—a spy shot at the wall—a truncated body shoveled under his own flower garden. Those others! Paul Emmerich clawed slender fingers through his gray-streaked hair. Friends turned into deadly foes. Villainy out of its ratholes at last. The Yankee would pay for some of this. That American knew—

"Major Emmerich!"

SPOKEN QUIETLY from behind him, his name interrupted thought, and he spun from the table to see a shadow paused in the sun and dust of the cottage door. A slim captain of Reichswehr infantry looking in from the street. The man saluted mechanically, stepped into the cottage, and closed the door behind him. Then he stood deferentially before his superior, the collar of his gray-green military coat drawn up to his ears, his eyes strangely dark and alert under the brim of his iron helmet.

"You have caught the Americans already, Herr Captain?" Emmerich demanded.

"I have caught you," was the unexpected response. "Raise a call to those men in the garden, lift your voice above conversation and I will blow you and all these *salopards* to perdition, Blow up Esperance, will you? Torpedo our homes? Kill my father before my eyes? But I've got you and the rest of your dirty general staff where I want you. *Non,* you dare not shoot. Enough high explosive in my pocket to lift the top of this mountain and your murderous Teuton officers with it at one jolt. And in good time I'm going to lift it."

The man in the uniform of a Reichswehr captain pulled a paper-wrapped parcel from his coat and balanced it on a palm. The collar flapped down from his jaws. Cat-green light raged in the man's narrowed eyes. Emmerich saw the livid scar on his cheek, and sucked an icy breath.

It was Raoul Dubail.

FOR THE space of a minute it seemed to Paul Emmerich as if the world had come to a stop on its axis. As if the air in that cottage room had become a lifeless vacuum. Conversation in the garden without was the voices of bees in a far-off infinity; the chug and mutter of traffic beyond the closed door came from another world. He could not look at the deadly package

in Dubail's hand. Madness in the man's eye held him mesmer-
ized. A drop of perspiration trailed ice down the side of his nose.

"How—how did you get here?" The whispered question was
as foolish in that moment of horror as a titter in a vault.

Dubail's mouth was laughing without making a sound. The
skin along his jaws was yellow, and his teeth looked dry. As
casually as if he were handling a loaf of bread, he returned the
package to his coat pocket, limped a step forward, stood with
folded arms.

"Herr Gott, Raoul, what are you doing in this masquerade?
The war is finished between your country and mine. What do
you want here? Another minute and my uncle, the staff generals
will be in here. This is headquarters of general staff—"

"Ah, *oui, alors,* that is why I am here." Again Dubail's teeth
shone in that silent laugh. "I wanted to find the generals. The
officers who command this machine that murders innocent citizens without warning. I, Raoul Dubail, rejected by my air corps
because I am lame, I came to fight you as a taxi driver. Ho ho!
Came to Switzerland in a little cab to kill you—"

Pain wrung Emmerich's mouth to a colorless twist. "Why
me, Raoul, why—"

"Because you are a Teuton and I would kill you and all your
monstrous kind to the last man, by the name of Jean of Luz, I
would! But since I cannot kill them all, I will slay those at the
top, the generals, the Neros who laugh at the burning, *mais
oui!* All through the night I drove Stehli in his cab. But he did
not recognize me, *non!* He did not know it was I who brought
him from our city. And then I waited until this fine young
Reichswehr captain walked by a certain doorway with a song
of victory on his swinish lips. He thought the war was over, eh?"
Dubail's hands pantomimed a wringing gesture, "So it was for
him. So it is for you—"

"Dubail, in the name of the *lieber Gott—*"

"Non! Non!" Lightfooted, the Esperenchman backed away.
"Do not touch your gun, Teuton. Shoot me and this packet hits

the floor—*pouf!* and this village is gone. Shreds you would be. Faceless shreds like my father on the floor of his little bake shop when the first torpedo struck. And now you will call your officers into this room. You will summon these butchering Teuton generals. Raoul Dubail has come with a reckoning"—he shook a pale fist at the windows—"a reckoning with the War Lords who killed my helpless father. And you, friend Emmerich, because of those murders at the Metropole—"

"At the Metropole?" Emmerich said huskily.

Dubail laughed soundlessly. "Who else but you could have done it? Who else could have slipped by the police detectives of that city? Did you know I discovered there was a transom between that dining room and the bedroom where the press—"

"Why should I do it, Raoul?" Voice brittle with desperation, Emmerich spoke with an eye to the windows. Any minute his uncle's staff would be coming in. He must stall, stall. "Why should I kill the statesmen?"

"Your father was bankrupt. I saw what happened on the exchange. Once you told me about your holdings in chemicals. Behold what a war did, then, for Emmerich Leather!"

HEAT SWAM in colored spirals before Emmerich's eyes. The floor was sinking and he must brace himself by gripping the table. *"Mein Gott,* you thought that of me? And I—I thought it was you!"

"Butcher! Swine! You dared blame me for those murders?"

"Ja," Emmerich whispered. "Because I knew you hated Gatreau. To kill Gatreau you must also kill Von Speer. And then I found your gun—"

"My gun?" Dubail spat. "Where?"

"It was after I turned in my story to the *Tageblatt* office," Emmerich said desperately. "I returned to the hotel. Your pistol was lying near that door with the full length mirror. It had just been fired empty. Because you were my friend I picked it up and fled, thinking you must have dropped it there and it had been overlooked when we entered the bedroom to write our accounts.

That is why I questioned you at the Café Guste. I knew our police would have held you for the assassinations. I was afraid for your life, and when I reached my home I threw your gun away, into a pond—"

"And I do not believe your lying words because you are a Teuton, a Boche, with the blood of murderers in your veins," was Dubail's condemnation, harsh through those dry white teeth, *"enfin* I will kill you all."

Then it seemed to Paul Emmerich as if everything in the world happened at once.

The cottage door lashed inward with a blurt of sounds, and a yelling cycle Uhlan officer charged across the sill. "Herr Major, the Americans got away. Even as we caught up with them their car crossed the frontier. The Yankee chauffeur leaned from the window and put a thumb at us to his nose. As we are not at war with Helvania my men could not pursue across the line—"

Raoul Dubail, uniformed as a Reichswehr captain, whirled screaming at the intruding cyclist.

Faster than he had ever moved in his life, Paul Emmerich snatched the repeating pistol from his belted holster, sprang at Dubail's back, crashed the gun barrel down *whack!* on the exposed neck-nape. Dropping the gun, he caught Dubail's sagging body by the armpits and held him upright, his voice going like talk out of nightmare.

"It is all right," he heard himself panting at his men, inventing frantically. "This is Captain Scheldt of the Bavarians. Shell shocked in this morning's battle. His mind had gone, but he will be all right although he may not know who he is—"

Popeyed with astonishment, the general staff was trooping in. Somehow his uncle was at his side, gesturing, shouting. "Shades of Friederich Wilhelm! is this headquarters a madhouse? Who is this captain? Who sent these cycle officers after that American car?"

"This is Captain Scheldt. He is sick. I sent the cycle Uhlans. The Americans in that car will try to spread the story we shot the Swiss spy without cause. One is a Yankee newspaper man who had a hand in the murder of Von Speer at the Metropole. My men could not pursue them across a neutral boundary into Helvania—"

And the radio officer, who had darted to his cackling wireless instruments, came rushing across the floor with wires and phones clapped to his shaved head, report blanks flagging in his hands, mouth going like a loud speaker.

"Herr General! *Offiziers!* It has come. Announcement from the High Command to all general staffs. Replacing *Feld-Marshal* von Reinmar, General Gottlieb von Neumann is appointed *Feld-Marshal* in command of the entire Teuton armies. In reason of Von Reinmar's assassination and its obvious inspiration in the Helvanian War Office, hostilities are to open at once in the east. August Schnitzler, himself, is coming to join our march on the Helvanian capital. With his own hand he has just signed the declaration. *Teutony declares war on Helvania!*"

HALF ASLEEP in the hot gold of noon (how'n hell could a growing man keep awake on an empty stomach?) Crazy Hooper had just sweated through the somnambulistic motions of changing his third tire while John Keats kibitzed and swore and got in the way. Crazy yearned to sit on the ferny mountain grass along this baking white roadside and snore. When had he slept last? When had he last eaten? Blinking warmth from his eyelashes, he made drowsy efforts to stow the tools and tire pump back in the kit, his hungry eyes on the gay wings of a yellow butterfly exploring some near-by laurel, fragrant under a signpost that read, *"Helva. E. 60 Kilo."* Reminded of a city and restaurants, his hands came awake and hurried.

Then a sound, a far-off disturbance in the crystal Alpine stillness, caused him to look backward toward that descending five miles of whitewashed road down which they had come. At first he could not discover what it was, and stood peering toward sunny distance, nibbling doubtful nourishment from a green fingernail.

"Snap into it," came John Keats' fatigue-cracked rasp. "We could've overhauled the Russian girl's crate if this tire—"

Crazy Hooper's yell took all the words out of Keats' mouth. "Holy Jerusalem—look at that!"

John Keats looked back. What had seemed at first glance to be a smoking pour of metal flowing down through the Pass became sunlight tipping a million moving steel-points with fire. Brightness coming eastward on that road in a high and rushing column of gold dust, like a funnel of shiny wind. John Keats shook the hair from hie eyes, and saw what it was. A wheel-jack fell from his nerveless hand. Great Lord!

It wasn't any cycle squad after them this time. The entire Teutonic Army was after them. The entire Teutonic Army, humming across the border of Helvania; and as far as John Keats could see there wasn't a single Helvanian soldier in sight to stop the flood!

But an old man in the black gaiters of a cleric had appeared in the road-bend ahead and came strolling up the middle of the concrete with a basket of cut flowers over one arm and a painted placard under the other. As the old man trudged past the Minerva, he gave its wild-eyed occupants a cheery nod. Crazy was pumping on the starter, and John Keats stared at the old man's sign. The sign said, "Welcome."

CHAPTER XI

INVASION!

"HELVANIA," SAYS YOUR Atlas Almanac of 1936, "is that little kingdom of Balkan extraction, bordered on the east by Rumania, its western frontier recently extended—by Treaty of 1935—through former Austrian territory to Godek Pass in the Franco-Swiss Alps. A benevolent monarchy, the crown passed at the death of King Gillam III to the present ruler, Queen Roberta.

"The palace of the Queen is in Helva; the state forum and the council chambers open to all who care to witness government sessions from the visitors' galleries. A broad new boulevard cuts through the heart of the city, boasted by its engineers as the widest avenue in the world. At the cost of many millions this avenue, which runs from west to east gate, is lined with great elms and cool parks, the scene of many carnivals and fiestas, and a traveler on this luxurious thoroughfare, remembering he is in one of the smallest countries in Europe, may well be amazed—"

JOHN KEATS, traveling on that luxurious thoroughfare, was more than amazed. The Minerva, dented, dusty and roaring, looked no more like a magic carpet than Crazy Hooper, at the wheel, resembled Aladdin. But here they were at Rainbow's End. Somewhere this racing limousine had outrun reality. At one o'clock of the afternoon this couldn't be a city awaiting the crash of an invading horde. Where had they left reality behind? At that place on the mountain road when Crazy had first spied the coming army and an old man had passed them with a basket of flowers and a card that said "Welcome"?

Keats glared through the windshield glassy-eyed. Five years ago he'd been in this Helvanian capital, but there'd been no boulevard like this. Had Crazy Hooper steered off the map into another country?

There was the same leisured passing of ox teams and creaky vans, shiny motors and busy bicycles. Screened sidewalk cafés, little islands in the flow of pedestrians where one might stop for coffee and an unhurried glass. Book stalls and courteous flower girls, people and dogs strolling in the public gardens, shoe-shine boys and newsboys and peddlers hawking along the curb. The city was cool, summery.

"Crazy, am I out of *my* head?"

"It's got me, buddy. I was wonderin' if an empty stomach had turned me nuts."

The car began to pass a file of statues, heroic figures in marble that watched their speed with no more excitement than the pavement crowds. Five years ago these men in marble had been captains and kings. Keats stared at the sculptured figures in deepening astonishment. The captains and the kings had departed. Like the boulevard's concrete, these statues were new. There was Shakespeare, colossal with Elizabethan ruff and pen. Then Pasteur, the healer. Plato and Aristotle from ancient Greece. Roentgen, discoverer of the X-ray. Lincoln. Cervantes.

What wizardry had put these people on the pedestals of kings? No Napoleons, no conquerors remembered on this boulevard. Here were artists, musicians, healers, philosophers, singers and players of a hundred nationalities, discoverers of medicine, men who had found time to tell tales to children. What kind of a nation's capital was this?

"I'm dreaming," Keats panted, "dreaming."

THEY FLED across a square where a new marble was rising in block and tackle. Five years ago an equestrian of King Leopold had stood above, those flower beds. Now the Helvanian ruler was gone; his place given over to a pyramid wearing another name. Argo Galenne, the young Helvanian poet.

The Minerva was slowing down. Keats pulled himself together with an effort. No time to stop in front of miracles.

"Step on it, Crazy! She can't be far. Frantsovna—"

"Gas," the lank one snapped. "Got to stop for petrol."

They slid into a filling station. Crazy sped from the car toward a restaurant stand while the pumps were working, and Keats, collapsed in the seat, could only continue to stare at the façade of the cathedral across the boulevard. Five years ago that edifice had housed the Helvanian State Church and its one-eyed bishop, as formal in its religion as its stony architecture. But the portal had been altered to a broad staircase open to the sun. A row of marble figures stood at the top step flanking the door. Above the door was a shining invitation in bronze: "Worship For All." The statues congregated there were the fathers of world religions, Confucius and Moses and Lao Tse, Zoroaster and Buddha, Christ and Mohammed, their shoulders touching in amity, their faces turned to the avenue in friendly appeal. On the walkways below, the passers-by wore expressions of cheer. Near-by buildings were in holiday garb. Flags and flowers, drapes and festoons and colored toy balloons. The city was red and green with bunting, the colors of Helvania. Peasants and carts everywhere. Children in frills. Kids eating peanuts. Furniture vans creaking by. Everybody seemed to be moving in from the country. Was this a national holiday, a national moving day? Cloth banners fluttered above the avenue. Signs and flags. "Welcome." "Greetings." "Helvania Invites All Comers." "Welcome."

KEATS WHISTLED at a newsboy, and the lad came on the skip.

"Read all about it—traffic bill passed—"

Traffic bill! The newspaper, Helvania's largest courier, cracked and quivered in Keats' hand. No news at all! Headlines about a bill going through the Helvanian Crown Council. Front page story featuring a council debate on the speed of motor cars.

*The gun pointed
at Schnitzler.*

Council had passed a bill that all automobiles must be controlled by an attachment that would cut motoring speed to fifty miles an hour. A precautionary measure to slow up joy-riders on the nation's new highways and prevent traffic accidents.

Headlining a bill to prevent traffic accidents, and not a soldier in those outlying fields to stop that avalanche! Well, it might be expected of a country that trusted its pedestals to philosophers and poets and invited the fathers of religion to stand together at the door of its cathedral. Unbelieving, Keats gaped at the newspaper in his fingers. Queen Roberta couldn't be responsible for this monstrous censorship of important news. Some ugly dictatorship over the press was hiding truth from the public in this country.

His hands shook through the printed pages; stiffened in new astoundment. Here it was! The latest press dispatches, on the next to last page, among the underwear advertisements. Reported in small type as of no more import than the story of a dog biting a man. *Teutons War On Esperance. March Through Swiss End of Godek Pass. Esperench Capital Destroyed by Aërial Torpedoes. Their Government Collapses and Armies Mutiny Before*

Teuton Advance. Capital of Teutony destroyed in reprisal. Gas, disease, fire ravages both great cities. War flames in all modern methods of horror after killing of statesmen in Metropole conference. But Swiss and Esperench are beaten in less than fifty hours' fighting. Thousands of citizens slain, Allied troops decimated before tremendous Teuton war machine—Schnitzler sets in motion greatest motorized army ever known—

IT WAS true, then! He wasn't imagining, for here was the latest noon release in the Helvanian papers. Relegated among the underwear ads, but honestly reported in black and white.

John Keats lifted his unbelieving glance from the newspaper to see if the city was still there. It was. He could look down the boulevard and still see the statues of poets and minnesingers under cool trees. He could look across the plaza at the amazing new cathedral. Bunting fluttered in the sunshine and Welcome signs floated in the breeze. Didn't they read the papers? That brown-skinned peasant in his embroidered waistcoat, conducting a tan and white ox along the curb, hadn't he ever heard of aërial torpedoes? Those two Helvanian mothers in frilly skirts walking arm in arm ahead of their scampering children, didn't they know what had happened in Esperance, in Teutony?

Dimly Keats realized Crazy Hooper was back from under the restaurant awning with two sandwiches in his mouth, a dozen more in his hand, juggling ham and bread as he paid off the filling station attendant.

"Crazy Hooper," Keats whispered, "did we see that army coming?"

The tow-head nodded soberly.

Keats snatched a sandwich. "Stop at that traffic policeman out there. Hurry, man! Hurry!"

THE MINERVA slid them across the boulevard, stopped at the officer's post. The red and green policeman eyed them incuriously and continued to wigwag his white gantlets. A procession of small girls carrying a daisy chain passed, laughing, before the halted foreign car. Consternation muddled Keats' tongue. Not a word of Helvanian could he muster. This cop must think he was strangling on a sandwich. Then the language came at a blurt.

"Officer—I—I want to go to the capital of Helvania!"

"But," with a smile at the flag on the Minerva's radiator cap, "you *are* in Helvania's capital, my American."

"This is the main avenue through the city?"

"The main highway going to points east, my American."

"A blue touring car," Keats gurgled. "Did such a car come this way? Driven by a woman in a khaki waterproof—"

"I noticed her because she was a foreigner," smiled the traffic man, "and driving very fast. But we do not arrest those unfamiliar with our local ordinances."

Then Frantsovna had gone through! And the rest of it was coming. Border communications must have been cut by the motorcycle Uhlans, and this city wasn't warned, didn't know it stood in a tornado's path! But the language wasn't made whereby you could tell a policeman that an enemy army was thunderbolting down his road and he'd better prepare to die. Not when the fellow stood smiling and adjusting his buttons and directing daisy chains.

"Crazy," Keats switched hoarse yelling into English, "they don't know there's a war. My God! Palace of the Queen, and make it fast!"

The Minerva started like a bullet. Streets, squares, parks, monuments blurred rearward in a rainbow streak. Crazy made it fast. A dozen blocks at hair-raising steeplechase pace, and the long car smoked up a gravel drive, through a tall open gateway to the marble columns of a ferro-concrete palace hatted by a gleaming white dome that stood like an Alpine snowcap against the sun. A vague glimpse of frock-coated functionaries strolling in the palace gardens. Uniformed dignitaries lounging along the terrace, discussing in little groups on the palace steps.

Every window, gallery, cornice of the palace was gala with flags. A tremendous banner, red letters on green gauze, floated above the marble portal. "Welcome To Helvania." Not a soldier

in evidence save the ornamental Household Guards too lazy to
challenge a foreign car.

BURSTING WITH bewilderment and panic, John Keats
dashed up the marble steps into the coolness of a broad, open
hall where his running boots made the racket of a colt on the
floor of a museum. Nobody stopped him. Courtiers who stood
at inner doors eyed him with composure. He must look like a
maniac, unkempt from hours on the open road, features black
with dirt and sleeplessness, darting into a palace with a half-
eaten sandwich forgotten in his hand; but the grizzled chamberlain in velvet who came forward to learn his business might
have been expecting him.

Keats choked, swayed on his feet. "The Queen—Queen
Roberta!"

"You have an appointment? Your name, please."

"John Keats—war correspondent Universe News! She—the
Queen will know. I—I must see Her Majesty—"

Apparently Her Majesty did know. "Her Royal Highness
has been awaiting your arrival," was the astounding response.
"This way, please."

Dumb, Keats followed the velvet chamberlain up a sweep of
staircase to bronze doors that opened into a wide bright drawing-room where a white figure—another marble?—stood alone
at room's end. The chamberlain was retiring, bowing at the hips,
and that solitary figure was not a marble. Posed at a sun-filled
casement, the girlish profile was unaware, eyes turned toward
the window in thoughtful contemplation of the boulevard below.

She was wearing the same white riding costume as when he'd
seen her last before her coronation; linen blouse open at the
throat, spotless whipcord breeches, milky leather boots silver-
spurred. Sunny hair bound with a cord of gold across her untroubled forehead. Seeing here there, Keats rooted to the carpet on
feet of stone. They'd deserted her already! Abandoned their
Queen! He clawed the hat from his head and miserably twisted
the article in nerveless fingers. Hearing, she turned with a smile,

and then, as if receiving seedy Americans was a habit of hers every afternoon, she extended both hands in informal greeting.

"John Keats, I am so glad. I knew you would come."

"Sire," he gasped. "Your Majesty—"

"You see I am not surprised." She spoke as if they'd left off visiting yesterday and the years between were not at all, "I had instructed my border outposts to watch for you, and they wirelessed me this morning when you crossed the border from Switzerland. I suspected your papers would send you to my country. Such a long time since you were with us. And just in time to report our greatest holiday—"

"Your Majesty," the tongue moved like a rusty bell-clapper behind his teeth, "I—I'm not here to cover any assignment. Europe—you must know Europe is at war! Esperance and Switzerland have fallen. I tell you, I—I've just come from Godek Pass—there was a disastrous battle—the Teuton armies—"

THE QUEEN continued to smile. "I was anxious to hear an account, and would have sent for you. Helvania needs an honest observer—"

The palace drawing-room spun in whorls of color at Keats' eyes. He cried, "You do not understand me, Sire. Teutony has crushed the Allies. Esperance is beaten. Your generals have deceived you, betrayed you, sold your country out—"

"No," she contradicted cheerfully, "my generals have not tricked me. I am in sole command of Helvania's troops. Every citizen will prove a loyal soldier when the time arrives."

"But the time is here!" John Keats could have wept. "I saw them coming over your border not four hours ago. Tanks. Cannon! The Teuton army—"

"We know that," the Queen said gently. "They declared war."

"But your national defenses," Keats yelled. "Your national defenses—"

"You have seen them," said Queen Roberta, smiling, "pictured along the city's boulevard. Tolerance, religion, friendship, education, justice. Those are Helvania's defenses. And laughter," she added as an afterthought. "Laughter. The holiday, the flags, it is for the Teutons. I radioed Herr Schnitzler to come ahead, and my subjects look forward to a wonderful parade. Let us join the welcoming committee on this outside balcony where we may see it better."

She had radioed her country's enemies to come ahead!

A low muttering tremor on the window casements grew in the blond day outside like a rising of wind. An undertone, beelike droning, the chorus of thousands of rolling wheels over-toned by a far-away, myriad-throated human outcry.

Sweat sprang in icy globes on John Keats' temples. "The Teutons are in the city. The people are screaming!"

"Not screaming," said the Queen, taking his arm. "Cheering."

IF HE lived through ten hundred incarnations, Keats told himself, he would never forget that afternoon's review. Bona-parte's entry to Vienna, Sherman at the sea, Von Moltke's strut across Paris—history was cluttered with the sagas of conquer-ors parading the cities of the vanquished, but there was nothing to match this parade of Teutonic might through the capital of Helvania.

Wedged into a silent little group of frock-coated Helvanian ministers, a girl Queen at his elbow, axle grease on his cuffs, he stood on the balcony with sunshine on his hair, refusing the evidence of his eyes.

These outriding motorcycle Uhlans must have had a shock when they were met on the border by a cleric in gaiters who bade them Godspeed. He could fancy the lookouts in the turrets of their armored cars mopping their jaws and beginning to swear.

Helmets ready to duck an ambush fusillade that hadn't come. Eyes wary for enemy patrols that weren't there. No logs felled across the highway, no cunning barb-wire traps in the fields, no secret gun pits or exploding mines or bridges smashed for their engineers to repair. Nothing to shoot at save a peasant girl who leaned on a white-nosed Holstein cow and gave them a hand-wave. Nothing but open road and mountain butterflies and an occasional small Helvanian boy who whooped and grinned. Signal cars deployed across this enemy landscape reporting: "all roads clear, full speed ahead"; officers glaring in incredulity; the High Command throwing down their charts and battle plans with nothing to do but sit.

Keats could imagine the veterans from Belgium and Alsace starting to look over their shoulders and fidget. Certainly the face of the first motor Uhlan who drove through the wide-open city gates saw clear boulevard ahead and eager Helvanians cheering along the curbs, and was struck by nothing more deadly than a handful of confetti—that first Uhlan's face was no whit more astonished than the face of John Keats who saw him come.

THEN, IN a blizzard of colored streamers, a snowstorm of ticker tape from roofs and windows, the Teutons marched in. Flashing and glittering, the columns of machinery thundered down the boulevard, wheeled in mechanical precision at the palace gates.

As if at a prearranged signal, every window, gallery and roof the length of that avenue had loosed a rain of flowers and flakes, and the huge iron flocks of war machinery made the appearance of steamrollers puffing through a florist conservatory. Man and boy, every Helvanian on the line of march had a rose, a carnation, a greeting card, a confetti bag to throw. By the time the infantry lorries were passing, the air was a blowing drift of petals, colored balloons, streamers and tinsel.

Under another blow of astonishment, John Keats saw that Helvanian women, stationed at intervals along the pavement, were passing wicker baskets up to grabbing hands. Showers of cigarettes joined the paper snow from above. Girls in tea gowns, in smart picture hats, in afternoon frocks leaned from rooftops, ledges, doorways, laughing and beckoning, waving, throwing kisses. Somewhere—it must have come from a near-by park, the music intensified by a battery of loud speakers—an orchestra started the "Blue Danube." Music drifted in rhythmic glissades above the crowd-roar, the *clank* and *tonk* of iron wheels, the *clop-clop-clop* of caterpillar tractors, the grinding of motors.

Flowers, ticker tape and cheering swirled across the torrent of the guns. Yellow daisies clung to the muzzles of giant Essen cannon. Wreaths and streamers fluttered from the throats of upturned anti-aircraft rifles, growling howitzers. Never had such an exhibit of death-dealing mechanism trundled before the eyes of a civil populace, and never was there such a reception.

The "Blue Danube"! Something seemed to have gone askew with this military Juggernaut. Its streamlined Teutonic perfection had slipped a gear. Beyond the helpless palace its advance patrols were having an argument, an armored car was out of line down the square, and a company of Helvanian schoolgirls were thronging against the wheel-guards, passing up lunch boxes and gifts. Work Troopers in lorries behind were jostling one another to catch cigarettes out of the sunlight, and a lissom woman in a scarlet gown blew kisses at the grinning men. Transfixed on the palace balcony, Keats watched a liver-faced staff officer dash down the line of stalled trucks, stand up in the motorcycle side-car, bellow at the troopers. But the woman in the scarlet gown swung from the curb to catch the officer's arm, and was laughing up at him.

"You begin to see?" a small voice whispered at Keats' shoulder. "You begin to understand?"

His fingers clutched the balcony rail. "See? Understand?"

"You see," the Queen whispered, "that is one of *my* generals. Tikita is her name, and they know her, for she has danced in all the great theaters of Europe. Every actress, chorus girl, peasant beauty, every girl and woman of Helvania is somewhere along the boulevard."

"Bravo!" Keats heard the roar. *"Gesundheit,* Tikita! Bravo!"

"We have planned for three years," the Queen went on cheerfully. "My people knew," she gestured at the steel columns blocking the avenue below, "it would come. My ministers saw the straws in the wind. We could never stop Schnitzler; afford no armament race with them. But our budget has prepared for this holiday, a million for flags, a million for flowers and wine."

He wondered if he was hearing this, so he turned his eyes at the speaker's face. Queen Roberta's expression was tranquil, amused. "Is it not cheap compared to an expenditure of billions for armaments? We have no cannon, no air force, no munition plants, and our city is saved. They do not bombard us, for we have nothing of danger for them to destroy."

"But your country—" Keats managed to gasp.

"Schnitzler has preached war. I have preached peace. You will learn my method of fighting is more modern than this dictator's. Instead of gas alarms, fear propaganda, bayonet practice, my people have drilled for holiday, flower brigades, flag exhibits, trained to remain cool under provocation. Rigidly as any Work Troop platoon, my subjects know what to do, how to distribute banners, cards, floral pieces, wine, to preserve order. It takes two to make the quarrel—"

"But if shooting starts—"

HER LIPS made a firm line. "The Teutons alone can start it. My police have long ago confiscated all firearms in the kingdom. A major crime to carry arms in this country. Detectives line the roofs watching for snipers. Our florists are the artillery here. Every garden in the country supplies the War Office." Her eyes glowed with the shine of sunlight on mountain water. "I depend on you," she breathed, "to report this to every newspaper of the world."

Cold fear melted the muscles around his heart. "It can't work! They'll loot the city, Sire. Enslave you and your people—"

"Wait," she cut him short, "and watch."

He was watching, all right. Sirens were shrilling through the madness below, and there was a mechanical tumult as lorries, tanks and machines were backing against the curbstones. A narrow path opened down the blossom-strewn boulevard. A corps of blue-steel sedans came speeding through the parade lines, snored to a halt at the palace gates. A van-load of men in canary yellow shirts brought up the rear, and as the sedans squealed to a standstill, the yellow-shirted soldiers tumbled across the pavement to erect a fence of bayonets leading to the palace steps. Officers whipped their bodies to attention. Arms slanted skyward. Keats knew what that bodyguard of Yellow Shirts meant, and swallowed a gulp of expectant fear.

"*Hala!*" the Helvanians were cheering. "*Hala!* Greetings!"

A *generalstabsoffizier* sprang from the first car, followed by a Field Marshal and his staff. The sedan doors clanged like the doors of steel safes. Coat skirts swishing, helmets a-glitter with spearheads and eagles, the staff generals hustled up the palace walk, then stood as if uncertain of the next move. One goat-whiskered colonel was scrubbing his forehead with a handkerchief; another pointed to the gallery where the Queen of the Helvanians watched with her ministers, but the others did not look up. Then whistles were shrilling everywhere, officers became images, the doors of the second sedan whanged open and a cordon of Yellow Shirts came rushing through cheering thunder.

But the man hustled in their midst was not under arrest. Nerves tightened under Keats' scalp when he looked down on that spare figure in its severe uniform, khaki breeches and brown cavalry boots, O.D. shirt belted across the breast, the familiar brown necktie, white band on the sleeve with its glaring, squared black Trefoil Cross. "*Heil!*" the city screamed, "*Heil!*" But the spare, hatless man ignored the tumult, angrily dusted confetti flakes from his sleeve, and ran quick-step up the palace drive. Keats had a momentary glimpse of that stern-chiseled face with its theatrical swoop of hair across the forehead, ascetic mouth downturned at the corners. August Schnitzler!

Then Yellow Shirts, *generalstabsoffiziers,* Field Marshal, *Der Meister* himself, passed into the palace. The boulevard whirled in kaleidoscopic colors that ached on his eyeballs, and Keats turned on sick legs from the balcony rail. Somehow Crazy Hooper was on hand with a vest-pocket camera, while the Helvanian ministers were moving off, patting on their tophats, self-conscious as senators after a newsreel pose. The Queen of Helvania came to take his hand.

"Come," was her royal command. "My cabinet and I go to meet him in the Council Chamber. I want you, my Americans, to report this historic meeting to the world."

CHAPTER II

ULTIMATUM!

JOHN KEATS HAD bungled the reporting of one historic conference in his journalistic career, but the minutes of this meeting in the palace of Helvania would remain forever indelible on his mind. Afterwards he could never quite recall how he and Crazy, outlandish in that Balkan setting, arrived there in the Council Chamber to sit like a pair of tramps at an offside press table under a domed ceiling full of misty light.

On a raised dais before this backdrop sat the Queen of Helvania with her cabinet ministers. Posed in her snowy riding costume behind a pulpit-like black-and-gold desk, her ministers seated glee-club fashion at her back, the little Queen seemed no more than a boy; a small and unafraid tribune confronting the highest delegation from Mars.

They might have come from Mars, the gray-green officers who stamped through the tall doors at room's end. Yellow Shirts and Storm Squadsmen clanked to guard stations in the outer corridor as the tall doors closed; and a harsh rustling of gray-green overcoats, clacking cavalry boots, the jingle of body harness and sidearms accompanied the spare, hatless man with his backstage haircut up the room.

Seeing a close-up of Schnitzler for the first time, John Keats could almost understand why an enlightened nation could throw aside reason and follow a human as a god. Nothing in common between this man and the military robots lumped behind him. When Schnitzler struck an attitude the chamber went quiet as

174

stone. His arms were folded in that daguerreotype pose of his photographs, chin lifted exalted as a Cæsar's; but his posturing was more than good theatricals.

The Puritanic simplicity of his uniform was a cunning ostentation against the braid and buckles of his generals. Fanaticism burned in those features. Mystery. Super self-belief in every line of that face. Anger was on it now, like a reflection of firelight on cold marble. The eyes appeared glazed, as if coated by a blue-black Chinese enamel. The sensitive, downturned mouth quivered like a girl's. In that attitude of conquering "super man" there was something half poetic, half grotesque, neurotic yet compelling as dynamite. This was a man, yet he could fling an arm at the sky and populations would salaam.

THERE WAS a minute when, watching Schnitzler, Keats was reminded of a magician whose act had bungled up his sleeve. Garlands for his guns and this calm little ruler in a riding habit! He couldn't have staged it better himself, and maybe she'd stolen his spot. Eye to eye she met the Schnitzler glare. Red color drained down the stern bones of his face, his eyes twinkled black, and his outburst came with the simplicity of fury.

"Madam, what does this carnival of nonsense mean?"

Midway to the dais Schnitzler's staff officers had halted in a sort of confused, watchful silence. The Helvanian ministers made no expression or sound. At the muffed rage in the Dictator's voice, John Keats could have uttered a nervous snicker, but he wanted to yell the same question, himself, to snap that thread of strain.

Queen Roberta stood up behind the high-topped desk with a pleasant smile. "On my part, Herr Schnitzler, I might ask the same of you? But it has always been the custom of Helvania to welcome visiting neighbors. Now that you are here, just what do you and your people intend to do?"

Visiting neighbors! Intend to do? Suspicious gutturals muttered from the Teuton officers. August Schnitzler stroked the swoop of hair out of his left eye to glare the more directly.

"Her former Majesty," he suggested in a sweetened snarl, "presents a very clever charade, a jest we do not fail to appreciate. Unhappily in the emergency of war, Teutony has no time for jests."

"I do not jest for my people," the Queen answered, her words a shade louder. "The Teutons are here with welcome. You have a million men in my country? Five million? Good. There is room in Helvania for all. Our countryside you have found at your disposal. Already my subjects have quit their homes in a gesture of hospitality toward your good soldiers. You will find quarters available for everybody, as my people are gladly transferring their families to the apartments reserved for this day, apartments built by public funds in this city. Our hospitals, libraries, hotels, farms are open, by my royal order, to all who wish to come."

John Keats heard a chuckle from the lank man at his elbow. But August Schnitzler and John Keats and the Teuton general staff were staring like fools, and only the Queen appeared sane in that aberrant chamber. Even an orator could lose his mind. Schnitzler's mouth jarred open.

"You have voted to abandon your allies? You propose an affiliation with Teutony?" he panted.

"Helvania did not abandon her allies, Herr Schnitzler," her reply was clear and calm, but there was an obvious sting in the "Herr Schnitzler" that a dictator could not fail to resent. "My country made military alliances with no other power. As for an affiliation, what matter the government so long as one's subjects are alive and happy? Let us, you and I, put aside confusing diplomatic speeches, and speak plainly for all to understand. As Queen of the Helvanians, I am responsible for the last man under my sovereignty. I do not wish my people to fight, to die for me. Life, that is what I wish for them. My subjects have no quarrel with yours. If your rule be just and fair, what matter the capital city? Regard," she threw out a small hand. "Here is my country, here are my subjects. Gladly I give them into your care. Can you heal their business depressions? So much the better. Can you collect the taxes, sell their goods, operate the farms, build the highways, conduct the labor reliefs, handle the Helvanian affairs—what matter the surname of the ruler? Better my subjects be live Teutons than dead Helvanians. The Teutons are a great, a noble race. I trust the heart of your people. Gladly I extend the responsibility of ruling to you, Herr Schnitzler, here is my country, a great country. Take it, and welcome."

WHAT A climax to a war that was! *Here is my country, my friend. If you can run it better than I, take it.* If Schnitzler's face was something to remember, if the faces of the conquering generals were a solid blob of amazement, John Keats would have wanted to see his own visage, right then. The press table was shaking under his elbows. Crazy Hooper was swallowing air with a sound like peanut brittle going down. August Schnitzler's reply sawed through gritted teeth.

"Her former Majesty fails to appreciate her situation. I am forced to remind her that the Kingdom of Helvania is no longer hers to offer up with such subtleties of meekness and good will." Thunder worked the muscles in his throat. "Teutony is not fooled by pious protests of friendship on the part of her beaten enemy. God is a mighty fortress and a sword in the hand of the righteous. It is the word of God that the Pharisees be driven from their temples without favor or mercy. It is His will—"

"Aren't you confusing yourself with the Deity?" the Queen asked in an unruffled tone. "You speak of God as an angel of vengeance, and talk of yourself as His emissary. In the words of Voltaire, I might ask to see your written credentials. And since we have gone into Biblical quotations, do you remember the commandment, 'Love your enemies'?"

Keats saw a plump staff general nudge an artillery commander with a whispered, "Not difficult if they were all so good looking," and the room tinted crimson against his eyelids. Schnitzler's face had shaded the hue of suffocation.

"Pious mummery!" he thundered. He slung up his arm at a slant. "As *Reichsmeister* of Teutony, I demand the unconditional

surrender of the Kingdom of Helvania and the immediate arrest
of the commanding general of the Helvanian army!"

QUEEN ROBERTA moved to stand beside her upraised desk.
"As commanding general of the Helvanian army, I offer myself
to your arrest, Herr Schnitzler. For my people I have spoken.
Might I ask on what charges I am to give myself up?"

"Her former Majesty, the Queen of the Helvanians, might be
referred to Article Two of our Declaration of War submitted at
seven o'clock of this morning."

She nodded. "But in ordinary relations of diplomacy one
country serves another with an ultimatum giving a time-limit
to answer the charges. My War Office was accused of complicity
in an act of war against your High. Command, and no chance
was offered for discussion through the channels of diplomacy
or the League."

Schnitzler offered curtly, "Teutony does not belong to your
League. Your ministers had pledged Helvania's neutrality, then
instigated a direct attack on a nation at war."

"You have proof of our complicity in Von Reinmar's murder,
Herr Dictator?"

"Proof enough!" Schnitzler hurled up an impatient fist. "I,
myself, listened to the trial by radio phone. Papers found on the
Swiss directly implicated Helvania."

"My War Office denies any hand in this crime. But I, Queen
of the Helvanians and commander of their army, freely offer
myself to your firing squads as indemnity for Field Marshal von
Reinmar's murder."

"Enough!" Schnitzler shouted. "Teutony refuses to be trapped
in a design motivated to turn public opinion against her. Do
warriors trade their commanding generals for members of a
tottering royalty? The Queen will give immediate orders that
her War Office surrender all men, arms, munitions at once to
Feld-Marshal Gottlieb von Neumann. Cabinet ministers and
all government officials to be placed under arrest. Her former
Majesty is given twenty-four hours to prepare for exile."

Facing that tumult of commands, the Queen stood in silence; Schnitzler's voice emptied itself into a chambered hush; and the Teutonic generals grouped behind their leader moved uncertainly forward. But there sounded a rattle of metal beyond the tall doors; voices snapped and barked; a Reichswehr officer and three Yellow Shirts broke into the room. Savage staff generals whirled at the intruders, and before the Dictator could go on with his capitulatory demands, he was called into a feverish consultation with his staff. John Keats caught fragments out of the whispered uproar. Things were doing out on the boulevard. A company of Work Troopers had deserted their trucks to dance with Helvanian girls on the square. There'd been a row with the officers who tried to call them into line. A captain trying to arrest an actress had been knocked down by one of his own men. These women were swarming all through the army. Soldiers were singing and drinking.

Reports from outside the city claimed artillerymen were strolling around with girls on their arms. Some Bavarian riflemen had openly thrown down their guns. A company of machine gunners had cheered the Helvanians. A Reichswehr officer was seen fraternizing with citizens in a near-by café. Troopers were heard to say they were sick of killing—

ALREADY STUNNED where he sat, Keats gaped under the spell of Schnitzler's new fury. The Dictator sprang among his staff officers, bawling, empurpled. "A plot! A plot to destroy our army's morale. We will stamp out this weakness at once! Put the city under martial law. The Bavarian riflemen to be shot as deserters. Arrest any soldier seen talking with these Helvanian pacifists!"

He spun at a white-skinned aide. "Clear the Helvanians from the streets and lock them in. Tear down all flags, signs, propaganda to hurt our morale. Those images of intellectual decadence that clutter the city, pull them down, do you understand? Sweep them out. Smash them. Wipe out every last sign of this Helvanian propaganda. That public library—burn every last book by nightfall. Indoors with the citizens, do you hear? My men will not be subjected to this scheming false hospitality designed to undermine their efficiency. Any girl or woman seen talking with a soldier goes under arrest. Any Helvanian male citizen caught speaking on common terms with our men is to be shot! Do you hear those terms?" he whirled at the Queen and her ministers. "My army will *not* be undermined by your cunning propagandists."

Hands open at her sides, the Queen gazed evenly into the dark points of the raging man's eyes. For a moment she had no answer, and the room was alive with the sound of breathing. Everything was like a play, and the echo of running cavalry boots that came in when the tall doors swung was like sounds offstage. The lavender face of August Schnitzler could not be real. John Keats could believe none of this.

Only the eyes of the girl on the raised platform seemed true, meeting this Teutonic dictator's glare with a contempt and anger of her own that was pure royalty.

"Are these the laws you would bring my subjects, Herr Schnitzler?"

"You will see them go into effect immediately."

Her white figure moved behind the tall desk; she, too, could stand with folded arms. Unafraid, she gazed at the man before her. "I do not like these laws. I was afraid of this. In your country the people are the servants of the Law. In Helvania the Law has always been the servant of the people. I said I would gladly turn my subjects over to your government provided it gave them a fair chance to live."

"Do you presume to argue the will of the Teutonic High Command—"

She derided, "We welcome you with open hands and you order my people shot for hospitality. In that light I refuse to surrender my people to your rule; refuse to sacrifice myself for a crime my country did not intrigue. I carry this matter to a higher court; the court of world opinion." Lifting her head fiercely, she swept a wide gesture with an arm. "I warn you, Herr Dictator, anything you say may be used against you. Microphones in this room are now carrying our voices to every corner of the world; my radio engineers have called a worldwide hook-up; I leave the listeners of humanity to judge these proceedings."

PULSES THUDDING like kettle drums, Keats sped a stare of comprehending admiration at the amazing ruler of the Helvanians. A gusty exclamation escaped Crazy Hooper at his side. But Schnitzler's fist was a dark maul waving at the ceiling frescoes.

"Know that my generals are not caught by this treachery. The radio engineers of my army have been creating static to eliminate the sending power of your secret Helvanian stations."

Pallor came to the Queen's lips, but she countered softly, "So we reveal our true stripes, you and I. Honesty is never afraid of being overheard. I have provided against the eventuality of a secret session with you, however. At our press table sits the representative of a news syndicate, an American citizen, neutral, unprejudiced. I count on this gentleman to report in exact detail each word of this meeting."

"Gosh!" It was the mildest expletive Crazy had ever used.

Breath chugged out of Keats' lungs in a cold gush that seemed to bring his heart up with it; the enameled eyes in Schnitzler's face wrenched toward him, jabbed like electric surgeon's knives that would cut him away.

The Dictator's voice was acid. "I am sure the presence of this alien reporter will not guarantee a press account of Helvania's humiliating surrender."

Above the marble desk the Queen's eyes flashed the color of sun on ice. "Helvania has made no surrender, humiliating or otherwise. Herr Schnitzler, I warn you and your Teuton generals. To avenge the murder of your statesman, Baron von Speer, you have caused the deaths of thousands," her cry rang down the room. "My unarmed populace shall not be pillaged to avenge the death of a general, slain at no instigation of ours. Be warned again! If one single Helvanian is killed by you or your men—"

On this wholly unexpected tone of warning, her voice paused on its note of threat, stunning every hearer in the room; and the consternation that traveled down the room might have been echoed by the commotion outside. Confused sounds, muffled words of command came faintly through the barrier; then, as everyone shifted startled eyes, the door snapped open, whipped shut at a sharp order, and a pair of Teuton officers were there like an interruption. Striding forward swiftly, they advanced toward the paralyzed staff commanders; one tall, slim, purposeful, the other spare and stooped, walking with the swing of a limp.

Something in the carriage of those rigid figures addled the eyeballs in Keats' head. Their gray-green field coats made a militant swish. Hard light glittered on their steel helmets. On stepping through the doors, the first man had whipped a machine gun pistol from his coat to cover the Teuton staff. Stepping sideways, the second man pointed a pair of black automatics at the Helvanian end of the room.

IT WAS August Schnitzler who first screamed. "Teuton officers! *Herr Gott!* What does this mean?"

"*Ja!*" The blurt spouted from the gray Field Marshal, leaping from the cluster of staff generals. "You, Major Emmerich! Are you mad?"

On no muscular effort of his own, John Keats was half out of his chair. "Paul Emmerich! Great—"

"Hold that pose!" The slender one's words cracked with the low ferocity of a whiplash. "Do not move, one of you, or you are dead men. That goes for you, August Schnitzler, and," he spun with the gun, "you, too, Uncle Gottlieb. Because I am your nephew they let me in, but I say it—"

"He is mad!" the Field Marshal squalled.

Schnitzler shook out with passion, "So! The Helvanians have brought on a mutiny! Some one will die for this—"

Keats drove his fist against the Swede's jaw.

Incredibly the second man growled in an accent, "Too many have died already and so a few more will make little difference—"

"That is the truth, someone will die," Paul Emmerich snarled, "and that is the next in this chamber who makes another move or utters a cry. For once August Schnitzler will keep shut his mouth. So will this Helvanian Queen, and the rest. You will hear what Raoul Dubail and I have to say."

"Dubail!" Keats whistled the name in his throat, and as he sank in his chair the second man dealt him a look from eyes of deadly jade, shifting a gun menacingly.

"Major Emmerich is sick, insane," that was from the white-lipped Field Marshal.

"Sick," nodded the slim man. *"Ja wohl,* uncle, I am sick. But sane as a blade. Thinking, once in my life, with a clarity. That colonel behind you will keep the hands in the air or I will blow off his head. All of you! *Achtzung! Ja,* I am sick. Sick to death of this war, this killing. My father, my mother, my friends—dead.

Our cities blown to ashes. A neighboring country mutilated. Thousands and thousands butchered. My friend's father killed before his eyes—gun fodder!" His chin sank on his breast, and the gun shook in his hands.

August Schnitzler stood livid. "Traitor! You bring an Esperenchman with you—"

The machine-gun pistol swung at the Dictator. "You! You and these generals of yours! Thousands you have killed in the last few hours. Thousands upon thousands of innocent men. Men on both sides. Why did we attack Esperance and Switzerland, her ally? Why did you bring us here to invade Helvania? Because," his tongue cracked on the scream, "because two men were murdered in the Hotel Metropole must humanity die in flames? *Nein!* And these dead have died for nothing. For nothing have we slaughtered the Swiss, the Esperench. It was not an Esperenchman who killed Baron von Speer! The Swiss did not kill Von Reinmar—"

"You," husked the ghostly masquerade of Dubail, "have falsely accused in either case. The innocent have died. You have slain the wrong men." His jade eyes glittered at Schnitzler.

"We have come to rectify the mistake," Paul Emmerich whispered. Chin on breast, eyes amber seeds in a face of parched bone, he wheeled slowly in mid room, and levelled his pistol straight at John Keats' forehead.

ONE OF the grudges John Keats had always harbored against fiction was the clean-cut American hero who could face a pointed gun without starting a sweat-bead, strike an attitude of complete (but wary) composure, go on talking without cracking into a tenor, and eventually (with a miraculous side jump) remove the weapon from the enemy hand.

He now wished he could copy this performance. His effort to grin pained his jaw. Covered by the lethal muzzle of that machine-gun pistol, his face streamed. The impossible room whirligigged at his vision, and he was atrophied in his chair.

"Keats," and Emmerich's voice was miles away, "it was *you*

who killed Von Reinmar. It was you who assassinated our statesmen at the Metropole—"

Queen Roberta's ministers were like a lot of clay busts of
the same man ranged on shelves before the purple velvet backdrop at that end of the room. The Queen was lovely marble
with spun-gold hair behind her tall desk. Centered on the floor,
August Schnitzler and his conquering generals, impossible to
begin with, looked as fatuous as a flock of wax idiots in Madame
Tussaud's London Exhibition.

"*Salopard!*" Turtle-fashion, Dubail's head thrust out from the
shell of his upturned gray-green collar. "Paul Emmerich and I,
we know. We know what happened at the Metropole. We had
accused each other, *mais oui*. But then he told me about the
British journalist found dead in the bathroom!"

"It had to be you," Emmerich whispered.

There were sounds of dismay deep in Crazy Hooper's chest.
With his lank arms in the air he resembled a held-up cowboy.
The room was a three ring circus; Schnitzler and his staff,
animals at bay; Queen Roberta and her Helvanian ministers
an astonished audience. It had to be you—wasn't that a gag line
from some Tin Pan Alley ballad of long ago? Keats felt as if his
brain had dried up. A taste of cotton wool in his mouth. The
muzzle of Emmerich's pistol was a fascination.

EMMERICH'S WHISPER went on. "Go on. Go on. Deny it.
But you are surprised. Maybe you thought the fire that destroyed
the bodies in the dining room would also destroy Philip Shepler, locked in the bathroom dead. *Nein!* Von Speer and Victor
Gatreau were cremated, but the fire did not reach the bedroom
bath. At four o'clock of that morning our police discovered the
body of Shepler. Because I had previously found his pistol, I
thought the killer was Raoul Dubail."

Dubail apologized in a sort of whimper, "And I, in my mind,
had been accusing my best comrade, Emmerich. Because I knew
a war would make him rich, save his father's bankrupt stocks."

"He came through our lines to kill me," Emmerich described

softly. "Luckily we put our stories together. We found out, Keats. *You!*"

"The truth. *You!* Was there not a transom between bedroom and dining room, M'sieu Keats? Were you not alone in the bedroom that night while Nielsen, the Swede, was in the shower?"

"*Ja,* Keats. You shot Gatreau and Von Speer. Later you returned and murdered Shepler. Perhaps he knew too much. It was just after I left the young Englishman there in that bedroom. Police who found his dead body questioned a sentry who said you had entered and left the room while Shepler was in there. Who else could have murdered him, then?"

"*Alors,* you fled to Esperance," Dubail snarled. "Myself, I made some discoveries in my home city. Our Foreign Office informed me Gatreau had visited Von Speer on a mission of peace. His object was a total disarmament between Esperance and Teutony. Also, from the *Etoile* Bureau, I discovered that you, M'sieu Keats, had been in Rumania the morning before this peace conference. In Rumania, closeted with Garganoff, the munitions king. A confidential source reported Vasil Garganoff had given you one hundred thousand dollars. Why?"

"Blood money! The munitions master paid you to kill Gatreau and Von Speer, to stop any peace talk," Emmerich snapped fiercely.

"Meanwhile you faked it to appear as a duel and planted, somehow, weapons in the dead men's hands."

"Next," Emmerich pursued, "you went from Esperance to Switzerland. You were caught on the pigeon house behind Anton Stehli's cottage. You claim you saw Stehli lower a back window. Von Reinmar was in the room behind the Swiss. Stehli did not see you. Stehli died for that murder, but no gun was found in his house. *You* shot Von Reinmar. Using a silencer. The opened window—"

POINTED GUNS. Jade eyes. Eyes of hot amber. Emmerich's whisper like a muffled file on iron. Dubail's tongue a thin knife slicing words through his teeth. Accusations that dropped in the stifled air like vitriol. The ugly Greek Chorus went on and on. Queer how the fury on the lips of these men exaggerated their individual accents. The Teuton's tongue had thickened; the Esperenchman hissed. The tone was a level droning. Under the rapid bombardment of their condemnations, John Keats sat dumb, nerveless.

Could he answer the iron certitude in their words with a fairy story about vanishing assailants and mysterious small boys? Frantsovna? The Russian girl's name formed in his throat, but he couldn't speak it. A suspicion was no good in this welter of circumstantial evidence. How had Dubail's news service learned Garganoff had offered him money? That was bad. Shepler's body found in that bath after he'd left the hotel was worse. Von Reinmar's assassination while he, Keats, hid behind Stehli's cottage was deadly.

Sweat poured in guilty streams on his forehead. He looked guilty. Strangely, facing accusations he felt guilty. Always had. Now, under this terrible arraignment he felt guilty as hell: sat paralyzed as a fly in a web. Step by step they were binding him in, using the very threads he'd tried to use against them. Emmerich's thick whisper was weaving a summation.

"—killed them all. The two statesmen in the Metropole. The young Englishman. Field Marshal von Reinmar. Indirectly Anton Stehli, *Lieber Gott,* and fostered a war that caused the death of thousands, thousands!"

The room dimmed and spun, and he heard Queen Roberta's choked sob. Dubail's lethal drone came as an echo, "What can you say, John Keats, before you die?"

Too much was happening in too short a time. Everything was merry-go-round. His windpipe clotted with desperation. He said nothing.

"My God!" Crazy's bawl numbed his ear. "Say something! They'll put you on the spot—"

"Tell them," a far-away voice screamed, "what I saw! *Tell them you did not do it, John-Keats*—"

Heads jerked like masks on strings. That smothered cry had echoed from Nowhere. Keats stared at the Queen. Then he saw the purple curtain at room's end was stirring. The glee-club of Helvanian ministers moved their chairs. Folds parted in the velvet, and a slim figure in a khaki trenchcoat slipped from behind the cloth, darted swiftly across the platform, down the room.

BROKEN AT this strain, the silence in Keats' throat burst to a yell. "Frantsovna!" There was a tight second when the mesmeric spell impelled by Emmerich's machine-gun pistol and Dubail's guns threatened to dissolve. Waxwork Teuton generals and clay Helvanian ministers almost came to life. But Dubail rotated sidewise with a limpy whirl, guns aimed.

"Stand as you are, *messieurs!* First officer who again moves, I will shoot."

"Stand!" Emmerich blazed out in a low tone. "We have not finished yet, *nein!* You, Keats. Arms above the head. Higher! Fräulein Frantsovna—what the devil are you doing—you— behind that curtain—"

It was Queen Roberta who answered from her place on the dais where she had stood in frozen immobility throughout Keats' inquisition. "Alexandra Frantsovna was in the Council Chamber at my invitation. I wired the Soviet newspapers to send her." She bowed coldly toward August Schnitzler. "You will pardon my precautions toward making public our talk here. Behind the curtain is an alcove where newspaper people may sit unseen to record the exact minutes of our Council meetings. It assures their privacy, allows them to write unbiased fact without chance of coercion."

"A spy!" Schnitzler spat from purple lips.

"You keep out of this," Paul Emmerich warned the Dictator bluntly from the corner of his mouth. "This is between Dubail and me and the American swine."

Throughout that moment's whirlwind of drama, jeopardized as he was, John Keats had to marvel at the iron nerve of the Teuton newspaper man who dared confront Schnitzler and the High Command like this. And the courage that had brought Dubail, an Esperenchman, in disguise through the lines. Two men holding up the Gods of War to avenge the death of Peace.

Emmerich was snarling, "All the rest of you will keep out of this." His slitted eyes swerved at the Helvanian Queen. "Sire, I beg Helvania's indulgence—this Esperenchman and I, we will die here—but you will learn the truth behind this war—if there are spies back of that curtain—"

Then Keats was aghast at the sight of Frantsovna, running boldly toward the levelled guns. "No! I was back there alone. I heard every word you spoke against John-Keats. I know about the murders. He is innocent!"

"Attend!" From his station near the doors, Raoul Dubail snapped at the girl. "You were with us there at the Hotel Metropole."

Emmerich waved her back with his gun, "And you were in Anton Stehli's cottage in Switzerland. Did the old Swiss kill Von Reinmar?"

"I could not believe Stehli guilty at the time," Frantsovna shook her head furiously. "Of Von Reinmar's murder I know nothing—"

Emmerich gritted, "Then stay out of this business, Fräulein. You left Switzerland on the heels of Kurt Nielsen. Did," his eyes narrowed suddenly, "Nielsen have anything to do with these murders?"

Dust shook from her khaki, belted coat as she cried, "Oh, I thought so at first. I was sure of it, and I did not know why, that night at the Metropole. But I know he did not kill Von Reinmar in Stehli's cottage. He was in the front of the house with me. Yes, I—I determined to follow him. Into Helvania. I trailed Nielsen's car—"

Dubail asked thinly, "Where is the Swedish reporter now?"

"Dead."

IT WAS John Keats' cue to launch a cry into this play of voices. Lining tore in his throat as he blurted, "Nielsen's dead?" and Alexandra Frantsovna's eyes were sapphire lights looking at him from under smoky lids.

"It was this morning. Perhaps a mile in advance of me, he was, and driving very fast. A gray roadster he had brought from the Esperench capital. You know the main highway. We were nearing the capital of Helvania. There was a bend where I lost sight of his car, and then I saw he had steered off the concrete to take a side road, a dirt road through a pine woods. I followed the tracks of his car."

Queen Roberta spoke quietly into the scene, "I know the place myself. There is a landing field for aircraft behind the woods."

"Nielsen may have been headed there, but he did not gain his destination," Alexandra Frantsovna recounted. "The dirt road crossed a deep culvert in the woods, underneath was a pond of black water. There was Nielsen's motor. Overturned. Completely submerged. Driving too fast, he must have lost control. It had gone off the bridge. A small boy stood on the bank weeping at the wreck. He said he saw it all. Nielsen was under the car, drowned—"

Emmerich rasped thickly. "The boy saw it happen, so?"

"He said the car nearly ran him down as it jumped the bridge. His white sailor suit was spattered with mud. It had occurred ten minutes before I came. The boy said Nielsen was under the water."

Keats crashed up out of his chair. "Frantsovna! A little boy, you say? *A little boy?* White sailor suit—"

The machine-gun pistol whipped up in Emmerich's hands. "Sit down, Keats! Too bad the Swedish correspondent is dead, *ja,* for we could hear his testimony about your doings at the Hotel Metropole."

"Emmerich! Dubail! I didn't kill those statesmen. Don't you see I—"

Frantsovna's cry joined his impassioned outburst. "John-Keats did not kill them. You must listen to me, please! I, Alexandra Frantsovna, was on the roof across from the hotel windows."

"On the roof of a building?" Emmerich was incredulous.

"Yes. I wanted to see the statesmen in conference. Perhaps get an angle for my news story. I *did* see into the dining room where they sat. Also into the bedroom where the presswriters were. I saw Keats enter the bedroom with Nielsen, and a while later I saw them leave together. After that I looked into the dining room where Von Speer and Gatreau were talking at table. They, Gatreau and Von Speer, were *alive* at that time. They were alive when I left the roof across from their windows and hurried down to the terrace—"

AIR HIT cold on the bottom of Keats' lungs. Was the Russian girl lying, now? Lying to save him? He saw unbelief on Paul Emmerich's ashen face; angry cynicism green in the eyes of Dubail. The Esperenchman's teeth glittered.

"A pretty story, *mademoiselle.* Do not believe this, Paul."

"You, Fräulein Frantsovna? You on the roof of a building?"

Dubail grimaced, "It is a lie. You were paged on the terrace to answer a phone call. Keats had already gone upstairs with Nielsen."

"Also," Emmerich reminded, "it gives no alibi for the young Englishman's murder. It does not explain how Von Reinmar—"

"She knows nothing to explain," Dubail scoffed, hitching on his bad foot, "nothing. The girl is stalling for time. She is lying to save the American cur. *Morbleu!* her every gesture betrays she is in love with this scoundrel. To save him she lies—"

Then, as if agonized beyond endurance, before the Russian girl could further any protest, Paul Emmerich flung his appeal to John Keats. "For God's sake, Keats, confess your crimes and die like a man! Speak! Don't let the people of these countries die

for what you've done. In the name of *Gott* and mercy! Confess,
and halt this terrible war—"

Confess and halt the war! The words stood Keats on his feet,
and the room was out of focus again. So that was why they'd
risked their blood to come after him. Could a phrase from his
mouth put a stop to impending slaughter? An eerie chuckle
started in his throat, and his hand shook across his eyes. Suppose
he took the blame for Europe's skullduggeries. Teutony couldn't
attack the U.S.A. Maybe the fool generals would go home satisfied.

Through this pinwheel of thoughts he could dimly see Alexandra Frantsovna signalling him with appalled eyes; she seemed
to be crying. If the Russian girl could lie to save him, couldn't
he lie to save others? Back in history a man had died for the
world—but had Golgotha ever done any good? Martyrdom
didn't eradicate evil; the influence boiling this bath of hatred
would carry on, a killer laughing up his sleeve, going free. But
where was that murderous hand? At the Metropole the motives
were a dollar a dozen. Emmerich for leather. Dubail for revenge
on Gatreau. Frantsovna for revenge on Von Speer. Stehli for
revenge on society. Nielsen—but Nielsen was, like Stehli, dead.
Had Frantsovna seen that small boy standing by the Swede's
wrecked car? And the Russian girl's volume of Shakespeare—
the secret gun—who *had* murdered those statesmen and young
Shepler—great God! if he, Keats, stood here and took the rap—

THE PLAY was wrested from his hands by a roar. Across the
room a leathery bellow split into a jangling, raging laugh. The
purpled countenance of August Schnitzler had split into wrin-
kles of furious black. In the hour of victory they would steal the
great man's show? Well, he was stealing it back again. Charging
forward, he started his voice going like a drum. He stamped and
flung back his hair, coming back in the scene like a star who had
been elbowed aside by spear-carriers.

"A plot! A plot to stop Teutony in her victorious hour! This
insubordinate major with his Esperench spy—this so-called

American—newspapers, eh?—another Helvanian trick to break down capitulation. Did you think," he squalled at Helvania's Queen, "our High Command would be fooled by your show of passive resistance? Did you think to bring an armistice by this insane mock-turtle courtroom fiasco you're trying to stage here?"

Screaming, he whirled at Emmerich and Dubail. "Shoot! Shoot, you fools! Kill *Der Meister!* Kill the General Staff! And in two minutes my army blows this palace to shreds. Helvania will smother under such a bombardment as the world has never known. So, it was a good act, but not quite good enough. You thought it would halt the Teutons, to sacrifice this dummy of yours? The Fatherland does not stop for tricks. Our destiny goes on. *Teutonland ueber alles!*" Flinging about-face, he struck Alexandra Frantsovna with an elbow, knocked her to her knees on the floor. His squall struck the dazed generals. "Dunderheads! Fools! Our artillery will open fire at once! Arrest that Queen—take the guns from these blathering swine—"

A thousand things began to happen. *Thud, thud, thud.* Hearing uproar, sentries were thumping on the corridor doors. The Helvanian ministers made a glee-club standing up, clearing throats to sing. Shoulder to shoulder, Emmerich and Dubail were swinging like panthers in a cage, weapons ready to lash at the first move. Crazy Hooper's drawl touched Keats' ear, "They're gonna fight; always did want a poke at a Boche general!" and he was gripping the table-edge with his big hands. The gray-green blur of staff generals swayed in two seconds of uncertainty; then Queen Roberta was speaking from the dais, her voice cut high and clear.

"Stop! One move from Schnitzler or his generals brings disaster. Helvania is going to fight for the cause of peace. In the cause of peace my people will give themselves to the last man, woman, child. On this desk beneath my hand is an electric switch. A touch on that switch and Helvania is flooded by tons of gas."

Her eyes blazed at the fury on August Schnitzler's face. "You thought my Public Works were digging subways? Those subways are also gas reservoirs. From border to border my country has been underlaid with hidden mains. Every highway, street and bypath, every field and house is mined. We make no war. It is our defensive measure. You are in our backyard. We invited you as friends, you come as enemies. Be warned, my engineers have prepared a chemical to destroy an invading army in a trice. There can be no escape. If Helvania smother in its own defense, my people are ready to pay the price. That is my ultimatum to August Schnitzler! A turn of this switch to release that gas and the Teuton army is annihilated!"

ANNIHILATION. HELVANIA undermined with gas. It froze the room with a cold that stood every listener as quiet as a reflection in a mirror. Quick as mercury the atmosphere came clear; the shock in Keats' mind was a leap to reality from dream. Passive resistance. Confetti, and welcome signs. What a trap. The Teutons had come to the party on a pass, but now they must dance. A telegraph wire in his head caught a forgotten message from long ago. He'd been kneeling at a door, and the words were coming vibrant through the wood. "The fate of Europe depends on us, Von Speer." And the guttural answer, "But we must obliterate this monster by another method—we cannot disarm when our spies tell us the Helvanian chemists are inventing a gas that can wipe out the biggest army of the world in one second—"

Obliterate what monster? This girlish Helvanian Queen who controlled that secret ultimatum? Gas! Von Speer had known of it, then, but August Schnitzler did not believe it now. The black wing of hair slid over his left eye. His right eye squinted in a slit of red. Wind filled his blown cheeks, but the voice that came was small in that chambered tomb.

"A ruse! A lie! You have no secret gas. Your dynasty is poor. You would have traded it for power, conquered Europe, sold it for millions to the munition kings—"

The Queen's hand was a white butterfly hovering at the marble of her throat. "Betray my own people for money? What human would be that small—who would be small enough to—"

Small enough! The mirror smashed in John Keats' head. Two

words had smashed it. In the thousandth of a second a thousand particles, remembered incidents, recollected gestures, puzzle-pieces dormant on the floor of his brain were swept together. Answer! Like a long-studied cipher suddenly unlocked by its wanting key. In that flash the back was gone from the mirror; he could see through the glass. Pieces were missing, but he knew! In that blinding flash of discovery he wanted to yell. The others didn't know it. Five more seconds were gone, and he could only run his tongue across the edges of glued lips. The room was running away. He couldn't stop it. His hands made motions in the air, he shouted, "My God! Wait!" but August Schnitzler was not even looking at him.

AUGUST SCHNITZLER was looking at Helvania's Queen. Veins were green on the Teuton Dictator's forehead; his exploding wrath sent him bounding at the dais, queerly bent in his O.D. uniform, cavalry boots off the floor as if jumping a hurdle, arms reaching to grab. *"Gott strafe* Helvania! At them!" his scream tore backwards at his staff. "Enough of this! Is *Der Meister* to be threatened by a madwoman Queen—"

Keats thought of a maniac hurled at a porcelain figurine. Posed fragile, white behind her marble desk, Queen Roberta made no move. Only her fingers galvanized on the desk-top.

"Stop!"

But Schnitzler's boots crashed on the rostrum, and it was not the Queen's cry that stopped the Dictator. Alexandra Frantsovna whirled where she knelt. Her fist bulged in a brown pocket of her trench-coat. Fired through cloth, the shot made a spanking sound. *Whack!*

August Schnitzler gave a funnybone howl, tripped on a punctured foot, crashed across the marble desk. Keats had an eye-wink glimpse of everything happening. The Helvanian ministers spilling across their platform like a pack of cards. A thresh of Teuton generals crossing the floor. Lüger automatics and helmet-spikes. Dubail's voice somewhere. Emmerich shouting threats behind his gun. Frantsovna coming across the room.

Crazy Hooper's hands picking up the press table and dumping it over for a barricade. A thousand fists were hammering the corridor doors.

All that Keats saw in an eye-wink, and then, just as Frantsovna's arms reached his, the tumult went black. Simultaneous with the vanishing of light, wind rushed around the room with the sound of a hundred droning propeller fans. A blowing scent, unnamable, stupefying, faintly peach-blossom, gushed at Keats' face. Afterwards he could remember thinking it must be four o'clock in the afternoon and what would this be like in the open sunshine. Gas shells were one thing with their crash and noise, but this invisible, rushing gale pouring through lamp-black a soundless sweet smell was more terrifying than the trumpets of doom. Pell-mell tumult turned to stone in that blackness of rushing perfume. But for the sound of breathing, he would have thought the others struck dead. Somebody made a sound like a giggle. Somebody dropped a gun. The walls seemed to be shaking, trembled by a hurricane. A girl's weight drooped in his arms. Other sounds died in the roaring of the gale, but there was a lot of noise far away somewhere and he was getting sleepy the way they claimed you grew drowsy when freezing to death.

He struggled to fight this sensation and another illusion that a hand was shaking fiercely on his arm, lips talking against his ear. "Quick! Quick! Can you hear me, John Keats? I've told your comrade and he has gone—"

He felt happy and chuckled. "Good ole Crazy—yeh—"

The fingers steeled in his sleeve. "Quick, I say. This is the Queen, do you hear me? Cover your face with your kerchief, it won't hurt you! A passage behind the purple curtain is safe. Take the girl with you. You'll find a biplane ready. Quickly, then! In the air you are safe! Report story to the world. Teuton army no more. Go! Go quickly—"

HE WAS moving in this rushing scented dark, bringing Frantsovna with him, and guided by the Queen's unseen hand. He knew she was screaming at him to go, but in the gale her cries were whispers. It was like blind drunkenness. Lumps of misery hardened in his throat, yet he heard himself break them into foolish mirth. "Queen Roberta—can't leave you—asphyxiate—"

Her voice was a Toledo blade. "My royal command—go—this way, through here—run—"

Velvet swished past him; in a dim-lit corridor he was running. Running out of a desire to laugh and sleep. Sprinting into clear-headedness. Coughing that narcotic sweetness out of his lungs. Faster. He was surprised to discover Alexandra Frantsovna running at his elbow, a lace handkerchief crushed to her nose and lips. The corridor made three sharp turns before he realized Roberta of Helvania was not behind them. His boots stopped.

"The Queen—back in that—"

"Go on!" the Russian girl breathed frantically. "Her Majesty's orders. She—told me what we must do—an hour before you arrived. The story must reach the press. Telegraph at Bucharest. We must hurry—"

"News!" he lashed at the girl. "Damn you—a nation dies and all you think of is your dirty headlines—"

"Don't be a fool," was her stinging retort. "A Queen has commanded. Delay, and we will be too late. Her orders, John-Keats! Come—"

He hated her to his teeth as he followed her rockily along the passage; through a sudden door. Sunlight slashed on his eyelids. Somewhere behind the palace they were out in the day. Blue sky clean as ozone, and a long cool sward of green lawn. Face yellow and puckered, Crazy Hooper sat in the forward cockpit of a sleek tri-motor biplane that was tuning for the takeoff, wings shining silver in the sun, propellers idling in circles of watery rainbow light. Crazy yelled, beckoned. Bewildered, choking on quinine fury, Keats swung Frantsovna to the after cockpit and vaulted to the seat behind Crazy.

The camera man did not wait. Full gun the plane wheeled down the fairway, thrummed, lifted. Sky closed around them in a zoom. Roofs, treetops slid beneath the fuselage, fell away. John Keats thrust an aching wet face over the cowling and looked down. At five hundred altitude with the slipstream shrilling at his ears, the sound was clearly audible—a roaring, babbling pandemonium, a braying, hooting, ya-ya-yahing Saturnalia of sound that bedlamed up through the sunshine, generated from the terrain below.

A strange fog blanketed the earth. In the cañons of the city a translucent electric-blue mist was hurrying to and fro, sweeping around corners, glimmering over avenues and parks. Tree tops waved in this luminous wind. Papers, stray rubbish, confetti spiralled and twirled along the pavements. Bunting fluttered in window drafts as if agitated by waves of heated air, and in the tinted vapor the iron helmets of soldiers flashed and sped like fish seen in running water. On corners they darted in schools. The boulevard was a torrent of helmets that raced about in currents of blue. There was a plaza where a battery of anti-aircraft guns had parked.

Keats stared down on the gleaming up-pointed rifles with their deadly threat, but the Archie guns remained silent while the plane traversed their sights. Men swarmed and boiled about the cluster of bright war machinery, milling, brawling, threshing over the ground. Under the shining mist, they ran in disordered throngs: some staggered, careened, caught each other, fell. Others were flat on their backs with sky-turned grinning faces. Everywhere the soldiers were falling. He could see a Potsdam officer galloping along the pavement, arms upflung as if in a macabre dance. As he watched, the man buckled double, seemed convulsed by an overpowering laugh. Then the scene was gone; the drunken streets sped tailward; at two thousand feet the plane was spanning a landscape completely a-wash in that swimmy, diaphanous water-color, overlaid with tint like a map.

John Keats did not look down again. His burning eyes focussed a stony watch on the east's horizon ahead. Frantsovna's voice reached him one time, but he refused to hear it; did not look back. He was thinking of a legend, a werewolf tale of Transylvania, a *loup-garou* who could drink child's blood on the dark of the moon and change himself to a girl or a little boy.

"Small enough," he whispered.

The answer was dead ahead, and someone was going to die.

CHAPTER XIII

GARGANOFF KEEP!

"I DON'T LIKE this," Crazy Hooper told him gloomily. "I don't like any part of it."

"Shut up and give me her gun."

The lank camera expert shrugged unhappily, "I reckon you know what you're up to, Jawn, but I wisht we wasn't doin' it on empty stomachs," and hoisted the bound girl to a sitting posture on the Mercedes sedan's rear seat. "Sorry, kid, the boss's orders." He extracted the pistol from her coat pocket and passed it to Keats.

Alexandra Frantsovna made no struggle, sitting mouse-quiet as she had sat throughout that night ride from Bucharest, Crazy's belt fastened about her ankles. Keats' necktie knotting her wrists behind her back. Only her eyes protested, large with fear, wide open and bright above the white smear of the hand-kerchief-gag. In the purple dark they sent a glance of fright at the black sedan window, then glowed at Keats in a way that almost evaporated his resolve. He could hear the panic of her breathing. The night was heavy, hot without wind. A cricket fiddled in the brush, and far on the mountain somewhere a timber wolf barked. His neck cords throbbed.

With a grunt of impatience he jerked his dry eyes from her dilated gaze; leaned through the car door, saying harsh-lipped, "No use pulling any sob stuff. You'll stay where you are and won't try to get away. If I don't come back in twenty minutes Crazy's got orders to run you back to town. You telephoned your super headlines from the airport office, didn't you?" He sneered, "Well, the Soviet papers got your wonderful scoop, so you ought to be satisfied, but I figured you wouldn't be and brought you out here to get a bigger one."

At the venom in his tone her eyes filled with a pain nearly convincing. These were his first words to her since leaving that afternoon's horror in Helvania. He had merely nodded when she'd left the plane to find the airport phone booth on their arrival in Bucharest; Crazy had spoken the invitation to ride with them to town in the hired Mercedes, and, following instructions, it had been Crazy who tied her up while Keats drove. Tears glimmering on her lashes moved him to sarcasm, mixed with a sort of fear. He slammed the car door on this piece of acting and spun at the shadow that was Crazy Hooper dim in the midnight of the road.

WITH THE girl's face out of the way bis purpose stiffened. He could feel the red of fury running up his neck and jaws to his eyelids. He snarled, "Watch her. Watch her like a cat. Don't move from this spot."

"Buddy, I don't like it."

"For God's sake, do as I tell you."

"Why can't you tell a fella why?"

"I can't tell anything yet." His fingers shook on the pistol taken from Frantsovna's coat. A Webley, by the feel. He snapped the weapon to see if it was loaded, and the metal made a small clash in the summer-night stillness. Shoving the gun into Crazy's hand, he jerked his own Colt from his hip. "Don't let her out of the car, get it?"

"This is givin' me goose pimples. We was on this road when they popped a shot through our windshield that day. What the hell."

"Remember, if I'm not back in twenty minutes drive like hell to Bucharest, give the girl to the cops and send the flying squad back here."

Crazy hitched his unbelted trousers. "Golden Jerusalem, ain't we had enough for one day? Lucky to get outa Helvania without sticking our neck out in Rumania. We been through war and hell and now you come—"

"All right, I'm going."

"You ain't going into that castle alone?" Crazy moaned. Already Keats had gone. A stir in the darkness, a whisper in the brush where the Mercedes hid. In the purple stillness Crazy stood alone. He shambled to the car, sat on the running board, and stared at the only light in that sleeping wilderness of black. Stone walls a quarter mile distant were shadows etched against night. A tower window made a single yellow pane, a square of moon high in the darkness. Crazy watched the window.

MOAT WATER gurgled from Keats' pasted clothes, and he cursed the squelch of his shoes on the mosaic floor. The gate guard had only sighed as the gun-butt struck his head, and swimming under the drawbridge had been easy. But this candle-lit hall was a tomb of echoes and the walls had a thousand eyes. He crept. His fingers sounded like gauntlets of chain mail on the anteroom door. The hinges screamed as his shoulder flung the door inward; and the secretary with the wen sprang yelling out of a chair.

Keats shot first and didn't stop to ask questions afterwards. In that cobwebbed midnight hour the gunshot crashed like calamity, echoes traveling in a hundred directions, as if a legion of unseen gnomes were firing toy pistols in galleried chambers beyond, trying to wake the dead. The secretary fell with a crash of his own, but didn't waken; and something beside gnome-fire would be smashing the castle silence any minute now.

Keats jumped the body with its wen, and took his dripping legs through the door beyond. He discovered more halls and grotto corridors. He ran through a succession of doors. Staircases, more doors—perhaps with all the doors in the place the shot hadn't echoed far.

Only his shadows were pursuing him, and he ran like a shade, himself, following ensconced handfuls of candleshine that clung like sick moths on the slab-stone walls. His squirting shoes whispered on flagstone steps, up and up, instinct alone retraced his passage through that medieval Gothic maze, and quite suddenly he stood with chugging breath at the foot of the tower stairs.

He paused to judge the distance, for there was light shining in the passageway above, a pencil of sulphurous yellow marking the door ajar at the summit. Voices were blattering in the tower room through a sound like popcorn and the overarched masonry was full of noise.

"This," a voice yelled through the tower, "is England!"

Thefting his way up the steps, John Keats had to repress a saneless giggle.

"England is calling over station GBS. England is calling over station GBS."

Thank God for station GBS and the radio that had tuned out his midnight gunshot with static. He prayed the little prayer as he took the last flight of steps with his heart pumping water through his pores.

"Stand by," the radio was bellowing. "Stand by for special announcement from Rumania!"

Beyond the door sawed a thin, falsetto whine. "Will you tune that devilish instrument quieter? There's going to be a special announcement from Rumania."

A MUSCLE twitched under Keats' shoulder blades, and the gun ached in his hand. His boot hurled the door wide, *wham!* and he crashed across the threshold screaming, "You bet there's a special announcement from Rumania!" but the word "Rumania" splintered shrill in his throat, ending in a choked cry—*"Nielsen!"*

The deep-shadowed room with its tall, funereal chairs and mortuary fireplace and ghostly chandelier aloft in the cavernous ceiling fluttered on his eyes like a mirage; and the tall, black-robed figure at room's end wheeled around so slowly, as if balance were difficult from wine and any moment it might fall down, that John Keats stared in mesmeric fascination. Then his gaze whipped back to the corner where Kurt Nielsen stood with his hand apparently frozen to the dials of the bellowing radio cabinet. It was cold enough for that. The Swede's gaunt body was shaken in its sack-suit of tweeds; the monocle in his face was a disk of ice. The radio yammered and howled reasonless syllables as Nielsen's fingers jerked from the dial; and the tower was freezing.

"Nielsen," Keats whispered hoarsely.

There were only the three of them in that tower room. The tall dark figure of Garganoff, turning slowly in its inky cape. The Swedish news correspondent unbending before the radio. John Keats rooted in a puddle in the doorway, eyeballs stony, measuring the scene.

Between himself and that shadow that was Garganoff, the flat-topped ebony desk and the invalid's wheelchair were placed as he'd seen them last. Three dove-colored envelopes were lying on the desk where he'd left them. There was nothing between him and Nielsen save an expanse of soundless carpet. He watched the distance, staring, swaying the gun. Things were going to happen in this Balkan backwater, and the radio uttered howls. Nielsen made a step from the screeching instrument to prove his own reality, stopped, blinked coolly at Keats through his eyeglass, fussed at the perfect knot in his tie. The Swede's forehead wrinkled in faultless recognition, surprise. He lifted his voice above the howling.

"My word, Keats, you gave me a jolt. D'you mind not pointing that gun at me and staring as if I'm a ghost? If you'll permit me to say so, you look a bit other-world, yourself. Why, you're sopping—"

"Keep up those hands!"

"Station BXFzzzzzzsputterwheeeeeee—" screamed the radio.

"But Keats, isn't this a bit irregular? Hurling yourself out of nowhere like this and—"

"Don't move, Nielsen! By God! Frantsovna said you were dead. Drowned in an accident—"

THE MONOCLE dropped from the Swede's pastel eye and slid down his tweed waistcoat. "Frantsovna? Me? Don't be absurd. I haven't seen the girl since—why, since we were chased out of Switzerland. Her car was about a mile behind me and—why, I haven't seen *you*—"

"Count Garganoff!" Keats shouted. "Get those arms out from under your cape and keep them high. You, Nielsen! She said you—"

"Yahoooooo," shrieked the radio.

"She said you were dead, Nielsen. Run off the road. She—"

"My dear chap, I haven't the faintest notion what or who you're talking about. As you see, I deserted the battlefields of Switzerland on advice of the Teuton High Command—did you know they'd shot Stehli for a spy—and came here to interview Count Garganoff. If you'll lower that gun—"

"I don't know why she told me you were dead, Nielsen. But you're not here to interview Garganoff; not at midnight, you're not. Nobody's going to interview Count Garganoff but me."

"Baaaahaaaaahaaaa," the radio yelled. Garganoff's voice came squealing like a rusty castor above this static, "Get that insane creature out of my castle. Get him out of here, I say." His tall figure tottered and shook the folds of his black cape. Whether palsied by rage or fear Keats was unable to tell, but the body under the fluttering shroud staggered violently as it turned to face him; once more Keats was shocked at sight of the munition maker's countenance. Colorless before, the man's features were now whiter than lime, the undersized head pulled like a turtle's into the rim of the Inverness collar, the chin buried in folds of the neck-cloth. The domed, youthful forehead glittered with sweat, while the features underneath were puckery, dry, screwed like one of those rubber toys that sticks out a tongue when pinched. The tongue came out, a pink flicker licking crust from an upper lip. A thousand kilowatt hate sparkled and burned in the lidless, chicken-like eyes. The monocle fixed in this mask glowed like an electric bulb. The pink tongue went like a lizard's, and the blood-red mouth was a quivering wound.

Keats heard himself screaming above the uproar, "It was *Garganoff!* He was behind those killings! He shot Gatreau and Von Speer in the Metropole. He was there in the hotel every minute of the time. I tell you, Kurt Nielsen, I know! It was Garganoff threw that knife at me while my back was turned. After I left the room with you, Nielsen, he shot the two statesmen, firing through the transom to get them. He set the stage in the dining room to look like a duel, but he lost a cufflink climbing the door, and luckily I found the exploded shells. Garganoff had recovered the knife out of my suitcase, and he tried to kill me again, sniping at me from the window. Down there in the alley he thought I was dead. He had to get back his cufflink and those damaging thirty-eights."

THE TOWER walls seemed to shake from the fury of his screams penetrant above the maniacal caterwauling duet of the radio. His voice went on, tearing his vocal cords, scarring his throat. "Then Garganoff crept back into the bedroom. He wanted to knock me off; he was sure I'd heard too much when I listened at the dining room door. Shepler came to the bedroom, and, when he had a chance, Garganoff shot Shepler in the back. Then he laid for me in the dark."

Keats' eyes blazed at the lidless balls of acid in Garganoff's scribbled, inhuman face. "I know, now, how you vanished in that room, Vasil Garganoff. I know how you disappeared when the lights went on. I know how you were there to plant a fire bomb in the dining room to destroy the evidence. I know you were on the train going to Esperance. You attacked Nielsen that night! You'd have killed me, too, if you'd had the chance. Then when we reached Esperance and the war broke, you thought your work was done. You'd left a batch of false clues to hide your trail, you decided I didn't know anything, and you hiked for home and safety. But you hated Anton Stehli for his writings, so you took time out to frame him. You were there in that Swiss cottage.

It was you who shot that Field Marshal. It was you who left evidence to bring Helvania into the war. You hated Helvania. You hated—"

"—War smashing across Europe," the radio cleared its throat to shout suddenly. "And most amazing report in the history of the world is just coming from Rumania where a fizzzzbang ow ow morning she zowwwwieeeee—"

"Hated the world," Keats screamed down the room. "You wanted to destroy! Destroy! Money means nothing to such monsters! You wanted murder—mass murder! Your hatred for mankind—"

Nielsen ran fingers through his Viking hair. "Keats," he screamed from his corner, "you've gone mad. Stark, staring mad!"

Garganoff swayed behind the black desk. His scarlet mouth loosed a parrot's shriek. The gloomed room screamed, squalled, banged. *Slam!* Flesh tore from the rim of Keats' ear. Blood spouted down his jawbone. He spun with his gun crashing, firing into explosions. The Negro servant whose eyes were like the dog's, and the Great Dane with its Negroid eyes were coming up the stairway. The velvet-liveried Senegambian hadn't waited for good aim. Keats fired at the whites of his eyes, and the black man dropped backwards out of view. The huge dog had been behind the Negro. It hurdled the body on the steps, and came upward, open jaws slavering, roaring. In the doorway Keats squeezed the trigger again and again. It seemed centuries before the Dane came to a stop. Continuous fire poured from the Colt; then the great animal halted in mid gallop, fell with splayed legs on the edge of the landing, somersaulted backwards sedately and rolled down.

THE RADIO offered no let-up to clashing sounds. Dizzy, jarred with pain, Keats sprang around from the smoke-clouded door in time to break the full force of Nielsen's dive. Head down, the Swede's long body came flying against his knees, throwing him heels over the crown toward the center of the room. Landing on his shoulders and the back of his neck, he made a spine-cracking corkscrew twist to his knees, somehow managing to keep hold of the automatic. Blood from the torn ear smeared his left cheek and eye; half blinded, he missed a shot at Nielsen, and they battled across the center of the room, locked together like jungle cats, pounding, clawing, rolling in and out of shadow on the silent carpet.

In its corner the radio chittered and brayed. Garganoff screeched across the desk-top, but made no move to join the fray. Keats strove with stabbing knees to break Nielsen's grip. The Scandinavian fought with an astounding ferocity, battering Keats' head on the carpet while his steely fingers, locked on Keats' right-hand wrist, twisted and screwed and forced Keats' arm upward in an attempt to wring the automatic from his clutch. Keats closed his left hand on the Swede's throat, shutting the man's windpipe with his thumb. Chameleon colors surged and faded on Nielsen's puffed face; his eyes, close to Keats' eyes, glazed and squeezed shut, but the screw on Keats' wrist continued its twist; Nielsen hung on.

Back and across the floor they floundered; pain in Keats' arm made him yell. This lasted a thousand years while his shoulder socket was taking fire. The Swede's wheat-shock hair smothered his nostrils. There was a sickening smell of damp flesh and wet tweeds. His thumb ached in Nielsen's throat, and Nielsen's face was violet. Extraordinary how long it took the man to suffocate. Nielsen's body cramped like rigor mortis. With an agonized convulsion he lifted Keats bodily from the carpet, spun him into an adagio, cranking the captured arm. A sword of pain cut the nerves in Keats' hand, and the automatic fell. He kicked the gun to the farthest wall, broke Nielsen's arm-lock with a shout, let go the Swede's throat, and drove his left fist smashing full against the Swede's jaw. Nielsen ran a dozen steps backwards, opening blue eyes. His face was green, and he flung a hand to the thumb print burned on his throat while his eyes hunted the gun that lay against the far wall, then sped to mid room where Keats stood nursing his lamed wrist.

Both men were equidistant from the discarded weapon,

and the same number of paces from Garganoff. All three were corpse-color to the eye. "Please stand by," the radio blatted. "Stand by, ladies and gentlemen—"

"For the love of God, Keats," Nielsen's mouth was swelling black as he chewed out the screech, "are you trying to kill us all? I'm not in this affair. How could Garganoff—how could Garganoff have been on that train as you say? Been in Switzerland— there at the Metropole—"

Then he stiffened erect, grinning skullishly. He saw where Keats' white-rimmed eyes were focussed. Keats' white-rimmed eyes were focussed down the room, focussed at something he hadn't noticed before, an object polished and bulky standing in shadow against the ebony desk.

As if sensible to melodramatics, the radio suddenly shut up. John Keats whispered, "That's how, Nielsen. I've only twenty minutes or I'd ask for a demonstration. Your traveling bag—"

Disdainful laughter shook from the Swede's injured throat.

Keats spat, "You're lower than a rat hole. You're worse than this maniac, Garganoff. You stood by and watched Anton Stehli die—"

Even at this moment of judgment the man's ineffable sangfroid was unshaken. "We've all got to die sometime, old chap. The Swiss was a born martyr, and it gave him his biggest moment. *I'm* not afraid to die."

"No," said Keats evenly, "you'd better not be."

Kurt Nielsen didn't see why. Deliberately he started to dash for the gun. John Keats made no effort to outrun him. John Keats merely stood. He was pulling a book, a copy of Shakespeare, from his pocket.

HE SHOT just as Nielsen's fingers snatched the Colt, firing without compunction and drilling the Swede through the back of the head. Then, turning at the waist, he caught Garganoff coming around the desk, moving in great long-legged strides that flapped the cloak in monkish swirls around his wrapped legs and stretched him to extraordinary height, like a disproportioned shadow come to life off a wall. Ungainly, towering, Garganoff rushed in a reasonless charge, the last semblance of sanity gone from the coals of his eyes, strange sounds squealing in his collar-muffled throat, tiny bubbles frothing on his ox's-blood lips.

Keats stood quite still with his left hand pressed on his stomach, the gun firm in his right. He waited till the creature was a pace away. Squarely and truly he sent four quick .38s crashing at the vampirish face. He wondered, while the munitions king fell, if the Hertha Gun Works had manufactured those bullets.

Garganoff seemed to come down in unjointed sections, breaking up in segments like a condemned chimney. Blood scattered the powder-scorched air. There was a sound of tearing cloth, a sound of splintering canewood, as if the man's dry skeleton was snapping to pieces, and he smashed on the carpet in a curious heap, a sickening mound of crape cloth with that bullet-gored head a rosette in the middle.

For all the world, Keats felt as if he'd shot down a marionette. His own frame was racked, unglued. His teeth pounded. Iced fury melted into nausea that almost turned to pity as he stared at what was left of Garganoff.

The absurdly venomous head had broken on its neck. There appeared to be no substance under the voluminous spread of the cape. Through a slit in the shoulder-folds, a frail, waxen, fin-like thing was protruding. It looked a little like a sprouted wing. He saw it was a tiny human hand. A hand no bigger than a child's.

Keats wanted to get out of there. In departure he stopped to grab the dove-gray envelopes from the desk where he'd left them last time (after all there was no use looking a Peace Prize in the teeth) and he lingered long enough to open Nielsen's yellow kitbag.

As he snapped the empty bag shut, the radio came on with a Choctaw yell. "It's come, everybody. It's come from Rumania. Special via world-wide Soviet announcement from *Izvestia!* Entire Teuton army defeated in Helvania today—disorganized, disbanded and disarmed. Helvanians in specially treated gas masks—destroying all war machinery. By nightfall—by nightfall, ladies and gentlemen—people taking to the streets, again—all Teuton soldiers en route for the Rhine. Schnitzler—August Schnitzler—slightly wounded—only casualty—ordering Teutons home. Never has a European capital witnessed so mad a celebration, so incredible an armistice—Think of it—a nation defending itself—there's so much noise in the studio, ladies and gentlemen, I can hardly get to the microphone—a nation defending itself by killing the enemy with kindness—destroying an invading army with a secretly prepared laughing gas—Helvania ending the war, ladies and gentlemen—flooding the country with a laughing gas—harmless laughing gas!"

CHAPTER XIV

LITTLE MAN, WHAT NOW?

THE CARD ON the doorknob was Rumanian for "Do Not Disturb," but there wasn't any peace for the winner of the Gobell Peace Prize that night. The airless hotel room was a hotbox of noise. Crazy Hooper, pale with near lunacy in his eye, groaned in his appointed corner. White, shadow-eyed, lips tense, Alexandra Frantsovna guarded the door. A purple fat man in shirt sleeves trotted up and down the floor, pawing the smoky dimness, threatening, cursing, lashing his victim with sinister hints of punishment to come. Somewhere in the city beyond the drawn window-blinds a Bucharest clock tolled four. The purple fat man snatched sheets of wrinkled paper from a table, shouted. "Faster! Faster!" tromping and swearing incoherencies.

John Keats looked over his shoulder with eyes dull as lead. He wanted sleep, but they wouldn't let him go to sleep. Propped in the rickety chair, he panted, groaned, shook the sweat of exhaustion from his temples, stared helplessly at the Russian girl's expressionless face and found no mercy for him there. His lame arm burned to the shoulder socket. Caught in the devilish intricacies of the torture instrument, his fingers were dislocating, nerveless, turning to thumbs; another quarter hour of this and his hands would come off at the wrists.

A bell clanged in the torture machine. The room blurred to a sort of alphabet soup, and his head must be swelling like a stratosphere balloon under the ice pack. Blindly he freed his hands from the instrument, inserting a fresh sheet, and his dislocating fingers were pounding again. The room spun. The typewriter chittered. He set his teeth together, bunched his shoulders, sprained his eyes and wrote:

"There is little doubt that Kurt Nielsen was the man your correspondent glimpsed that morning in the reception hall at Garganoff Keep. We may never learn the exact details of the Swedish correspondent's affiliation with the Rumanian munitions master, but there is evidence that Nielsen had been for some time operating on the Hertha Gun Works payroll. As news correspondent, Nielsen had access to all the back halls of Europe, and unquestionably his inflammatory writings and exaggerated income were inspired by Garganoff's interests. Unconfirmed rumor reports that Count Garganoff made numerous attempts at bribery among individual journalists whose writings threatened an expose of armament intrigues."

Keats stopped to pull his knuckles and grin at the typewriter, and the pinguid man behind his chair voiced a wrathful bellow.

"Go on! Go on! Just tell the facts; you don't have to write a masterpiece. Go on!"

"I'm just telling the facts, Sour Puss; does it read to you like a masterpiece?"

"It's just about the lousiest newswriting I ever read—"

"Write it yourself, then—"

"Go on, for the love of Buddha! It'll never make the morning editions. Listen, Keats! When you mention yourself didn't I always tell you to say Universe News? In capitals! Write it, damn you! Go on."

KEATS WROTE: "Papers in the possession of Count Garganoff's secretary, at present in the hands of Bucharest police, revealed the object of Victor Gatreau's inexplicable conference with Baron von Speer. Both the Foreign Minister of Esperance and Teutony's Iron Premier had been secretly approached by Count Garganoff, offered enormous bribes and fortunes in Hertha Gun Works securities, in a plot to have them throw their nations into a European war, assuring the Hertha Works large orders of munitions.

"Seeking private interview with Von Speer, the Esperench minister, anticipating Garganoff's refusal to attend, undoubtedly hoped to publish abroad the nefarious intrigue, at the same time laying the groundwork for total disarmament between the two Great Powers on the Rhine.

"Vasil Garganoff *did* attend that meeting in the Hotel Metropole. It was Nielsen's influence which arranged the press room adjacent to the conference chamber; Nielsen who, supposedly in Stamboul, was visiting at Garganoff Keep the fateful morning of the proposed conference. While your correspondent (UNIVERSE NEWS) was traveling to Teutony on the afternoon airliner, Vasil Garganoff and Kurt Nielsen were journeying northward together, probably by private plane.

"Together, under the very eye of the police, in the gaze of the crowded hotel terrace, watched by secret service operatives and a coterie of newspaper men, Nielsen and Garganoff entered the Hotel Metropole. They go unobserved, in the company of John Keats (your correspondent writing) to the fatal bedroom. I observed that Kurt Nielsen refused the services of the bellboys and porters, but I made no note of it at the time. It was while Nielsen was shut in the shower-bath and my back was turned on the room—"

KEATS PAUSED to stare at the reeling typewritten sheet. He chewed a thumb, then wrote, "I was kneeling at the door to the dining room with my back turned on the bedroom—" then scratched that out, and wrote savagely: "Nielsen went into the shower and I walked down the room with my back turned. That morning, on leaving Garganoff Keep, a bullet had mysteriously smashed the windshield of my car, nearly killing my chauffeur; and now a second attempt was made on my life. By throwing a knife, Garganoff probably attempted to create an air of mystery that would confuse the local police and in no way tie up with the intended murdering of the two statesmen next door. Missing its mark, the blade, hallmarked with a Russian Imperial eagle, appeared to have come from nowhere.

"No blame can rest on the shoulders of the Teuton police guards in the hotel suite. Efficient as they were, they could not possibly have conceived the workings of the crime that followed. I left the room with Nielsen, and Vasil Garganoff was free to carry out his fiendish plan. Armed with a .38 caliber automatic equipped with a silencer, the madman crept from his hiding place and found the bedroom to himself. The transom above the door to the dining room simplified his maneuver, although he was doubtless equipped with tools to force an entry. At the same time the transom proved an undoing. Circumstances otherwise played in his lethal hands. A convention shouting through the lobby. Noise in the corridors. He levered the transom without being heard, and delivered a deadly fire, his first bullet striking Von Speer. The Iron Premier, however, managed to draw his gun and fire a single shot at the transom. Gatreau had no such chance. Whirling out of this chair, the Esperench minister was felled by a bullet in the brain.

"Working with such diabolical ingenuity as only a madman could contrive, Garganoff dropped into the dining room and set the stage. He arranged their own weapons in the hands of the dead men, emptying Gatreau's gun by firing at random, perhaps muffling the shots with a cushion which could later be destroyed, firing a number of shots at Von Speer's already dead body, bullets certain to be extracted by the police and traced to the Esperenchman's pistol. He fired another shot from Von Speer's Lüger to account for the bullet in Gatreau's head. Now the setup was a duel, and a European war would almost certainly be the result.

"Undetected, Garganoff returned by way of the transom to the bedroom. In scaling the door he lost a link from his cuff, but apparently failed to notice it at the time. Before returning to his hiding place he recovered the Russian knife; then he must have discovered his cufflink missing, and there was the matter of the exploded cartridges. The discovery of the murders in the dining room gave him no chance to repair the flaw; he must wait in hiding.

"He sees the suite fill with frantic police. Guards look in at the door on constant watch. The newspaper men return to the bedroom where he hides, and frantically write their dispatches. Garganoff must have had a bad minute when he saw me inadvertently stumble across his dropped cufflink and at the same time discover those used shells. He could not follow me out of the bedroom while the corridor was alive with secret service men, but he did watch from the window, catch me running along the street, shoot me down. Taking a desperate chance he scampered out to the mezzanine, perhaps under the very eyes of the Reichswehr guard.

"On the storming mezzanine, in the lobby crowd, Garganoff passed unnoticed. Easy for him to deceive the sentry in the outer court; back in the hotel he slipped through safely again, returned to the bedroom and waited. Shepler, next to die, was in Garganoff's way. I was the one he was after. He ambushed me in the dark, slashing out with a knife where he might have missed with a gun. A close call for him, that time. I had the knife, again, and what was more dangerous to Garganoff, a certainty outside forces were at work and the deaths of Gatreau and Von Speer were not caused by a duel. Garganoff's hand was forced. He must destroy the bodies in the dining room before a detailed inquest was established and the bullet in Gatreau's brain examined. Counting on Nielsen's return at a moment probably prearranged, this death-dealing megalomaniac waited until the coast was clear, then flung a fire bomb into the dining room. The flames in the Hotel Metropole touched fire to Europe. Garganoff the recluse, the mystery man, the Rumanian arms king, set those flames. But the motivating mania of this sadistic fiend had its roots in something deeper, more horrible, deadlier than avarice.

"Nielsen, himself, so necessary, to Garganoff's machinations, could not have guessed as he speeded his dreadful master from the burning hotel, the inhuman depths of Garganoff's design.

For Vasil Garganoff was not a man. Locked recluse in the dark tower of his lonely Transylvanian castle, held prisoner by his mother, shy, miserable as a boy, bitterly wretched in old age—the soul of this millionaire who was poorer than his lowliest peasant must have alchemied to iron. Were-wolf. *Loup-garou.* Drinker of the blood of children. So any munitions master might be named. Garganoff was more. A terribly wronged human whose mother had left a tremendous weapon in his hands. Swallowing for years the acid of hatred against life, the master of Garganoff Keep would take a revenge on life, revenge on the society he could never join.

"But a stranger force than hate would stop the guns of Vasil Garganoff. A force unknown to the killer's contorted mind. A force to turn back the loosened hordes of war, to stop the officers of hate, to shout down the generals, the Schnitzlers, the guns. No army or dictator, no medal-flaunting soldier or scheming diplomat or preacher or propagandist can stand against it. It will always antidote the wrongs, break up the strutting drill fields, scatter the old grudges, heal the new wounds and defeat the Garganoffs of the world. Laughter!"

KEATS THOUGHT that last paragraph was pretty good. He flung himself backwards in his chair, snatched the paper from the machine, shied it into the fat man's purple hands, and closed his eyes.

"That's that. There's your story, Major Asprin. I'm through. Get it? Through!"

"Through is right," was the corpulent bellow. "Nobody asked you to write an editorial. If this ain't done in time for the morning editions, I'll fire you. Yah!"

"It's done," Keats snapped with finality. "My fingers are broken. Get to hell out of this room, all of you, and leave me alone."

The Major sorted the manuscript wildly. "Where's the rest of it? Where's what happened to you on the midnight train and in Switzerland and in Helvania—"

"That's all in the lead-off page." Keats dragged an arm across cindery eyes, tottered up out of the chair, glared blindly at Alexandra Frantsovna. "Nielsen and Garganoff were together in that Wagon-Lit compartment, see? I think they planned to kill me and heave me out the window. The express going fast, it would've made a nice looking accident. Nielsen tried like anything to decoy me into his sleeping room, but lucky for me I stopped in to talk with you first."

Alexandra Frantsovna smiled. Little crinkles around her eyes. She said, "You didn't believe a word I told you, did you, John-Keats? About me being on that roof across from the Metropole and seeing—"

He jammed hard fists into his pockets; growled, "I'm sorry."

"You don't need to be," the Russian girl told him. "You weren't watching me any harder, these past three days, than I was watching you. Naturally you'd suspect me after a Russian knife had been—"

He denied, "I was sure you didn't toss that blade. It was stamped with the double-headed Imperial Eagle, old Romanoff crest. A citizen of Soviet Russia wouldn't own one of the things; they're scarce as hen's teeth in the U.S.S.R. I knew it must be an heirloom from a wealthy collection. My first real clue on Garganoff. The Czar had sent him gifts."

"I'm glad you didn't think I would murder *you*, John-Keats."

He could feel his neck reddening, and lied, "Not for a second. Saved my life on that train, going in to have a chat with you. Then Garganoff and Nielsen must've had a terrific quarrel; maybe Garganoff gave the Swede a beating for not trapping me. Nielsen was nearly brained, anyhow. Maybe it was just a set-up."

"A set-up?" the Russian girl inquired.

"A trick. Fake attack to throw guilt off Nielsen in case any questions were asked. Same reason he tore that quotation out of your Shakespeare book, clutched it in his hand to make it seem—"

THE GIRL said breathlessly, "He heard me read that line aloud on the terrace in front of the hotel. Yes, and he must have entered my hotel room at the Metropole when I was out dispatching my news story. He found the line and tore it from the page."

"Well," Keats rattled out, "Garganoff and Nielsen tried to put suspicion on you. But in Esperance the war broke faster than they expected. With all hell loose they were safe enough, and lit out for the Alps."

Frantsovna smiled soberly. "And I lit out, as you say, after Kurt Nielsen. But, John-Keats, I did not know this Garganoff was with him—"

"No!" Major Asprin's egg-plant colored face seemed to explode the word. He flourished the typewritten pages in his hand. "And how the devil is anybody else going to know, Keats? You've written a lot of stuff that hasn't explained a blasted thing! How'd Garganoff come with Nielsen to the Metropole? How'd Garganoff hide and vanish and what not in that bedroom? How'd he disappear on that train? And in that cottage in Switzerland where he killed Von Reinmar, and you have this Stehli sayin' he was alone with Von Reinmar in the room. What the thundering Hades does it all mean?"

Keats lit a weary cigarette. "Sorry, Major. You can write it in for me, then. Thought you'd guess why Nielsen wouldn't let the porters carry his bag. How else could Garganoff get around like he did without ever being seen? That's how he got in and out. That's where he vanished. Sure. Garganoff was hiding in Kurt Nielsen's traveling bag. Some air holes concealed along the bottom and peep holes near the hinges at each end. He could pop out and back like a jack-in-a-box. He—"

"Garganoff!" The Major's mouth yawped. "In Nielsen's *kitbag!*"

"And room for the Swede's change of underwear, besides. Nielsen had a drag with the frontier customs. Nobody'd bother to examine his—"

"But Jumping Judas on a raft!" the Major squalled. "Vasil Garganoff was a man six feet tall. I've seen a photograph of him. He always wore a long cape, stoop shouldered, thin, a man over six feet tall—"

"Or a little boy about five years old, with his goatee shaved off," Keats said. "A little boy in a white sailor suit who said he was my son and picked my pockets in the rain. A little boy hiding in a yellow kitbag with a .38 and a Russian knife and a fire bomb in his blouse. That's where he was in the hotel and on the train and in Anton Stehli's cottage. And Garganoff had been trying to sell munitions to Helvania. The War Office wrote back they wouldn't buy. That's where he got hold of Helvanian War Office stationery, and how that faked document came in Stahli's cottage. Garganoff was the same little boy who ordered Nielsen to run his roadster into a culvert when Frantsovna got too close. The little boy who stood there saying Nielsen was drowned, while the Swede ran ahead to a flying field in the woods and got hold of a plane—"

"Keats," the Major stood on tiptoe and thundered, flapping his arms like a crowing bull. "Keats, are you mad?"

"No," Keats said, "but Count Garganoff was. You'd be, yourself, if you'd spent your life locked in that tower room. A lot of them are born in this corner of Europe, they say. Think of it! Hiding himself in that monstrous cloak, playing the invalid, standing up in that wheelchair and creating the illusion he was sitting down. God! Walking about on stilts! I tell you, he was the smallest I've ever seen—hardly two feet tall. Garganoff was a *midget!*"

MAJOR ASPRIN, shaping his course for the door, fell down twice. His resiliency was amazing in a newspaper owner of his age and embonpoint. His howls for a telegraph boy rattled the hotel to the roof and started a radio in the lobby. America, England, China and Pago-Pago fought for supremacy in the Bucharest air. America won. A New York nasal dinned through concert.

"Thank you, Graynie. Folks, this is Walter Busby, the Bad Boy of the Atmosphere, back on the mike again. Graynie and I been handing out the news for the last three hours. Some excitement in Europe! *Some* excitement. And I just got a tip that this certain American correspondent that's been in the middle of the show over there has been seen a lot in company with a certain Soviet news-getter, the same little lady who took a pot-shot at Schnitzler, they say, and it looks like the Universe Newsboy bachelor may be catching himself a Russian bride according to—"

Keats shouted, "What a nerve! What a nerve!" and shut the hall door with a savage kick. His glare turned at Frantsovna, and the Russian girl seemed to be smiling.

"How'd that get to America? How'd that damned snooper—"

Alexandra Frantsovna shook her head. "I didn't tell a soul."

"You knew?" Keats hollered.

"All the time," the girl said cheerfully. "From the first. I knew you loved me, the same way you knew I was in love with you."

Women always had a way of startling him, and Russians in particular. He bawled, "How about that judge you kissed in Spain to get off—"

Her gray eyes shimmered. "So long ago? But I had to. They were putting me in jail. I had to do that or I wouldn't be here."

Keats shouted, "What makes you think I love you after the way I treated you? Didn't I tie you up, almost kill you? Didn't I chase you—"

"You couldn't help that, John-Keats. You didn't know."

"I know I love you, all right," he rasped, "but I always said I wouldn't marry out of my class. You're 'way out, Alexandra Frantsovna. 'Way out. I lose my head. You're always on the level. You wouldn't want me—"

"John-Keats," she smiled, "you know I would."

"Say," Crazy Hooper yawned the drawl from his corner. "I knew this sort of thing would happen."

Keats spun at the gaunt camera man in fury. "Shut up! Everybody seems to know about everything that's going on around here but me!"

"Golden Jerusalem," the lank one sulked, "have we got to hang around and draw you diagrams? Listen, I'm getting out of here. I want a sandwich. I'm starving."

"How would you like," John Keats snarled, "to help us eat a wedding breakfast?"

Made in the USA
Middletown, DE
22 December 2020